Beyond
the Sea

MYSTERIES *of* MARTHA'S VINEYARD

MYSTERIES *of* MARTHA'S VINEYARD

Beyond the Sea

JANICE THOMPSON

Guideposts

New York

CHAPTER ONE

Eliza Jamison bought a . . . what?"

Priscilla shifted her cell phone to her left ear to answer her cousin Trudy's question. "A 1954 surf-green Bel Air convertible. I can't believe I'm telling you this. It's supposed to be top secret. But I'm going to bust if I don't tell someone."

"My goodness." Trudy's pause felt elongated, and Priscilla wondered what she might be thinking. "I know she loves classic cars. She and her fiancé both do. I've seen them cruising up and down the island, struttin' their stuff, Carson in that blue Jaguar and Eliza in her red Corvette. But why get a new one this close to the wedding? They both already own classics, after all."

"Right." Priscilla struggled to maintain her hold on Jake's leash as he pulled her along the cliff's edge. "I guess it doesn't make sense when you consider what they already have."

"Exactly. Why spring for a new—er, old—convertible?"

Priscilla shivered as she waited for Jake to do his business. Her teeth chattered, and she fought with one hand to pull her jacket tighter to ward off February's chill. "It's all part of a big surprise. Eliza's been planning this for ages. They'll drive off into the sunset—rather, to the Harbor View hotel in Edgartown—in this brand-new-to-them car. Carson has no idea she's purchased it, so he's going to be wowed, for sure."

"Happy wedding day, I bought you a car!" Trudy laughed. "That's some present, don't you think?"

"You can say that twice and mean it." Priscilla glanced out over the water, catching a glimpse of the early-morning sun dancing across the ripples. "Anyway, the car arrived yesterday afternoon from the mainland. Eliza hired a transport company to bring it all that way so Carson wouldn't suspect anything. You wouldn't believe what we had to go through to get it here."

"We?" Trudy's question was laced with curiosity.

"I've been helping," Priscilla explained. "Long story. Don't want Carson to catch on, you know."

"I see. Wow, she's taking this present very seriously."

"Wouldn't you, if you spent that much money on a surprise gift?" Priscilla shifted the phone back to her other ear, never releasing her hold on the leash. "Anyway, Eliza's been communicating back and forth with the restoration company in Boston over the past month or so. You wouldn't believe how much work has gone into that vehicle. It was a mess when she bought it, but you should see it now. It's been completely transformed. She sent me pictures every step of the way. I've never seen anyone so proud. You'd think this was her baby, learning to walk or something."

"Sounds like you two are really getting close."

"We've become good friends, yes. You know I'm helping out with her wedding. And even though I'm not much of a car person,

I feel like I've had a vested interest in this one, since it means so much to her."

"I was wondering how you figured into this story. Then again, you manage to find your way into a great many stories in Misty Harbor, don't you, Priscilla?"

"That seems to be the case, whether I want to or not." She paused to think through her cousin's words. "In this instance, she asked me to help her find someplace to hide the car after it arrived on the island, someplace Carson would never stumble across. I was happy to help. Or should I say, Gerald was happy to help. It's in his garage, safely tucked away until the wedding on Saturday. Eliza and I went by last night. I wanted to see it in person, and she wanted to make sure the restorations were done correctly. Just three more days. It'll go by fast."

"So, Gerald has played a role in this too." Trudy's voice took on a suspicious tone. "Very interesting."

"Just loaned us his garage is all."

"Right. So, how did the car turn out?" Trudy asked. "After the restoration, I mean."

Priscilla paused as memories of the gorgeous vehicle flooded over her. "It looks amazing. I could almost see myself driving along the coast in that gorgeous convertible, my hair whipping in the wind."

"In February?" Her cousin laughed. "Remember that big winter storm that just blew through?"

"I don't mean I would drive it with the top down in February, silly. Only in the spring or summer. Anyway, I can definitely see the appeal. A car like that would make me feel young again."

"In that case, I'll take one, myself." Trudy chuckled and Priscilla could almost see her expression. "But I'm really surprised you were able to keep all of this a secret from us. You really are turning out to be quite the sleuth—you know how and when to keep secrets and you're able to solve crimes, to boot."

Priscilla managed to coax Jake back toward the house. "Nah. Just trying to keep Carson from finding out, which is why I didn't let you ladies know about the goings-on. It's all top secret as I said, so mum's the word."

"So, now you're a sleuth and a car aficionado?"

"Hardly." Priscilla laughed as she thought through her cousin's choice of words. "As I said, I know zero about old cars. Zip. Nada. But Gerald seems to. I only know what I see with my eyes—a gorgeous old classic."

"Are you calling Gerald O'Bannon a gorgeous old classic?" A girlish giggle escaped from Trudy's end. "My goodness."

"No." Though Priscilla had a hard time not smiling as she thought of how comfortable things had become between the two of them. Of course, it didn't hurt that the man had gorgeous eyes and the perfect laugh lines. Perhaps he could be called a classic after all.

"Did I lose you?" Trudy's voice startled her back to reality.

"Um, no. I'm still here." Priscilla was glad her cousin couldn't see her face over the telephone. Her warm cheeks must be beet red.

"Sure you are. Well, you must admit, he's easy on the eyes, a lot like that car you're describing. And runs well for his age too."

"Trudy, please."

"I do believe Gerald would be there for you, no matter what you might need." Trudy sighed. "Just sayin'. The two of you are as thick as thieves."

A delightful shiver ran its way up Priscilla's back. Or was that just the cold wind off the water? She watched as Jake paused near the garden, coarse and brown from February's chill. "C'mon, Jake. Do your business and let's get back inside. I want to watch the morning news and then get this day started."

"Yes, get inside where it's warm," Trudy echoed. "We're supposed to have another cold snap over the next couple of days. The weatherman said to stay inside."

"If only I could. I have to help Eliza with last-minute details for the wedding. I sure hope we don't end up with another nor'easter like the one we just went through. Brr."

"That's one party I wasn't sorry to miss."

"You and Dan went south just in the nick of time. Anyway, this wedding will happen, good weather or bad. Eliza's so excited about having the ceremony and reception at the Bluffs B&B. She and Anna have gotten closer than ever." Jake tugged at the leash and then took off after a squirrel. Priscilla fought to keep up with him, nearly losing her grip on the leash. "Do you m-mind if I p-put you on speaker, T-Trudy? I'm having a hard time keeping the phone next to my ear. Jake keeps dragging me around the yard."

"Sure. I don't mind being on speaker. There's no one there but you and Jake, right? Not that it would matter. I'm an open book."

"It's just us. I'd just fixed a cup of coffee and turned on the TV to watch the news when Jake decided he couldn't wait one minute longer."

As she rounded the side of the house, the crunch of tires on her gravel driveway caught Priscilla's attention.

"Hang on, Trudy. Sounds like someone just pulled into my driveway." Priscilla made her way to the front of the cottage and saw Gerald O'Bannon's Coast Guard vehicle. As he opened the driver's side door and stepped out, she couldn't help but smile. Fully decked out in his Coast Guard uniform, he looked like a hero from another era.

Unfortunately, the somber expression on his face did little to bolster her enthusiasm.

"Um, Trudy...it's Gerald."

"Ooh-la-la. You two going to drive off into the sunset in that new convertible before Eliza and Carson have a chance? Sounds like fun."

"I'm not so sure he's in the mood for fun, judging from the body language."

"Oh no. Well, keep me on speaker. I'm dying to hear what's going on."

"Trudy, I can't do that. I'll call you back later." Priscilla hastily swiped her finger across the screen and slid her phone into the front pocket of her hooded sweatshirt.

Gerald took several steps in her direction, and now she could see the pronounced wrinkles in his brow.

"Everything okay?" she asked him.

He pulled off his hat and waves of hair fell across his forehead. "No. There's something I need to tell you, but it's probably a good idea if you sit down first. Can we go inside?"

"Of course. But, sit down? Why?" Her heart raced. Had something happened to a family member? Uncle Hugh, perhaps? After his recent heart issue, she worried about him.

Priscilla tugged Jake toward the front door of the cottage. She opened it and stepped inside. Gerald followed closely behind, then shut the door.

"Is it Uncle Hugh? Please tell me he's okay."

"He's okay. Just do me a favor and sit down, Scilla."

So she sat. Like a compliant child, she dropped down into her favorite living room chair, grabbed the remote, and muted the television.

Gerald paced the room, which only caused her blood pressure to rise even more. When he finally turned her way, she could hardly believe the words that tumbled out of his mouth.

"I hate to be the one to tell you this, but Eliza's newly restored Bel Air convertible...has been stolen."

CHAPTER TWO

The car is gone?" Trudy's voice pierced the air.

"What?" Priscilla had jumped at the sound of Trudy's voice. "I thought I hung up with you." Apparently she hadn't actually ended the call. She reached into her pocket to grab her phone out. "I'll have to call you back, Trudy."

"Wait! Keep the phone on speaker so I can hear what Gerald's got to say about that car. Please? I'm dying to know!"

Priscilla sighed and turned to face Gerald. "Sorry. I shouldn't have told anyone, and I thought I ended my call with her." This whole thing was supposed to be top secret, after all.

Gerald paced the room, clearly distracted. "No idea how it could've happened. I went out to the garage to check on the car last night before bed and everything was totally fine." A smile tugged at the edges of his lips. "Okay, I did a little more than that. I sat in the driver's seat and tried to imagine what it would be like to drive the car. I don't mind telling you, my imagination kicked into overdrive."

"Sounds more like the car kicked into overdrive," Trudy said.

Priscilla did her best not to fret as she caught Gerald's attention. "You didn't drive the car, right? Not that it would matter. I know Eliza wouldn't care, but I'm just wondering if anyone saw you out for a spin in it and decided they had to have it for themselves."

"Nope. That car never left my garage when I was behind the wheel. For that matter, I didn't even open the garage door. I just sat in the driver's seat, wowed by that amazing interior. Those vinyl seats are—"

"Stellar. I know. You wouldn't believe how much she paid to have them reupholstered. And now someone else is sitting on them...somewhere." Priscilla released a slow breath. None of this made any sense. How could someone steal a car they'd so carefully kept a secret?

"Right." Gerald cleared his throat and took a seat on the sofa. "The point is, everything was fine at that time. So, I did my usual thing. Went to bed around eleven. Woke up at three because I thought I heard a noise, but it sounded more like wind hitting against the garage, not a car engine or anything like that."

"Probably the sound of the garage door opening." Trudy's voice rang out from the phone. "Whoever stole it probably opened the door, put the car in neutral, and pushed it out."

"Maybe." Gerald didn't sound convinced.

"That's how I would've done it, anyway." Trudy paused. "Not that I stole the car. I didn't. In fact, I didn't even know about it until just now, so don't point any fingers in my direction."

"No one was supposed to know at all." Gerald glanced Priscilla's way, as if to ask, *Why did you tell Trudy?*

Another sigh escaped Priscilla's lips.

Trudy continued to share from her end of the line. "Gerald, if what you're saying is true, then we're talking about two people working together. At least. One lone person would have a hard time pushing and guiding the car. Unless it was a big, burly person with lots of muscles. Do we know anyone who matches that description?"

"I'm sure it was a team." Priscilla rose and paced the room, finally coming to a stop directly in front of Gerald. "Have you told Eliza yet?"

He looked as if he might be sick. He picked up his Coast Guard cap and fingered the edges. "Um, no. I was kind of hoping you would tell her."

"Gerald!" Trudy's shrill voice was back. "You have to tell her. It's her vehicle. She deserves to know."

He dropped the hat and leaned forward, putting his head into his hands. "I know, I know. And I will. I just have to think of how to tell her. And when. This is a terrible time to present her with bad news, just three days before her wedding. What am I supposed to say? 'Happy wedding day! I lost your car.'"

"Let's not jump the gun." Priscilla sat down next to Gerald. "Maybe we'll locate it before she realizes it's gone." She thought that through. "We can always tell her after it's returned to your garage."

"I sure don't want her thinking I had anything to do with this." Gerald gave Priscilla a pleading look. "I'm a fan of old cars, like most every other guy on the island."

"She would never think that."

"But no one else even saw the car." Gerald's eyes widened. "Hey, wait a minute." He snapped his fingers. "I just thought of something."

"What's that?" Priscilla asked.

"Victor Fox."

"Ugh." Trudy's voice sounded from the phone. "Don't tell me you think he's involved. Didn't we already suspect him of kidnapping his wife a few months back?"

Gerald rolled his eyes. "Yes, but he wasn't guilty, remember?"

"He pushed her away with his obsessive treatment. That's almost as bad." Trudy paused. "Anyway, what were you saying about him, Gerald? He saw the car? That can't be good."

"I was saying that he pulled up just as I was closing my garage door yesterday afternoon. I think he caught a glimpse of the car. He asked me about it, but I avoided the question."

"He is a car guy," Priscilla said. "That would make sense, that he would be interested."

"Right. And from what I've heard, that used car lot of his isn't bringing in as much money as he'd hoped." Trudy's voice had a suspicious edge to it. "Very in-ter-es-ting. Maybe he took the car and plans to sell it."

"Even Victor Fox knows he couldn't sell a stolen car." Priscilla shook her head. "Certainly not on his lot for all of Tisbury to see. Makes no sense."

"Agreed." Gerald nodded. "Besides, I'm not a hundred percent sure he even saw what kind of vehicle it was. He came across as nosy, not shady."

"But the point is, he saw enough to ask a question about it," Priscilla countered. "And, since he was the last one to see the car besides you, we have to assume he's a suspect."

Gerald sighed. "I can't believe we're making a suspect list. This is just nuts. That car only arrived yesterday, remember?"

"And disappeared last night." Priscilla paused and rested her hand on his arm. "So, do we tell Eliza right away or wait?"

Gerald paled. "I've rarely been called a coward, but the idea of calling her up to tell her that car was stolen while under my care makes me feel sick inside."

"I can't keep it from Eliza," Priscilla said. "She has to know."

"Whoa, whoa!" Trudy's voice sounded from the phone. "If I get a vote here, I vote no. She seems pretty overwhelmed with wedding plans."

"Yes. And aren't you the one who just told us she deserves to know?"

"Well, I've changed my mind. It's a woman's prerogative. Didn't you tell me just yesterday that she's still got a dress fitting, one last meeting with Candy to talk about the cake, family members flying in, a wedding rehearsal, and so on?"

"Yes."

"Priscilla, think about it," Trudy said. "You can't possibly add more stress."

"I won't be adding it. The situation will be. But I can't avoid the situation. And besides, don't you think she deserves to know? It's her property."

"I once had a friend whose husband was cheating on her, only she had no idea he was cheating on her." Trudy's voice grew more animated. "The only reason I knew was because I actually saw him with the other woman on the ferry. Well, at least I thought she was the other woman. Anyway, the point is, I found myself with a dilemma—tell my friend what I knew about her husband or forever keep my mouth clamped shut, knowing she would kill me if she ever found out I'd known all along. I don't mind telling you, I sweated a lot of bullets."

"Wow, that's a tough one, Trudy."

"You're telling me."

"So, what did you do?" Gerald asked.

Trudy giggled. "Well, it's the funniest thing. I told her. Turned out the woman I saw him with on the ferry was his sister. She was coming to the island to spend a week with family, and he met her in Woods Hole so she wouldn't have to ride over alone."

Priscilla clasped her hands together. "I see what you mean. What happened to your friendship?"

"If she hadn't been a very forgiving woman, it probably would've wrecked it. But how could I know the man was faithful? He looked like a cheater to me."

"I hardly think this story fits our current situation, Trudy." Gerald glanced Priscilla's way and rolled his eyes. Clearly, he found Trudy's story an interruption. "One thing's for sure. We have to tell the police."

"Well, what are you waiting for?" Trudy said. "Let's get this show on the road. Give me five minutes to brush my hair, and I'll meet you at the police station."

Priscilla tried to interject a bit of common sense into the conversation. "Trudy, you're not a witness to anything, so I really don't think you need to—"

"Try and stop me!" Trudy ended the call with a click.

Priscilla looked at Gerald and shrugged. "She's in, whether we want her to be or not." She rose from the sofa.

Gerald put his cap on. "I say we hit the road and get to the police station first. You need to take care of anything before we leave?"

"I just walked Jake, so I'm good to go." She reached for the remote. "I'd hoped to catch the weather report, but I don't suppose that matters now."

As she started to turn off the television, a commercial came on. Priscilla almost groaned aloud as she saw Victor Fox's face splashed across her TV screen. "Ugh. Speak of the devil. It's that commercial again. Victor Fox, advertising his used car lot. Have you seen it?"

Gerald glanced at the TV. "Yeah, just the other day. I don't know why you're so hard on Victor, Priscilla. He's come a long way since he gave up politics."

"Gave it up? He lost, Gerald. That's not the same thing. I honestly think the man sounds more like a politician now than he did when he was a politician. He wants us to vote his car lot number one on the island? No way."

"He's just trying a new marketing strategy."

"Hmm. You would think he'd learn from his loss not to take a politician's approach on this latest venture of his."

"I honestly think it's all he knows." Gerald's brow rose.

Priscilla found herself distracted by something in the commercial. She caught a glimpse of Victor standing in front of a classic car in a lovely shade of lemon yellow. "Whoa. Did you know he sells classics?"

Gerald shook his head. "Nope."

She clicked off the TV and turned to face him. "It's just weird. I didn't realize he was in the classic car business too."

"He might be looking for some new way to make money. He's divorced now. Probably paying alimony. But we don't really have time to talk about Victor. Let's get to the police station, shall we? I want to ask the chief some questions about the ferry service. We'll probably have to get the Steamship Authority involved."

"Mm-hmm." Priscilla grabbed her purse and followed on Gerald's heels to the door. She couldn't stop thinking about Eliza. Should they call her...or not?

With Gerald now sprinting across the front lawn, she decided that would have to be a question for another time.

CHAPTER THREE

Ten minutes after leaving her house, Priscilla and Gerald arrived at the police station. She parked her car in the spot next to his SUV and climbed out.

"Brr. I'm glad I brought my heavy coat." She pulled it tight and followed him inside.

Gerald went ahead of her to ask to speak to Hank Westin, Tisbury's police chief, and she waited, making small talk with Gabrielle Grimes, who manned the front desk. Priscilla could hardly believe her eyes when all three of her cousins came marching in.

Joan rushed her way. "Oh, Priscilla, Trudy told me about the car. I can't even imagine how I'd feel if I lost my new car. Awful."

"Someone stole it from Gerald's garage?" Gail asked. "How did it happen?"

"I see bad news travels fast around here." Priscilla fought the temptation to slap herself on the forehead. "Trudy, I really wish you hadn't—"

"Oh, I didn't tell them on purpose." Fine lines formed around Trudy's eyes. "See, Joan showed up at my place just as I was pulling out of the driveway."

Joan nodded. "I could tell from the look in her eyes something had happened, so I wouldn't let her leave until she told me. Then

I called Gail right away. We didn't want you to go through this alone, Priscilla. You need our help."

"What am I, chopped liver?" Gerald approached and stopped directly in front of them. He put his hands on his hips as he faced the ladies.

Trudy laughed, then turned her attention to Priscilla. "But, really, you need our support right now."

"What we need is discretion." Gerald lowered his voice to a whisper and leaned forward. "The fewer people who hear about this, the better. We don't know who we can trust at this point."

The front door of the police department swung open, allowing cold air to rush inside. A couple of officers walked in with a big white box from Candy's bakery. They brushed by Priscilla and the others, deep in conversation.

Trudy leaned against the wall. "Well, this is a fine kettle of fish. Is that an accusation, Gerald O'Bannon? You know you can trust all of us."

Before he could respond, Priscilla's phone rang. She pulled it from her purse and swallowed hard when she saw Eliza's name on the screen. She whispered a prayer asking the Lord to guide her. If the right opportunity came up to tell her friend about the missing car, she would do it. But the timing had to be perfect.

"The strangest thing is happening on this end, Priscilla." Eliza's words sounded a bit breathless. Rushed.

"What's that?" Priscilla half-expected Eliza to dive into a story about the car going missing.

"Remember Sally Jenson, the lady who transported the Bel Air to the island for us?"

Priscilla's heart skipped a beat. "Of course. I met her at Gerald's place yesterday afternoon. Nice lady."

"Very. This is so fascinating. She stayed overnight at the Bluffs."

"Anna's place? Where the wedding is being held?"

All the cousins leaned in a bit closer, as if trying to hear the conversation. Priscilla shooed them away.

"Yep. She's staying a few extra days for some R&R. Isn't that funny?"

"R&R at the B&B. Cute."

Eliza laughed. "Okay, you got a laugh out of me, Priscilla, and I really needed that today. I think I've been getting too wound up these past few days. Feels like I've been working on wedding plans for years, yet here we are in the eleventh hour and the list seems longer than ever. Stress will do that to you, I suppose."

"Yes, relax, honey. Remember I'm here to take the stress for you."

"Oh, Priscilla, you don't know how much I appreciate that! I'm so scatterbrained right now, I don't know if I'm coming or going."

"You're going…to be the prettiest bride on the island. You just relax and enjoy the next few days."

Priscilla decided right then and there she would tell Eliza about the missing car. No point in letting this drag on. She would get this off her conscience right away.

"Eliza?"

"Yes?"

"Listen, there's something I want to tell you. It's really important I let you know that—"

"Oh, Priscilla, I have to go. That's Carson calling. I was talking to him earlier and our conversation was interrupted. We ran into a little problem with the marriage license. They spelled his last name wrong. Can you believe it? Anyway, I don't want to leave him hanging."

"Of course. We'll talk later."

Priscilla ended the call, shoved the phone in her purse, and looked up to discover the cousins and Gerald staring at her.

"Well?" Trudy asked, hands raised in questioning fashion.

"Everything okay?" Gerald asked.

"Yes, everything's fine. One item of interest—the gal who delivered the car is staying at the Bluffs B&B, so we don't have to worry that she might've taken the vehicle."

"Maybe she stayed to throw off suspicion," Joan suggested.

"Yes, maybe she's getting in line right now to board the ferry," Gail added. "This makes me more nervous than ever."

"That doesn't make a lick of sense to me," Trudy said. "If she stole the car—and who knows if she did or didn't—why not just flee the island yesterday afternoon when she had the chance? Or, better yet, under the cover of darkness on the final ferry yesterday evening?"

"For that matter, if she wanted to steal the car, why did she deliver it to the island in the first place?" Gerald asked. "She could've just taken it in Boston."

"Good point." Priscilla released a slow breath.

"How did she leave your place, Gerald?" Trudy asked.

"In a cab," he responded.

"Maybe I should contact the cab company to see if they took her anyplace else before going to the B&B," Priscilla suggested. "That might be a good place to start."

Joan rested her hand on Priscilla's arm. "It's not your problem. Leave it to the police."

"I would love to see that car returned before the wedding day, that's all." Priscilla sighed. "I can't bear the idea that Eliza put so much time and effort into the restoration only to have it stolen out from under her just before the big day."

"You're a good friend, Priscilla." Gail gave her a sympathetic look. "That's all I've got to say about that. You've got a stick-to-it spirit that I admire."

"I just care about Eliza, that's all. She used a big chunk of her savings on that car. And don't even get me started on how much the renovations cost. You would be shocked. She went with one of the top restoration companies in Boston—Romano's. You don't want to know how much she spent there. A lot more than planned, for sure."

Joan sighed. "The car must mean a lot to her then."

"More than you know. It's a lifelong dream. And remember, ladies, this is her first—and hopefully only—wedding. She wants it to be perfect. Giving a gift like this car is something she's been passionate about from the get-go."

Before she could say anything further, Hank Westin, the Tisbury police chief, showed up. He took one look at the crowd and his eyes narrowed. "Folks, I hear you want to see me?"

All the ladies started talking on top of one another.

Hank put his hand up. "One at a time. Could you name a spokesman, please? That should simplify matters."

The cousins pointed to Priscilla, and her heart skipped a beat.

"Fine." Hank gestured to his office. "Come with me, please."

Priscilla released another slow breath and tried to calm herself as she followed on the police chief's heels toward his office. Hopefully he could help them straighten this thing out in a hurry.

CHAPTER FOUR

Priscilla and the others traveled as a team to the police chief's office, a tiny space with a cluttered desk and dusty framed certificates on the wall. Judging from the pile of papers on the desk, this was one busy man.

Gerald and Gail opted to stand, offering the three chairs to Priscilla, Joan, and Trudy. Hank took his seat then brushed crumbs from his desk and tossed a dirty napkin in the trash. "Now, let's start at the beginning."

Priscilla spent the next several minutes telling the tale. She started with the purchase of the vehicle, then shared about the renovations, finally adding information about the transport to the island. Gerald finished up where she left off, offering details about the car's disappearance from his garage.

"So, let me get this straight." The police chief reached for a pencil and rolled it in his fingers. "You have reason to believe a car—"

"A 1954 Bel Air convertible, surf green with white interior," Priscilla chimed in. "Gorgeous, by the way. You'd love it."

"Right. A 1954 convertible has gone missing, possibly taken off the island. And you need our help to contact the Steamship

Authority to make sure a car matching that description hasn't been taken off the island via ferry. Did I get this right?"

"That's it, exactly." Priscilla leaned back in her chair. "I'm available to assist you as well, though my time is more limited, now that I'm coordinating Eliza and Carson's wedding."

Chief Westin's eyes narrowed and he leaned forward to put his elbows on the desk. "Mrs. Grant, as I have told you so many times in the past, these matters are best left in the hands of trained officers. I really don't think—"

"Don't think you can manage this in time to get that car back before the wedding day," Trudy interjected. "Without Priscilla's help, I mean. Now, admit it, Hank, Priscilla has more than proven herself over the last eighteen months. How many times has she figured out something that had you guys stumped?"

"Well, I certainly don't see—"

"Right. I don't think you see her value, either." Trudy crossed her arms at her chest, as if daring the poor fellow to speak. "But trust me, she's going to figure this out. She'll get that car back in time for Eliza and Carson's big day. And you know she'll somehow wheedle the information out of the Steamship Authority, with or without your help. So, you might as well work with her so you can receive at least partial credit for solving this crime. You don't want Priscilla to get all the glory, do you?"

Hank rubbed his forehead, as if dealing with a headache. "Are you done now?"

"I could go on." A quirky smile tipped up the edges of Trudy's lips. "But I think that will do for now."

All four women stared at the police chief until he tugged at his collar. "Is it warm in here, or am I just feeling the effects of being cornered by you four?"

"Not warm to me," Gail said. "But then again, my body acclimates well to the weather, hot or cold."

"I'm fine," Joan added.

"I'm perfectly comfortable," Trudy said.

Gerald just offered a shrug.

"Now, how are we going to fix this, Hank?" Priscilla asked. "What can we do? Besides contacting the folks who run the ferry, I mean."

"Let's start with the person who delivered the car." Hank turned to face his computer and started typing. "I'll need her name and contact information. I would also like to know how she left the island. If she arrived in the Bel Air, how did she leave?"

"Funny you should ask about her. I just got a call from Eliza letting me know that Sally Jenson—that's her name—stayed on the island last night. She got a room at the Bluffs B&B, same place the wedding is set to take place. Don't you find that coincidental?"

"Not really. Getting on and off the island is a lengthy process, what with having to make appointments to take the ferry. A lot of people stay overnight because day trips are complicated, and there are only so many places to choose from, especially in the off season."

"Especially if you don't have a car." Priscilla paused. "Now that I think about it, it's a little strange that she didn't have someone follow her on delivery day in a separate vehicle."

"Maybe someone did but they didn't want to pay the fee to bring the car onto the island via the ferry?" the officer suggested. "Maybe she plans to walk on board the ferry, cross the Sound, then meet someone in Woods Hole to drive her back."

"Good thinking, Chief." Trudy pointed at him. "Extra points for you."

"Definitely a possibility." Priscilla paused to think this notion through. "But at any rate, her name is Sally Jenson and she's with a company called In Motion. Very nice lady. Nothing about her seemed off. And like I said, she's at Anna's B&B right now. Or at least she was."

The chief shifted his gaze from the computer to Priscilla. "Do you have her information?"

"I do. She gave it to me when she dropped the car off." Priscilla reached inside her purse and fished around until she located Sally's card. "Here you go."

"I'll give Anna a call first and ask a few questions. Then I'll call..." He glanced at the card in his hand. "I won't let her know the car is missing. I'll just see if she spills any information."

"Great idea," Priscilla said.

"Can you describe this Sally Jenson?"

"Sure. She's in her mid to late forties, I would guess. Short blonde hair. I notice she tucks it behind her ears a lot. She was wearing a dark gray coat, unzipped, and I could see a T-shirt underneath with some band name on the front. Of course, this was yesterday. I have no idea what she's wearing today."

"Sally is a little…" Gerald's brow wrinkled. "Rough around the edges."

"Yes." Priscilla nodded. "But not in a bad way. Just tough. Sure of herself. Not delicate or prissy, that's for sure. Oh, and she was wearing jeans. I forgot to mention that."

"Okay. Anything else we need to know about her?" the chief asked. "Any distinguishing marks?"

Priscilla thought about it before responding. "Oh, yes. I remember now seeing a tattoo on the inside of her wrist. Not sure which wrist. But it was a tattoo of a bird. I think. Didn't get a close look at it."

"I'll let my guys know so they can be on the lookout for her. And we'll check with the Steamship Authority to make sure a Bel Air convertible hasn't left via ferry. As I'm sure you're aware, no cars come or go from this island without a record from those folks. If that car left by ferry, there will be a paper trail."

"And if it didn't?" Gerald looked concerned.

"Then one can only surmise that the car is still on the island." Hank paused and turned back to his computer to type something else. "And if it's here, we'll find it, I can assure you. Martha's Vineyard is only so big, after all. And we're talking about an unusual-looking vehicle, so it won't be hard to spot."

"Unless the thief paints it," Gail suggested. "Did anyone think of that?"

"It's been gone less than twenty-four hours," Gerald said.

The police chief continued to type. "Yes. Hopefully no changes have been made to the vehicle."

Priscilla pulled her phone out of her purse, swiped to a photo of the car, and showed it to Hank, who released a whistle. "Wow. A lot of work went into that one, for sure. It would never cross my mind to paint that vehicle. It looks brand-spanking new."

"I once painted a car," Trudy said. "Ugly rust-colored Ford Pinto."

"Was that the before color or after?" Gerald teased.

"Before. I painted it bright green. My husband always hated that green, now that I think of it. Which makes me wonder how Carson will feel about the color Eliza chose. Might be quite a ruckus if he hates it as much as Dan hated the green."

"I love the color of my new car," Joan said. "It would be a shame to cover up something so pretty. Makes no sense at all."

Hank raised his hand. "I apologize for interrupting this little chat, but are you telling me that the groom-to-be, who owns said Bel Air, doesn't know that he owns a Bel Air?"

"Oh, that's right." Priscilla clamped a hand over her mouth, then pulled it away. "And he can't know, either. Eliza would kill me if he found out."

Hank typed something into his computer then faced the group. "So, I can't ask one of the owners of the MIA car about his MIA car until after his wedding?"

"Well, even then I'm not sure I'd mention it, because Eliza probably won't tell him until later." Priscilla paused. "Then again, she doesn't know yet, either."

"Doesn't know she owns a 1954 Bel Air convertible, or doesn't know it's gone missing?"

"Doesn't know it's gone missing." Priscilla twisted her hands together, her nerves getting the best of her. "I know this is all very confusing."

"Sure is." The police chief scratched his head. "But I've come to expect that with you, Priscilla, if you'll pardon my saying so."

"Eliza Jamison definitely knows we had the car yesterday," Gerald chimed in. "She came to my house yesterday afternoon to check it out before it went into the garage. She wanted to make sure everything was perfect."

"Yes, that's right. She paid for it and arranged all the details regarding the restoration and transportation." Priscilla paused for breath. "But she doesn't know it's missing, and we'd like to keep it that way, at least for now."

The worry lines in Hank's forehead deepened. "I don't recall ever having a case like this, where the owner didn't know his or her car was missing."

Priscilla shrugged. "But if we tell her we've lost it already, she might have a nervous breakdown. Have you ever worked with a bride three days before her wedding?"

"Never. Nor do I plan to." Hank asked several more questions, including a few about the transport company. And though he didn't seem to understand everything Priscilla shared—what with her words coming out so quickly—she kept going. No point in leaving anything out, just in case.

The chief gave her a pensive look when she finally came up for air. "So, just to reiterate: I can't ask Eliza or Carson anything about this car?" He closed his notebook. "That's what you're saying."

"Correct. Or you'll spoil the surprise."

"And/or run the risk of Eliza having an emotional breakdown before her big day," Trudy chimed in. "A brokenhearted bride is not a pretty sight."

"Well, I certainly don't want to be responsible for a bride-to-be having a nervous breakdown," Hank said. "So, for now I will agree to turn over other stones and avoid the car owners. There might come a day, however, when I have no choice."

"By then I will have worked up the courage to tell Eliza myself," Priscilla said. "I really feel like it needs to come from me, since I've been her confidante."

"Right." The chief squinted as he gazed her way. "And just for the record, Mrs. Grant, where were you last night? If you don't mind my asking."

"I was at home in bed, of course."

"I can attest to that," Gerald said. "I called her home phone last night and we spoke at length."

"Mm-hmm. I see." The officer scribbled something in his notebook.

"So, now what?" Priscilla asked. "Does the investigation begin right away?"

"We'll do the best we can to get right on this." Hank rose and walked to the door, as if nudging them all out of his office. "I'll be sending a couple of officers to look over your garage, Gerald. Say around four?"

"Sure." Gerald nodded. "I'll make a point of being there. I've gone over it with a fine-tooth comb, but maybe I've missed something."

"Hope so." The chief turned to face the ladies. "I'll be in touch. Have a nice day."

They walked to the front hallway, where Gerald paused. "I'm so sorry this happened on my watch, ladies. I feel really bad."

"What could you have done?" Gail asked. "Put an alarm on your garage? Padlocked it?"

"Maybe." He shrugged. "Anyway, I'm sorry I can't be of more assistance, but I have to get back to work." He glanced Priscilla's way. "Just promise me this: you ladies won't go to the Steamship Authority and ask a bunch of questions. Let the police do their job."

"Us? Interfere with police work? How dare you suggest such a thing?" Trudy laughed.

"We won't, Gerald. I promise." Priscilla gave his hand a squeeze, and they said their goodbyes. She turned her attention back to her cousins. "So, where do we go from here?"

"I don't know about the rest of you, but I'm ready for an early lunch." Gail put her hand on her stomach. "I fixed breakfast for Dad but didn't get a chance to eat it."

Priscilla was suddenly struck with the most wonderful idea. "Hey, I know. Let's go to the Black Dog. That way we can keep an eye on the cars coming and going from the ferry. If we spot a surf-green convertible, we'll—"

"We'll what, Priscilla? Jump the driver and insist he or she give the car back?" Joan shook her head. "We can't do that. Besides, we promised Gerald we would let the police do their work."

"We are letting them do their work. We're just having an innocent lunch out, is all. And keeping our eyes wide open."

"They have the yummiest chowder at the Black Dog. And the views of the ferry landing are terrific." Trudy rambled on and on about their upcoming lunch, but Priscilla didn't hear much of it. She couldn't stop worrying about the missing car and wondering if she should call Eliza to share the news.

Maybe a few more hours wouldn't hurt. Perhaps, with a little help from her cousins, she might just locate that missing Bel Air. One could hope, anyway.

CHAPTER FIVE

P oor Hank. I think we really confused him." Priscilla shook her head as she thought back over the conversation they'd just had with the police chief.

Trudy nodded as the waiter gestured for them to take a seat at their table. "Right. I'm not altogether sure he believes the car even exists."

"But I showed him a picture. It's real, all right." Priscilla plopped down into one of the chairs with a sigh, and her gaze shifted to a man at the next table who was eating a lobster roll. Yum. "Though, I'm beginning to wonder, myself. I mean, the car was on the island less than a day. Was it just a figment of my over-active imagination? Maybe I dreamed the whole thing."

"If it's a figment, it photographs well." Gail sniffed the air. "Now, what are we going to have for lunch, ladies? My stomach is turning inside out. Gumbo? Lobster rolls? Fish tacos? The food here is amazing."

They opened their menus, but Priscilla had already made up her mind. The delicious aroma of gumbo permeated the room, overwhelming her senses. Then she found herself distracted as a waitress delivered a large platter of fried shrimp to a young man at a nearby table. "On second thought, I'll have what he's having."

"And plenty of it," Gail said, laughing.

The waiter returned a couple of minutes later to take their orders, and the cousins dove into a conversation about the weather. Priscilla couldn't seem to stay focused, however. She found herself torn between wanting to call Eliza to tell her about the missing car and hoping it would turn up. What was Chief Westin doing at this very minute? Calling Anna at the Bluffs? Talking to the Steamship Authority? Chatting with Sally Jenson, playing it cool?

Thank goodness the food arrived in short order. It served as a lovely distraction, especially the french fries, which were crisp and golden, still hot to the touch. Priscilla picked one up and bit off the end, sighing as the salty goodness hit her taste buds.

Perfect choice. She looked around the table at the various offerings. A little bit of everything.

Through the window she caught sight of the cars lining up to get on the ferry. It still mesmerized her that so many vehicles could squeeze into such a seemingly small space. Priscilla kept her eyes peeled for the Bel Air convertible, but nothing resembling it joined the line of cars headed to Woods Hole. A little farther away she saw a cluster of pedestrians lining up to board. Was Sally in that group, perhaps? She squinted to get a better look but didn't see anyone familiar.

"Did we lose you, Priscilla?" Joan asked before taking a spoonful of her gumbo.

"No. I'm just distracted. I feel like I let Eliza down. That car means so much to her."

"It's not your fault. And it's not Gerald's either, though I can tell he feels guilty. These things happen."

"Not to me, they don't. Automobiles don't go missing from garages in my world." She sighed and took another bite of her shrimp.

"Maybe we should change the subject," Gail suggested. "Let's talk about Valentine's Day. Anyone have any big plans for tomorrow?"

This led to an upbeat conversation among Priscilla's cousins about how they planned to celebrate.

Joan fussed with her napkin, then dabbed her lips. "What about you, Priscilla? You haven't told us your plans yet."

"Who, me?" She shrugged.

"Sure, you." Joan flashed a smile. "Has Gerald asked you to be his valentine yet?"

Priscilla shook her head. "We're not in junior high, silly."

"You don't have to be in junior high to have a Valentine," Trudy chimed in. "Dan and I are still romantic, even after all these years."

"Well, yes." Priscilla brushed a couple of crumbs from her blouse. "But you gals know Gerald. He's not overly mushy. That's just not a side of him I expect to see."

Even as she spoke the words, Priscilla realized Gerald did have a romantic side. It showed in the gentle way he spoke to her, in the way he held her hand. It was apparent when he shared pieces of his heart with her in quiet conversation.

Not that these ladies needed to know any of that.

Still, she had to wonder if Gerald had forgotten about Valentine's Day. It hadn't come up in conversation at all. Likely, he just thought she was too busy with all the wedding plans. Yes, surely that was it.

"Ladies, it's not like that with us. We're just..."

"Friends?" Gail asked.

"Well, maybe a little more than that."

Trudy quirked a brow. "Boyfriend and girlfriend?"

"That sounds too high-schoolish."

"Exactly." Trudy rested her palms on the table. "So, why don't you just say what it is, Priscilla? You're falling for him. He's falling for you."

Despite her best attempts to change the subject, the rest of the meal was spent talking about Valentine's Day. Priscilla continued to eat, her gaze firmly planted on the vehicles lining up to get on the ferry. After a while, the car-watching grew tiresome. She found it difficult to stay focused. The same yummy smells that had drawn her in now made her feel a little nauseous.

Joan looked her way, fine lines forming around her narrowed eyes. "You okay over there?"

"Yeah. I think I'm just exhausted. And disappointed about the car, of course. I'm letting Eliza down."

"On the contrary, you've gone above and beyond." Gail wiped her lips with her napkin. "I would argue with anyone who says otherwise."

"Just pray that the police locate that car, ladies."

Joan nodded. "You know we will, Priscilla."

Trudy pushed her plate away and leaned back in her chair. Her gaze shot to the window. "We've been here for over an hour, and I haven't seen anything that even remotely looks like a classic car."

"Me neither." Gail swiped one of Priscilla's french fries. "But the food is great. You have to admit that."

"Very good." Priscilla wiped her hands on her napkin, then took a sip of her water. "I must confess, I've never been much of a car-watcher before. There are a lot of vehicle types out there."

"If you could choose to drive off into the sunset in the car of your dreams, what would it be?" Trudy asked.

"Oh, that's easy—a limo." Gail's eyes took on a dreamy look. "I've always wanted to do that, just for fun."

"I'm taking careful notes." Priscilla winked. "What about you, Joan?"

"When Allan and I got married we just drove away from the church in his sedan. It wasn't much, but our friends fixed it up with shaving cream and toilet paper and stuff like that. The usual wedding paraphernalia." A brief smile flitted across her lips, and Priscilla wondered if her cousin was reminiscing.

"If I had it all to do over again, I'd take a cab," Trudy said. "That way no one could mess up my beautiful car. Speaking of which, if we ever locate this Bel Air, how are you going to keep folks from decorating it?"

"Oh, that's easy," Priscilla countered. "No one knows it belongs to the happy couple. It's a complete surprise."

"Unless we don't find it. Then it's going to be a surprise of a different sort."

Before Priscilla could get depressed once more about the missing car, the waiter showed up and asked if they wanted dessert.

"I couldn't eat another thing." Joan ran her hands across her stomach.

"Me neither." Gail swiped another one of Priscilla's fries and winked.

The waiter left to prepare their checks, and Priscilla resumed the conversation. "We'll find that car, and Eliza and Carson will have their sunset moment." She spoke with as much determination as she could muster.

"If anyone can do it, you can." Gail reached for her tea glass. "You're an old pro now, cuz."

Priscilla laughed. "Well, you're half right."

This response got everyone tickled. Then the waiter returned, bills in hand.

"I have a question." Joan reached for her purse and pulled out her wallet. "Might be a little bit off the subject, but where do you suppose this whole concept of driving off into the sunset came from, anyway?"

"No idea." Trudy set her purse on the table and started fishing through it. From what Priscilla could tell, she was having a hard time finding her wallet.

Priscilla pulled out her debit card and laid it on the table. "I think it comes from the days of old westerns when the cowboy would ride off on his horse into the sunset."

"Was there a woman on the horse next to him?" Gail asked. "Riding sidesaddle?"

"I don't really remember," Priscilla responded. "I just seem to equate sunsets with cowboys."

"Sunsets are nice," Gail said.

"So are cowboys." Trudy winked.

This, of course, got the ladies tickled again, just as the waiter arrived to take their payments.

"There won't be any cowboys at this wedding to my knowledge," Priscilla said. "But the sunset is supposed to be glorious on Saturday. According to the weatherman, it's due to set at 5:17 p.m. Eliza's wedding starts at three with half an hour for the service and another hour and fifteen minutes for the reception. The bride and groom will leave the building at exactly 5:10 so she can reveal the car and climb inside by exactly 5:17. Trust me when I say everything is planned out to the minute."

"Except the part where there is no car because someone stole it." Gail put her wallet back in her purse. "Couldn't have predicted that one."

Priscilla returned her gaze to the line of cars on the other side of the window. "We're counting on getting the car back in time so she can have her moment."

"I sure hope so. Though I'm not sure how I feel about that whole riding off into the sunset thing, myself," Joan said. "Too lovey-dovey, and we know from our own personal experiences that marriage isn't easy." She shifted her gaze to the table. "Not that being a widow is any easier. I wouldn't have wished this on anyone."

"Me neither." Priscilla patted her cousin's hand.

Trudy shifted her position in her chair. "I do find it a little odd that love stories always seem to end at that moment, with the couple driving off into the vast unknown, toward a glorious sunset, filled with color, filled with possibilities. Why don't stories show the stuff that happens after the fact? Like when he leaves the toilet seat up in the middle of the night only you don't know about it, so you go in there and sit down and almost fall in?"

"That's not very romantic, Trudy," Gail said. "I can understand why authors leave that part out."

"I just don't get why they lead readers—or viewers—to believe that everyone lives happily ever after, that's all. Marriage is tough. There are bills to pay, differences of opinion, and lots of other things. And don't even get me started on politics. It's a struggle to keep a united front sometimes. Yes, you're in love, but sometimes that love looks different twenty or thirty years later. It morphs."

Priscilla understood where Trudy was coming from, of course. Her marriage to Gary had certainly changed from the day she'd walked down the aisle as a doe-eyed bride. Life was hard. She and Gary had faced some serious challenges together, especially after his diagnosis. But she wouldn't trade any of it, blissful or painful.

"I think the point of the sunset is to offer people hope," she said after thinking it through. "When you're gazing over the horizon like that, you're trusting that God has the unseen things under control. He knows what's on the other side. And, as long as you walk hand-in-hand, everything will turn out okay."

Her cousins turned and stared at her.

"Wow. Being in love has turned you into a philosopher," Joan said.

Trudy winked. "Or a romantic."

"I think it's sweet." Gail rested her hand on Priscilla's arm. "And you're right. If anyone needs hope, married couples do."

"Or soon-to-be-married couples." Trudy's eyes narrowed to slits as she glanced Gail's way.

"Has Eliza decided on shrimp scampi or salmon puffs for the first course at her wedding?" Gail asked. "Tilly tells me she's taking forever to make up her mind."

"Tilly's catering the wedding?" Joan looked surprised by this news. "I had no idea."

"Smooth move, changing the subject like that." Trudy elbowed Gail. "But I do hope Eliza chooses the shrimp. I'm so burnt out on salmon puffs. If the salmon isn't fresh, they can be just awful."

"Might not be the best choice to choose shellfish." Joan's brow wrinkled. "Remember what happened to Tom Winthrop at the Sizemores' wedding a couple of months back? He ate the blackened fish, not realizing there was shrimp in the cream sauce. They had to use an EpiPen."

"Okay, salmon puffs it is."

"I heard she's having red roses," Trudy said.

"On the menu?" Gail looked stunned.

"No, silly. The bouquets. Do you think it's overdone to have red roses in February?"

"Just because it's Valentine's weekend?" Joan said. "No way. Red roses are always in style."

"That's what I told her when she asked," Priscilla said. "She doesn't want to come across as cliché."

Gail shook her head. "Trust me, she's one of a kind. There's nothing cliché about her."

The waiter returned to finalize their bills, then thanked them for visiting the Black Dog.

As she pushed her chair back, Gail glanced at her phone. "Oh, I can't believe how late it is. I need to get home and check on Dad. He's still a little weak, and I don't like to leave him alone for long periods of time."

Trudy put her hand up. "Just one more question before we go, Priscilla. If you don't mind."

"Sure." Priscilla brushed her palms on her slacks. "What is it?"

"It's none of my business, really, but it's been bothering me." Trudy opened a compact and looked at her lips. "Eliza worked for Victor Fox for years. We all know he paid her very little. And now she works for Carson in a secretarial position, right?" Trudy pulled a lipstick tube from her purse and carefully applied it to her lips with the precision of a master artist.

"Right." Priscilla rose and grabbed her purse.

The other ladies followed suit.

Trudy slung her purse strap over her shoulder and took a couple of steps away from the table. "So, I'm guessing her salary's not huge, certainly not big enough to purchase a car like that. Not that it's any of my business."

"Oh, I see," Priscilla said. "Well, I wondered the same thing, to be honest, but I think I've got it all figured out. Not that it's any of my business, either. And what I'm about to say is pure speculation, so I hope we can keep it between us."

The other ladies all nodded in agreement as they worked their way through the tables to the door. Priscilla took a mint from the common bowl at the front desk.

"Eliza was a caregiver for her mom during the final months of her life." She unwrapped the mint and popped it in her mouth.

"Right," Gail said. "She and I spoke about that many times. Both of us being caregivers and all."

"Understandable," Joan said. "If I recall, Anna rented Eliza's mom a room at the B&B so she could avoid going into a nursing home."

Priscilla nodded. "That's one reason Eliza decided to get married at the B&B, because Anna was so kind to them during that season."

"Bittersweet." Joan pushed open the door of the restaurant, and the ladies stepped out into the sunlight.

Priscilla reached into her purse for her sunglasses. "Eliza's mom has been gone a few months now and, from what I can gather, had a hefty life insurance policy in place. She left quite a sum to Eliza, who's an only child."

"Oh, I see." Gail shielded her eyes with her hand. "Makes sense."

"Eliza invested some of it but used quite a bit to purchase and restore the car."

"Wouldn't Carson know, then?" Joan asked. "Doesn't he handle her investments? That's his line of work, right?"

"Right. I haven't quite figured all of that out, but, as I said, it's not really my business." Priscilla shrugged.

Trudy's eyes narrowed. "I don't know Eliza as well as you do, Priscilla. Do you suppose there's any possibility—any at all—that she insured the car and then arranged for it to go missing so she could collect on the insurance monies?"

The very idea shocked Priscilla. How could anyone accuse her friend of such a thing? "Trudy, if you knew her as I do, you would know that's impossible. First of all, why would she go to all the trouble to fix up a car only to have it stolen? And why have it stolen before the wedding instead of after? Wouldn't the insurance scam scenario make more sense if the groom had already seen—and fallen in love with—the car?"

Trudy shrugged. "I guess. Just thinking out loud."

The ladies parted ways, but Priscilla couldn't stop thinking about their discussion. She turned her attention, one last time, to a new line of cars preparing to board the ferry. Had the police contacted the Steamship Authority yet? Were there any leads on the missing Bel Air? Was there even the slightest of chances that she would see that car again in time for the big day?

Perhaps she could do a little snooping on her own. Contact the restoration company in Boston for a chat about Sally Jenson. Talk to Gerald's neighbors to see if they'd noticed anything unusual. Maybe, if she worked hard enough, she'd find that missing car so that Eliza could celebrate in style Saturday evening.

CHAPTER SIX

Priscilla left the ferry landing at two o'clock, ready to head home. There were still so many details to take care of, but first she must swing by Eliza's place to share the news about the missing convertible. It would be hard, but she had no choice.

As she drove down Harbor Lane, Priscilla caught a glimpse of Gerald's SUV. She waved, and he turned his vehicle in her direction. Thinking he must have news to share, she looked for a place to pull over. Out of the blue, her car began to sputter.

"Oh no! Not again!"

The sputtering continued, and even grew worse.

"What in the world?"

She gripped the steering wheel and prayed the vehicle wouldn't stall. Why would a four-year-old SUV start acting up? Didn't make sense. On the other hand, with the risk of a stall now becoming very real, she'd better get off the road.

Aha. Just ahead she saw Victor Fox's Pre-Owned Cars coming into view. Perfect. She eased her way into the right lane, taking note of Victor's brightly colored banners waving in the afternoon breeze. The wind whipped the flags back and forth, their colorful triangles in constant motion.

As she drew close, Priscilla tapped her brakes to read the various signs he'd posted along the entrance to the lot: *A Car for All Budgets.* Not bad. *Bring in a Lemon and Take Out a Peach.* A little cheesy, but typical Victor. *Eye It— Try It— Buy It!* Nope. *Don't Dream It, Drive It!* Okay, now he sounded like a politician once again.

Her gaze landed on the one next to the entrance. *Find Your Own Road.* That one really left an impression on her. Wasn't that what she had done—traveled all the way from Kansas and discovered a new path for her life on Martha's Vineyard?

She drove into the lot and found a place to park just as her car began to sputter once again. Gerald pulled into the space next to hers.

Priscilla climbed out and gave him a curious look. "Everything okay?"

"Yes. Just wanted to let you know that Hank talked to the Steamship Authority and found out that the Bel Air hasn't left the island on the ferry."

"Yet," she added.

"If they do see it, they'll stop the driver immediately." He took several steps toward her. "Was that your car I heard as we pulled in?"

"Yes." She did her best not to sigh aloud. "It's still making that noise. I've had it at the mechanic's shop three times, but they still can't get it in working order. I'm tired of throwing good money after bad."

"I could look at it for you," he said. "Maybe after the wedding, when things slow down?"

His compassion warmed her heart. Priscilla couldn't help herself. She wrapped her arms around his neck and gave him a hug. "Thank you for coming to my rescue."

He hugged her back. "You're welcome. If this is my reward, I'm happy to be of service."

Priscilla released her hold on him and stood back to take a closer look at the car lot. "I didn't really have plans to stop here, but maybe it's fate."

"Fate?"

"Sure. You know I've never trusted Victor. He deals in used cars. That Bel Air was a used car. Maybe he—"

"C'mon now, Scilla. You don't really think he had something to do with this."

"Well, you did say he saw the car in your garage."

"For a second. Maybe two."

"I wouldn't put anything past that guy, that's all." She pointed to the sign by the front door of the showroom. "See that? 'We stand behind every car we sell.'"

"What's wrong with that?" he asked.

"Mildred told me she has a friend who bought a car from Victor and it broke down on the second day. So, the slogan just makes sense. There's no other choice but to stand, since the cars break down almost as soon as you buy them."

"That's not very nice, Priscilla. He's working really hard to rebuild his credibility. We've been praying to that end."

"I know, I know." Shame washed over her. "I'm sorry, Gerald. I know your hopes are very high for Victor. I'll catch up."

She stared out at the vast expanse of vehicles in front of her. She took a few steps farther into the car lot.

"What are you doing?" Gerald asked.

"Just looking. If there's anything to hide—and I'm not saying there is—maybe we'll find it."

"Just be careful. Victor might see you and—"

Gerald didn't even get the words out before a salesman approached and offered to help them.

Priscilla waved him off with a dismissive, "We're just looking, thanks." The fellow disappeared back into the showroom, a frown on his face.

She and Gerald walked among the cars. Her gaze traveled to a dark blue SUV. She ran her palm along the shimmering hood and then peered in the window.

"That little beauty can be yours today for just twenty-nine nine."

"Wh-what?" She turned to discover Victor Fox standing behind her. "Oh, no thank you. I'm not here to buy a car."

His bright smile faded at once. Just as quickly, he seemed to nudge the edges of his lips up once again. "Well then, how can I help you folks?" He extended his hand and offered Gerald a nod. "Good to see you, my friend."

"Good to see you too, Victor. We're just coming by to ask a few questions about a car. Not one on your lot, but one that's gone missing."

Creases formed on Victor's forehead. "That's intriguing. Would you like to come into my office?"

"Sure." Gerald nodded.

They followed behind Victor, who waved at an incoming customer and then hollered to one of his salesmen to take care of the shopper. Minutes later, Priscilla found herself sitting inside Victor's office. She couldn't help but notice the peppy slogans all over the place. The guy might've come a long way in some areas, but he was still a politician at heart. No doubt about that.

"Now, how can I help you fine people today?" Victor leaned back in his oversized chair, hands behind his head.

Gerald paced the room, then stopped. "I don't know if you heard, Victor, but a beautiful classic car—a 1954 Bel Air convertible—went missing from my garage yesterday."

Victor sat up straight in his chair, his eyes growing wide. "Is that the car I caught a glimpse of yesterday? Surf green and white?"

Gerald nodded. "Yes."

"Are you telling me you bought a 1954 Bel Air from someone other than me?" Victor's eyes clouded over. "Why didn't you let me know you were in the market for a classic? I could've gotten you a better deal than anyplace else in the state. I sell classics too, you know. And I've got a lot of connections."

"It's not my car. Let me explain." Gerald told him about the vehicle's origins, and Victor settled down.

"So, you see, Victor, it's not Gerald's car at all," Priscilla chimed in. "He was just kind enough to let us store it in his garage."

"What does this have to do with me?" Victor asked. "Wait, let me guess. Because I knew where the car was, you think I stole it? Is that how this story goes?"

"We're not saying that." Gerald cleared his throat.

Victor laughed. "If looking at a car makes a person a suspect, then toss me in jail and throw away the key. For that matter, you'll have to arrest all of my customers too. I'd be hard-pressed to look away from a classic car, Gerald. Anyone would be. The only reason I lingered in front of your garage was because I was curious. I'm a car guy. You know that."

"This isn't an accusation, Victor," Priscilla said. She fought the temptation to add, "At least not yet."

"Actually, I was wondering if you noticed anyone else around my place when you were leaving yesterday," Gerald said. "Maybe someone suspicious passing by? Something like that?"

"I saw nothing except a two-second glimpse of a car that looked like a real beauty. Where did your friend get it, anyway? Online?"

"Eliza bought it from an individual online then had it fully restored at a shop in Boston," Priscilla explained.

"Eliza?"

"Yes, she bought it as a wedding gift for Carson. He knows nothing about it, so don't share any of this information, please." Gerald gave Victor a knowing look.

"I just wish she had come to me for help, that's all." Victor shook his head. "Have I pushed away everyone who used to be close to me?"

Priscilla chose not to say anything. Instead, she shifted her gaze to the showroom floor, where several customers were gathered around an oversized red truck, oohing and aahing.

Gerald put his hand on Victor's arm. "Look, all that matters now is that you've got a thriving new business. You've come a long way over the past several months, Victor. Don't let anyone convince you otherwise. I'm proud of the progress you've made, and I know the Lord is too."

Victor nodded, albeit slowly. Then his frown shifted into a slight smile. "Thanks, Gerald. I needed an atta boy today. I just lost a big sale this morning. Really thought I had that one in the bag. Kind of a blow to the old ego."

"Sorry to hear that, my friend. But don't give up. Remember that scripture I shared with you last week: 'He who began a good work in you will carry it on to completion until the day of Christ Jesus.' God always finishes what He starts. Don't forget that."

"Right." Victor's smile was genuine now.

She and Gerald said their goodbyes and headed across the parking lot. Along the way, she caught another glimpse of that dark blue SUV. It shimmered underneath the afternoon sun, and she couldn't help but be drawn back to it. "Do you mind, Gerald? I want to take another peek."

"Really?"

"Just for fun, of course. Not to buy."

"That's what they always say."

She walked over to the car and took a good, long look inside. What would it feel like, she wondered, to sit in the driver's seat?

And look at that monitor on the dash. It was definitely a step up from the car she now drove. Before she could give it another thought, Gerald gestured for her to take a seat inside. He joined her, sitting in the passenger seat.

"Feels good," she said. "Perfect fit." She placed her hands on the steering wheel. "Not too big. Not too small."

"Okay, Goldilocks. Should I wrap it up and have it sent to your house?"

She giggled. "Not just yet, thanks. I have another car on my mind right now—a 1954 Bel Air convertible, to be precise."

"Hey, that reminds me. I thought of something after we left the police station today."

"Oh, what's that?" She rested her right hand on the gearshift.

"I thought of someone else who has a key to my garage."

"Who?"

"Beau Ortmann."

"What? Are you sure? Why does he have a key to your garage?"

"Because he's a handyman, Scilla. He was working on my leaky garage roof a few months ago, remember? That's where his materials were stored, so he locked up every day. I gave him the key to get in and out."

"Ah. Surely you don't think Beau would—"

"I can't imagine it. He didn't even know the car was in there, after all. But I should probably ask him for my key back. It's been months."

"Right. One more thing to consider, I suppose."

She spent a few more minutes looking over the SUV but finally got herself to climb out. "I think I'd better get back to reality here."

She pointed to her vehicle. "I've got a ton of work awaiting me at home. Centerpieces are calling my name."

"Then you must answer." He walked her to her car and gave her a kiss on the cheek. They parted ways; he headed back to work, and she turned her vehicle toward home. As she reached the turn-off, her cell phone rang. The call went to Bluetooth, and within seconds her daughter Rachel's voice greeted her.

"Mom! How are you?"

"Great, hon. Happy to hear your voice. How's the wedding planning going?"

This led to an enthusiastic monologue about bridesmaid dresses from her daughter, whose voice rose a couple of decibels with each ensuing sentence. From the zeal in her tone, Priscilla could sense her excitement. The words pink, rose, and blush came up in the conversation multiple times.

Rachel finally slowed down, speaking on a more even keel. "Mom, I'm enjoying this process so much. Is that weird?"

"What do you mean?" Priscilla asked.

"I never pictured myself as the kind of girl who would get this excited about planning her wedding. I mean, some girls start when they're in junior high. I've got friends who've had their wedding dresses picked out since seventh grade. I was never like that. It was the last thing on my mind. But I'm loving it so much."

"I'm so glad, honey. This should be an enjoyable experience for you."

"It is. Are you enjoying it too? I know you've been working hard to help Eliza pull off the wedding of the century. Feeling more like a wedding planner now?"

"If you'd asked me a few months ago, I would've said no way. But I guess it's like riding a bike. It comes back to you. Not that I plan to take up bike riding anytime soon, so don't get any ideas."

"I won't." Rachel laughed. "But you're bringing back some memories of my childhood."

"Truth is, I'm enjoying helping Eliza with her wedding," Priscilla said. "It's been fun."

"Good. You're definitely hired to help out with mine." Rachel sighed. "It's all so overwhelming. So many details. Food. Cake. Dresses. Order of service." She paused and then shouted, "Oh! I almost forgot to tell you!"

"Forgot to tell me what? And don't scare me like that."

"You'll never believe it! A.J.'s father is springing for a honeymoon in Bermuda."

"Bermuda? Wow. That's amazing."

"Yep. A full week of glorious fun in the sun. I can hardly wait." Rachel dove into a detailed list of all the clothes she planned to pack for her honeymoon. A couple of minutes later she shifted gears and started talking about wedding flowers. Then, about five minutes after that, they had a lengthy conversation about caterers. From there, they dove into a discussion about the wedding party and guest list.

"You know how frugal I am, Mom. We're only having a matron of honor and best man. Keeping it simple."

"That's my girl."

Rachel dove in again, barely coming up for air. After a couple of minutes, she grew quiet. "Mom? You still with me?"

"Hmm?"

"You're kind of quiet. Usually when we talk about wedding stuff, you're fully engaged. Have I lost you?"

"Oh, no, honey. I am a little distracted this morning. Eliza's been on my mind." That was putting it mildly, of course. "Her big day is coming up in three days, you know."

"Oh, that's right. Mom, I'm sorry. I shouldn't have distracted you so close to one wedding by talking about another."

"It's okay, I—"

Rachel went off on a tangent about all the tasks on her plate, but Priscilla didn't hear half of it. She was far too engrossed in the sound of joy in her daughter's voice to worry about all of that just yet. And the fact that Rachel had finally found the love of her life? That notion brought so much joy to Priscilla's heart that she could barely keep the tears from slipping over her lashes.

"Where are you now, Mom? Still driving?"

"Going through town now. I was at Victor's car lot when you called."

"I can think of a thousand places I'd rather be than a car lot." Rachel laughed.

"Me too. I—"

She never got the rest of the words out. A man stepped out into the street directly in front of her car.

CHAPTER SEVEN

Whoa!" Priscilla slammed on her brakes, barely missing the man.

"Mom, you okay?" Rachel's voice reverberated through the car's Bluetooth speaker.

"Yes." Priscilla willed her heart to slow down. "It's the craziest thing. A man stepped right out in front of my car. Didn't even look before leaping."

"Wow."

"Scared me half to death. And I still don't think he realizes what he did. I could've hit him, and he probably wouldn't have known. He was that oblivious." She grew silent, her gaze following the man as he continued across the street. She realized she'd seen him before.

"Have I lost you, Mom? You've gone quiet on me."

"Oh, no. Sorry. Just people-watching."

"Well, Martha's Vineyard is the place for people-watching. My favorite is the guy who wears the sandwich sign promoting snow cones."

"We only see him in the spring and summer. He won't be out for a couple of months."

"Every time I see him I get a craving for a Very Cherry snow cone."

"I prefer the banana."

"Look on the bright side, Mom. If you ever decide to write a book, you'll have lots of material."

"Yes, I will." Priscilla grew silent, keeping her eyes on the man she'd almost hit.

"Hey, I should let you go so you can focus on the road."

"Good idea." She ended the call and pulled her car to the curb, ahead of the man on the opposite side of the street, then tried to slow her heartbeat. The close call had shaken her to the core, but something else had her even more shaken.

"I know you." She whispered the words as she looked into her rearview mirror and watched the man meander down the sidewalk. "Tony Romano. From Boston." She recognized him from the many car photos Eliza had sent her over the past two weeks.

He was a long way from home. What was he doing on Martha's Vineyard on the very day the car he had restored went missing? She had no clue, but was certainly ready to find out.

Priscilla gave the man a closer look. His dark hair provided a stark contrast to the receding hairline. And the scruffy face spoke of someone who hadn't taken the time to shave this morning. Either that, or his facial hair grew at double-speed. In so many ways, he came across as stereotypical—a white T-shirt under a black leather jacket. Loose-fitting jeans. Dark shoes.

These things did nothing to distract her from the somber expression on his face. The Tony Romano Eliza had described was upbeat, pleasant, and focused. Smiling all the time. This guy looked more like someone she would dread meeting up with in a dark alley.

A shiver ran down her spine as she watched him walk into a building with several businesses advertised on the outside, including a dentist, a gift shop, and a Realtor's office.

"What are you up to, Tony Romano?"

Only one way to find out. She pulled her vehicle into the parking lot where it began sputtering again.

She really needed to get her car looked at one more time. Maybe when things slowed down.

Priscilla located a spot near the door. She slipped the car into Park, pulled out the key, and put the poor sputtering thing out of its misery. Then she climbed out of the car and stood there.

"Now what?"

Should she walk inside the building and act like she was interested in looking at a property at the Realtor's office? That tactic had worked at Victor's car lot, but she suspected it would be a bust here.

She could casually walk inside, maybe pick up a brochure for a friend. Maybe she would stumble across the perfect home for an acquaintance.

Or see what Tony was up to.

She reached the door and walked inside. The hallway was long and narrow with doors on both sides. Tony had obviously disappeared through one of them. She turned left down the hallway toward the Realtor's office and was startled by a woman brushing past her.

A blonde woman.

A woman with broad shoulders and a heavy red coat.

Sally Jenson.

Her movements were quick, her stride purposeful. This was definitely a woman on a mission.

Priscilla slipped into the ladies' room. No sooner had she caught her breath than her cell phone rang. Trudy.

"I can't talk right now," she whispered.

"Why not?" Trudy whispered back. "What are we doing?"

"It's a little hard to explain, but I'm tailing a couple of suspects at the moment."

"Shoot. I knew I shouldn't have left you alone. I wanted to spend the rest of the day with you. Now I'm missing all the fun."

"Not. Fun."

"Who are you tailing?"

Priscilla cupped her phone with her hand and whispered, "Tony Romano, the guy who restored Eliza's car."

"No way. He's on the island?"

"Yes. And so is Sally Jenson. Maybe one of them is tailing the other."

"Do you think she suspects him, or something like that?"

"The 'or something' part might apply," Priscilla said. "I don't know how Sally would know that the car is even missing—unless she had something to do with it."

"Crazy," Trudy breathed. "Tell me more."

"I don't know any more."

"Maybe she and Tony are in cahoots. You know?" Trudy started talking about a television show she'd recently seen with a similar scenario, but Priscilla found herself distracted. She opened the bathroom door and tiptoed out into the hallway just in time to see Sally slipping into a dentist's office next door to the Realtor's place.

"This gets stranger and stranger. She just went into the dentist's office."

"The dentist? Maybe she has a broken tooth. That would explain why she stayed on the island."

"Who knows? But the dentist is Conner Jenkins."

Trudy groaned. "I wouldn't send my worst enemy to that guy. You don't even want to know what he did to me the one and only time I went to his office. I was in pain for days, and the bill was outrageous."

"Pretty sure she's not there for a dental checkup, Trudy." Priscilla watched as Sally exited the dentist's office and tiptoed back down the hallway toward the Realtor's door. Is that where Tony was? "She moves like a private eye. Wow."

"Priscilla, have you considered the fact that they might be working together?"

"I'm thinking about it this very moment, in fact."

"How much did Eliza know about this duo when she hired them?"

Priscilla slipped back in the bathroom. "She's a car enthusiast. She knows the right people in the business."

"Or, in this case, the wrong people in the business. Maybe this Sally chick just wants it to look like she's following him to throw you off."

"Are you saying she knows I'm in the ladies' room watching her? She didn't see me at all."

"I think maybe she's got you and Eliza hoodwinked, Priscilla. She and Tony are a team. I'd be willing to bet money on it."

"I don't know, Trudy. It's impossible to say if she's working with him or following him. I'm not a PI. And my antennae are way down. I think I'm off my game because I'm so tired. Have I mentioned I'm coordinating a wedding?"

"Yes, and you sound a little cranky, if you'll pardon my saying so."

"I'm the one everyone's counting on, and right now that feels a little overwhelming."

Priscilla worked up the courage to leave the bathroom. She walked to the front door just in time to see Sally get into a cab and pull away from the building.

"What am I missing?" Trudy asked.

"She's gone. In a cab. I'm going back to the Realtor's office to see if that's where Tony went."

"Good idea. Make sure it's really him. Maybe it's someone else."

"I got a really good look at him when I nearly ran him over with my car."

"What?" Trudy let out a squeal. "I leave you alone for an hour, and you almost kill someone?"

"Well, sort of. I—"

Just around the hallway corner, she heard Tony's voice with its familiar thick Bostonian accent. He was definitely talking to someone about purchasing a property, but what kind? She listened closely.

"It's just a matter of time," Tony said. "Things back home are tumultuous right now, but they're going to straighten themselves out."

"How long are we talking?" the other voice said. "A few weeks? Months?"

"Probably a couple months before I can get my hands on any money. Things are...tied up. But they can be untied, as soon as I can manage it."

Priscilla's breath caught in her throat. Tony's voice grew closer. She ducked in the dentist's office, then peered out the door.

He disappeared down the hallway and walked out the front door. Priscilla left the dentist's office and followed him.

"Looks like he's leaving too. Should I tail him in my car?"

"Sure, why not. But maybe you should call Gerald or the police to let them know, just in case you run into trouble."

Priscilla kept a watchful eye on Tony, who headed across the parking lot. When the coast was clear, she got into her car and attempted to turn it on. Unfortunately, the sputtering noise put her on display for all to see. She turned the car off and waited until Tony was out of sight. Then she tried again. This time, the car started. Priscilla backed out of the parking spot and pointed her car in the direction she'd seen Tony go. But just two blocks away, she lost sight of him once again.

Now what?

Priscilla released several short breaths in a row and tried to stop trembling. This was all too much, too fast. She didn't have time to chase suspects through town, not with so much to do. There were still wedding centerpieces to put together, napkins to fold, a seating chart to update. Sleuthing would just have to wait for another day.

CHAPTER EIGHT

Less than five minutes after losing sight of Tony Romano, Priscilla pulled into her driveway. She could hardly wait to get inside, feed the dog, take him for the shortest walk in the history of walks, and get into a nice hot bath.

No sooner had she entered her living room than the house phone rang. She plopped onto the sofa and took the call.

"Hello?"

"Priscilla, did you forget something?" Eliza sounded worried.

"Forget something?"

"Our five o'clock meeting with Tilly to finalize the catering? It's already ten after, and you're not here. We were both worried. I tried and tried to get you on your cell, but it kept going to voice mail."

"Oh, Eliza, I'm so sorry. I've been terribly distracted today, and I've been talking to Trudy and Rachel for the past half hour. Please forgive me."

"I understand. I suppose I can do this by myself. I've been so torn about the salmon puffs, but the main course is really what's throwing me off. I'm afraid I'm changing my mind again, and I'm not sure how Tilly's gonna take it, but I'll give it my best shot."

"No, no. I'll be right there."

"Are you sure?"

"Of course." Priscilla rose from the sofa, gave Jake a sympathetic look, and headed to the door. Seven minutes later she walked into the Colonial Inn, which was abuzz with customers. Eliza and Tilly sat in a booth on the far side of the room, a generous spread of food in front of them.

"Glad you could make it, Priscilla," Tilly said as she took a seat. "Eliza is still struggling to make up her mind."

"I know, and I'm so sorry." Eliza shrugged. "You've been so patient with me, Tilly. I just can't decide on the appetizer."

"I say go with salmon," Priscilla said. "Too many shrimp allergies out there."

Eliza nodded. "Okay."

"See how easy that was?" Tilly scribbled down *salmon* on a piece of paper then looked at Eliza. "I'm not trying to be hard on you, Eliza, but I've never had a bride change her mind so close to the event before."

"I'm so sorry, Tilly." Eliza sighed. "I'm not trying to be a bridezilla."

Tilly grunted. "Now, I know you were also concerned about the chicken cordon bleu, so I've created two more chicken dishes as options." She shoved a plate in Eliza and Priscilla's direction. "Try this one, ladies. Chicken picatta. And when you're done with that, have a taste of the chicken Alfredo."

Tilly rose to greet incoming customers, and Eliza looked Priscilla's way and sighed. "I truly didn't mean to make this so hard on her. She tried to sell me on the chicken cordon bleu weeks ago and I agreed at first, but I just couldn't stop thinking about how old-fashioned that sounded. Help me, Priscilla. I don't know what to do."

Priscilla scoped out the options in front of her. She sampled each one. "I vote for the chicken Alfredo. Tasty, and it comes with pasta, which will fill up your guests in a hurry. It's a cheaper option. Less meat, more noodles."

"You sure?"

"Very. Now, what else can I help you with?"

"She's got a bunch of questions about warming trays and that sort of thing. I don't know all the answers to her questions, but I told her to talk to Anna."

"I'll run interference, if you need."

"Thanks. How was your day? You stayed busy?"

"Yes. But I'm glad we're finally alone and can talk. I wanted to let you know that—"

"What did you think of the Chicken Picatta, Priscilla?" Tilly's voice sounded from her left. The tiny woman crowded into the spot next to her.

"We've settled on the chicken Alfredo," Eliza said. "But thank you for going to so much trouble, Tilly. I'm sure it's going to be great."

"I have a list of questions about the setup for serving. Should I chat with you about that, Priscilla? Eliza seems to be having trouble deciding on that too." Tilly gave her an inquisitive look.

"Sure." They spent the next several minutes finalizing details, but Tilly kept getting up and down to greet customers. After one particularly lengthy trip away from the table, she returned with a scowl on her face.

"It drives me nuts."

"What?" Eliza asked. "The wedding prep?"

"No. Couples on their cell phones. Everywhere I look, cell phones. I mean, you wait all your life for Prince Charming, finally catch him, and then…bam. You trade him in for a cell phone. There he sits, staring at his phone while you stare at yours. Endless potential for romance is lost, and all because of social media."

"Tell us how you really feel, Tilly," Priscilla said and then laughed.

"I just did. It makes me crazy, running a restaurant, because I see this every day. I'd like to place a box at the front of the store for people to toss their phones into."

"Now that's a clever idea." Eliza took another bite of the chicken Alfredo.

"But what if they had an emergency?" Priscilla asked. "I mean, what if one of the parties had a heart attack and no one had a phone to call 911?"

"I have a landline. I'll call 911." Tilly sighed. "And yes, I'm exaggerating a little bit. Just saying, people can't see what's right in front of them. They're too busy catching up on the latest gossip or political wranglings on social media to nurture real relationships. That man sitting across from that woman over there…" She pointed to a man in a suit who appeared to be glued to his smartphone. "He once made her swoon." She pointed to the woman with him whose thumbs were typing a mile a minute on her own phone. "Now they don't even know the other exists. They're too busy catching up with people they could be chatting with later on, when they're not together."

Priscilla's gaze traveled to the woman. "Yeah, I get it. You're very perceptive, Tilly."

"I notice things, that's all, and not just people with phone addictions."

"Oh?" Eliza's brow wrinkled. "Like what?"

"Like that blonde woman who came in here for lunch. Forty-something. Kind of big-boned. Dressed a little man-like, jeans and a non-descript red coat. No makeup to speak of. Now, I never met the woman before in my life. Might never see her again. But it was painfully obvious to me she couldn't take her eyes off a certain gentleman in another booth, who also happened to be a stranger to me."

This sent Priscilla's radar up immediately. "What did the man look like?"

Tilly pursed her lips. "Hmm. Well, dark hair. Receding hairline. Olive skin. Maybe Italian? He was wearing a dark jacket and jeans. White shirt."

"Wow, you really do notice the details," Eliza said. "You could work as a private investigator."

"This man," Priscilla interrupted. "Was he tall or short?"

"Short. In fact, when he stood up, I remember thinking he was just a bit taller than me. I'm no giant, you know. Why do you ask, Priscilla? Do you know the man?"

"Oh, I...well..." She wanted to ask about the scar above his right eyebrow but knew this would tip Eliza off. Then again, maybe it was time to tip Eliza off. Maybe she should tell her everything.

Not that Eliza seemed to be paying attention. The woman looked a bit lost this evening. Her gaze kept shifting from one plate of food to the next.

"You okay over there?" Priscilla asked after a minute.

"Yeah." Her friend looked up and sighed. "Just thinking about how much my life is getting ready to change. I've never been married before."

"Oh, I see." Priscilla gave her an inquisitive look. "You're not getting cold feet, are you?"

"No. I don't think so." Eliza set her fork down and leaned back against the booth. "I think I'm just scared."

"Of what?"

A long pause followed. "I've been single a long time, Priscilla. A really long time."

"Ah, I see."

"There will be a lot of adjustments. I'm not saying I'm not looking forward to them. Most of them, sure. But I've been pretty independent." She paused once more and her tone changed. "Obviously, I wasn't completely independent when I was working for Victor Fox. He tried to control my every move. These last few months, though, I could come and go as I pleased, set my own hours, eat the foods I love, watch the movies I enjoy, that sort of thing."

"Ah. Gotcha. Well, there will be some adjustments there."

"Yes. I guess I'm a little spoiled too."

"You? Spoiled? I highly doubt that."

"Well, spoiled in keeping my own hours, my own schedule, my own mealtimes, and so on."

"Right." Priscilla nodded.

"Did you know that Carson likes football?"

"Most men do." Priscilla couldn't help herself. She took another bite of the pasta.

"Yes." Eliza released a slow breath. "Just one more thing I didn't think about. I'm not a fan. I mean, I can tolerate a game or two here or there, but to watch it all the time? What if he's one of those men who always has to have the game on? And what if he snores?"

"It's possible. My husband Gary snored like a freight train."

"I haven't even asked him what side of the bed he sleeps on. What if he sleeps on the left side? That's my side."

Priscilla laughed. "You're overthinking this, Eliza, I promise."

"I tried sleeping on the right side one night last week—just in case it comes to that—and I ended up lying awake all night. Couldn't sleep a wink. Oh, and I sleep with the TV on. Weird, I know."

"The noise doesn't bother you?"

"I mute it. Just use it to throw off burglars."

"I have no idea what that means." Priscilla glanced over at another couple on their cell phones.

"If a burglar looks in my window and sees the TV running at two in the morning, he'll think someone inside the house is wide awake. So, maybe he'll move on to the next house."

"Interesting strategy."

"Just one of my many quirks."

"You really have given this a lot of thought."

Eliza grew silent. When she finally spoke, her voice trembled. "I just hope I can do this, Priscilla."

"Eliza, you're worried for nothing. Everyone faces these little concerns when they marry after being single for a long time. But trust me when I say that God will take any wrinkles and iron them out as you go along. And who knows—maybe you'll fall in love with football. Stranger things have happened."

"Um, no. I can't see that happening." She giggled. "But I promise to try."

"You need to focus on the things you have in common. You both love classic cars, for Pete's sake. Do you know how rare that is?"

"True."

"And you are both compassionate people, interested in missions."

"Right."

"And you're both very nostalgic. You love things from yesteryear."

"True."

"Instead of honing in on the things that are different, enjoy the similarities. Before long you'll have plenty of opportunity to see what you're made of."

Eliza laughed. "You think?"

"I know. That's what being married for forty years to a man who's your polar opposite will do for you."

Before she could say anything else, something distracted Priscilla. The man in the booth behind Eliza was reading the newspaper. On the side opened to Priscilla, an oversized headline boasted an upcoming classic car show in Edgartown. She squinted and tried to make out some of the text but couldn't.

"You okay over there, Priscilla?" Eliza asked.

"Yes. Just noticed a headline about a car show."

"Oh, right. I could tell you anything you want to know about that. I'm a member of the local club." Eliza sighed. "I can't believe I planned my wedding on the very same day. This will be the first time in years I've had to miss it. Not sure how I got my wires crossed on the date, but I did. So sad to miss out." She went back to nibbling on a piece of chicken, then wiped her fingers on a napkin.

This led to a conversation about the kind of people who frequent car shows and, before long, the ladies had completely veered from the topic of the wedding. And it became clearer with each passing moment that Priscilla wouldn't have a chance to tell Eliza about the Bel Air going missing. She did, however, manage to free herself from the conversation around six thirty by telling Eliza that she needed to get home to work on centerpieces. Barring any more interruptions, Priscilla would get one thing off her plate, at least.

CHAPTER NINE

After what felt like the longest day in recent history, Priscilla finally climbed into bed. Jake whimpered from the floor next to her. She reached down to pet him.

"I'm sorry, fella. I've ignored you all day, haven't I? It's not much of a life when I'm not around, and even when I'm here you're surrounded by craft projects. I promise, I'll give you a good long walk tomorrow. Maybe we'll go up to the Beekman place. They have the best view around."

Jake's tail wagged, as if he understood every word. Priscilla's heart went out to the poor dog. He craved attention and she hadn't offered him much over the past few weeks, thanks to the wedding plans.

With everything now slowing down, Priscilla placed a call to the Vineyard Cab Company and inquired about Sally Jenson's whereabouts after leaving Gerald's place yesterday. It took a couple of minutes to explain the reason for her call to the night dispatcher.

"No, I'm sorry, I don't know the cab number," Priscilla said for the umpteenth time. "Like I said, this individual—a woman in a red coat—was picked up at a home in Misty Harbor at approximately four in the afternoon on Tuesday." She shared Gerald's address for the second time and then paused as the man on the other end of the line asked if she knew the name of the cab driver. "No, I'm sorry, I don't. I do know that Sally Jenson was taken to the Bluffs B&B and arrived sometime late afternoon or early evening. I'm calling to find out if she made any other stops along the way."

"Are you a police officer, ma'am? This would be considered an invasion of privacy, so we only give out information like this to the police."

"No, I'm not a police officer. And of course I don't want to be guilty of an invasion of privacy. But are you sure you can't tell me anything? Anything at all?"

"The minute you start working for the police department I'll be happy to talk to you. Even then, you would have to have a warrant."

"Okay, got it." Priscilla ended the call with a deep sigh.

"Forget it," she said aloud to the dog. "No one wants to help me today."

Not that she needed to be solving any crimes right now. What Priscilla really needed—and desperately—was sleep.

Just as she reached over to snap off the lamp on the end table, Priscilla's cell phone rang. She saw Gail's name on the screen and answered right away.

"Hey, this is late, especially for you."

"I know, and sorry, but Dad just told me about a guy over in Edgartown who heads up some sort of classic car club. Marvin Freemont. They're setting up for a big show this Saturday inside the pavilion."

"I saw that in the paper."

"Want to take a drive over there tomorrow morning?"

"I've got a meeting with Candy and Eliza at nine to talk about the cake, but maybe after that? Say, eleven? And only if we can stop at The Perfect Fit. I want to ask Claire some questions. She's helping with décor."

"Claire?"

"Sure. She's Carson's daughter, remember?"

"Oh, right, right." Gail laughed. "I can't believe I forgot. Happy to stop by her place."

"You're not dragging me into some store." Uncle Hugh's voice rang out in the background.

"You can stay in the car, Pop," Gail assured him.

"Okay, want to meet me at the bakery?" Priscilla asked. "I'm sure Eliza and I will be done with our meeting by eleven."

"Sure. See you then. And by the way, Priscilla, you're doing a great job with all these wedding plans. I know Eliza appreciates you."

Priscilla drew in a deep breath. "It's all a little overwhelming, if you want the truth. But I'm happy to help her. She seems a little indecisive, so I've been there to help finalize plans."

"I know it's a lot, but think of the memories you're making for Eliza. She could never have pulled this off on her own. And don't worry, Priscilla. We're all here for you. Candy's got the cake taken care of. Tilly has the menu planned out perfectly. And Anna has been on the phone with vendors for days, working on the details of the reception. Remember, it's not all meant to fall on you."

Priscilla released a lingering sigh. "Thank you for the reminder. I don't know why I feel so overwhelmed. I guess I just want it to be perfect for her."

"Weddings are rarely perfect. The more important thing is that it's memorable, and that the bride doesn't carry the stress on her shoulders."

"True. I'm doing what I can to keep any concerns tucked away. Well, except for the missing car. She's going to have to know about that. There's no way around it."

"Speaking of the car, any leads on that yet?"

"Not a one. It's the craziest thing. One minute the vehicle was there, the next it vanished into thin air."

"Hey, you're a poet. You just made a rhyme."

"I'd rather be a magician and make a 1954 Bel Air convertible appear from out of thin air." She fought the temptation to groan. "Anyway, I appreciate the reminder that I have help. I know this isn't all on me. We're a team."

"Yep. And if you need more help, just ask. We all want to do what we can to make this day memorable for Eliza and Carson, trust me."

"Right." Priscilla just hoped the day would be memorable for all the right reasons, not the wrong ones. If only the car would turn up in time, then perhaps Eliza could have the wedding of her dreams.

Before she could hang up, another call came through. Priscilla smiled when she saw Gerald's number, said goodbye to Gail, and then answered with a cheerful, "Hey, you."

"Hey, back." His voice put her at ease right away. "Just wondering how the rest of your day went. After I headed off to work, I mean. Any leads on the car?"

"You mean that beautiful blue number I saw on Victor's lot?" She couldn't help but sigh aloud.

"You're really enamored with that one, aren't you?"

She laughed. "Nah. I mean, yes, but it's out of the question."

"What did I miss after we parted ways? Fill me in."

"Well, I almost ran over a man at the corner of Harbor and Leeway."

"What?" The tone of his voice changed immediately. "Are you serious?"

"Yes. And you'll never believe who it was." She spent the next several minutes filling him in, and Gerald scolded her for entering the office building alone.

"Promise me you'll call me next time, Scilla. Please. This bravery of yours is giving me a heart attack."

"I'm sorry."

"You're sure it was Tony? And Sally?"

"Hundred percent. No idea why they're both on the island. Sent my radar up, though."

"It's doing the same to mine, now."

"I don't know if this is way out there or not, but I have some suspicions that Tony might be linked in some way to mob activity in Boston."

"That's so...Godfather of you."

"I know it sounds nuts, but this guy was talking just like you'd expect a mobster to talk. He said something about tying things up."

"Things...or people?"

"Who knows? And then he told whoever the other guy was that he needed two months to get his hands on money."

"I wonder if this is all has to do with drugs," Gerald said.

"Oh, I never thought of that. What if Tony hid drugs in the car—like, inside the upholstery or something—and stole the car just long enough to take back what he really wanted."

"Stranger things have happened, but usually in big towns, not tiny places like Tisbury."

"True, but still within the realm of possibility, wouldn't you say? He can't get his hands on money right away? That might explain why."

"Have I mentioned that I never want you to tail anyone again when I'm not with you?"

"Yes." She appreciated his concern. "I made it out of the building okay, and I think I did a pretty good job of scoping out the place while I was in there. I can tell you anything you want to know about the ladies' room, including the brand of hand soap they use."

"Scoping out the place." Gerald laughed. "Now you sound like a P.I."

"Do I?" Priscilla pulled the covers up. "That's funny."

"I can be funny on occasion."

An extended pause followed on his end. When he spoke again, his voice had a softer tone. "Hey, kind of last minute, but I wondered if you might like to go out to dinner tomorrow night."

"Tomorrow night?" She paused. "There's so much left to do with the wedding and all. I'm not sure if I can—"

"It's Valentine's Day, Priscilla. The traditional, 'Let's go out to dinner and a movie' night."

"True. That would explain the big banner advertising Tilly's special at the Inn and Victor's new commercial offering a ten percent off V-Day special." She laughed.

"I've been dying to try out that new steak place, Fleming's, in Edgartown, but I've been afraid to ask you because I know you're swamped with wedding stuff. That's the only reason I didn't ask before tonight. I've been too worried about your exhaustion level."

"Thanks for caring about me." She couldn't help herself. A yawn escaped.

"So, what do you say? Do you think you could step away from the wedding plans long enough for a quick meal?"

A thousand excuses rushed through Priscilla's mind as she yawned once more.

"C'mon, Scilla. Pretty please? I won't distract you too much, I promise. And maybe I can even help you out after."

"In what way?"

"I don't know. Surely there are some napkins I can fold or some RSVPs I can weed through. Something like that."

She laughed. "Well, there are a lot of last-minute details, but I've done a fine job of farming out the various tasks to others. So, yes, I will go out to dinner with you. But don't be surprised if I fall asleep at the table."

"You have been looking a little bleary-eyed, if you don't mind my saying so."

"Gee, thanks a lot."

"Well, it'll be a quick dinner and then I'll get you home so you can sleep. And by the way, thank you."

"For what?"

"For helping me out. It's been pretty awful for the past few years, spending Valentine's Day alone. This will be the first time in ages I've had a V-Day date."

"Happy to be of service, especially if steak is involved. Oh, one more thing…"

"What's that?"

"We'll have to take your car. Mine is giving me fits."

"I know, and I promise I'll look at it after the wedding."

"I should probably go to sleep, Gerald." She leaned back against the pillows and stifled a yawn. "See you tomorrow night."

"Sleep tight, Scilla."

"You too." She reached over and snapped off the lamp on the bedside table, and her eyes fluttered closed. Just as she felt herself drifting off, her cell phone rang again.

"Did you forget something?" she asked upon answering.

"Wh-what?" A female voice greeted her.

"Oh, sorry, Eliza. I thought you were Gerald."

"Ah." Eliza laughed. "I can see why you would get us confused. I know I'm probably wearing you out, but I just wanted to remind you that we have our final meeting with Candy tomorrow morning to wrap up details on the cake. Remember?"

"Right, I haven't forgotten. I'll be there."

"Awesome. I'm really excited about it."

"Sure." Priscilla felt her eyes growing heavy, and she forced them open.

"Oh, and don't forget, you promised to come with me on Friday for my final dress fitting." Eliza squealed. "I can't believe it's Wednesday night already. Before you know it, Carson and I will be driving off into the sunset in that beautiful new car, straight into our happily ever after."

"Mm-hmm."

"Okay, I can tell you're half asleep. See you in the morning. And in case I haven't said it a thousand times already, thank you for everything. I don't know if anyone's ever told you, but you're an amazing wedding planner."

"Thanks."

"Hey, I forgot to tell you one last thing. Sally Jenson's still at the Bluffs."

This certainly got Priscilla's attention. "No way."

"Yes. We visited for quite some time. I really like her."

"Did she happen to mention her plans for today?" Priscilla sat up and dangled her legs over the edge of the bed, now fully awake.

"Nope. Not a word. She was at the B&B this evening when Carson's family arrived. She settled right in with the rest of the wedding crowd, like she belongs there. Carson's mom and stepdad seem okay with it. Here's the weirdest thing of all—she really gets along with Carson's mom. I mean, nobody gets along with Carson's mom, from what I understand. She's pretty standoffish. But there's some sort of fascinating connection between the two women. Carson is beside himself. In a good way, I mean. His mom isn't the sort to have friends, I guess."

"Until now." Priscilla paused to think through her response. "So, maybe Sally's unwillingness to move on has been a God-thing. You think?"

"Maybe. I guess we should go ahead and invite her to the wedding. She's been part of my car journey from the get-go."

This raised all sorts of red flags for Priscilla, but she didn't voice her concerns just yet.

"Maybe Carson's mom has already invited her," she said. "She's probably decided you and Sally are good friends or something."

"I am getting to know her better, that's for sure. And she's really nice. I get the feeling she's a bit of a loner, in need of a friend."

"Maybe." *Or maybe she's hovering close because she stole your car and has some sort of master plan to sell it and make a bundle.*

"I guess I'd better let you go." Eliza paused and then giggled. "Hey, I might try sleeping in the middle of the bed tonight, just to mix it up."

"I suggest you sleep on the side you always sleep on," Priscilla countered. "You need your rest, Eliza."

"Okay."

"And I'll see you at the bakery in the morning." She paused. "Oh, wait…tomorrow is Valentine's Day. I wonder if Candy's going to be busier than usual."

"Too late to worry about that. We've already arranged to meet her."

They said their goodbyes and ended the call.

Priscilla settled under the covers and looked over at the left side of the bed, which was completely empty. She stretched out her hand and ran it along the comforter on that side, feeling the emptiness more than ever. A bittersweet feeling washed over her, one she couldn't put into words. Unexpected tears brimmed in her eyes, though she did her best to force them away. Probably just exhaustion.

Things would be better after a good night's sleep.

CHAPTER TEN

Priscilla slept long and hard. When she awoke on Valentine's morning she felt completely refreshed and excited to face the day—until she remembered the missing convertible. It only took a second for all of her concerns to come flooding back. Of course, she didn't have long to fret over it, what with the meeting at the bakery. She managed to squeeze in a quick walk with Jake but not as long as she'd hoped.

After getting him settled back inside the house she left for the bakery. Thank goodness, her car didn't give her any fits this morning. When she pulled into the parking lot, her cell phone rang through the car's Bluetooth speaker. The voice on the other end of the line surprised her.

"Mrs. Grant, this is Hank Westin at Tisbury PD."

Her heart skipped a beat as she anticipated what he might say.

"I've already spoken to Captain O'Bannon, but wanted to call you as well."

"Oh? Have you found the car?"

"No, I'm sorry. There's been no trace of it, in fact."

"I see." She did her best not to sound disappointed. These officers were working on her behalf, after all.

"At this point we have to believe that the car is still here on the island. Someone's doing a great job of hiding it. But our officers are keeping their eyes wide open, I assure you. It's just a matter of time before the thief slips up. They always do." He paused. "We have to consider one more possibility, that the thief has broken the car down and is selling off the parts."

Priscilla's heart felt heavy at his words. "I hadn't considered that."

"We've got our detectives scouring the internet to make sure no one on the island is selling parts that match the ones from that make and model."

"Good idea."

"Like I said, we're on top of it. We want to return this car to Ms. Jamison as badly as you do, especially with the deadline of a wedding coming up."

"Thank you for your help. I'm very grateful."

They ended the call, and she made her way inside the bakery. Priscilla caught a glimpse of Eliza sitting at a table in the far corner. The bride-to-be waved her over.

"Priscilla, you made it!"

"Of course, Eliza."

"You sounded so tired last night, I wasn't sure you would be here."

Priscilla smiled at her. "Right. I wasn't either, to be honest. But I slept like a rock and now, here I am."

"I went ahead and ordered for both of us," Eliza said. "My treat. I know how much you love Candy's scones, and her seasonal coffee is divine. Sound good?"

"Perfect."

A couple of minutes later Candy showed up at the table with their order. "Hey, gals. I'm sorry it took so long, so I wanted to bring you your food myself. As you can see, it's nuts in here." She set their plates and coffee mugs on the table.

"It's okay," Eliza said. "We're just here to meet with—"

Candy took off across the room to take care of another customer.

Eliza turned to face Priscilla, concern registering in her eyes. "Do you think she forgot?"

"If so, we'll remind her later. Right now, let's visit and eat these goodies."

"Sure." Eliza nibbled the edge of her scone. "It's just that she seems rather out of sorts. I've been noticing it for a while now."

"Me too." Priscilla took a sip of her coffee.

"You don't suppose she and Beau are breaking up, do you?"

"No, not at all. Maybe the lengthy engagement is getting to her. I honestly think she's been so busy taking care of everyone else's big day that she hasn't had time to focus on her own. That has to be frustrating."

"Poor girl. I do hope they go through with it." Eliza doctored her coffee and gave it a stir. "They're a match made in heaven. And I can't picture the bakery without Beau in it."

"Me neither." Priscilla sighed. She caught a glimpse of Beau working the cash register. He didn't seem to be in the happiest frame of mind, which seemed odd. The fellow was usually really cheerful.

"I know he and Candy have already had to postpone their wedding twice because she's so busy at the shop." Eliza shrugged. "I think it's getting to him. I know it would bother me, if I were in his shoes."

"Of course. Me too."

"He told me the other day that if he had the money, he'd hire someone to take his place here so he could take on more construction jobs. The cost of living on the island is, well, you know. Crazy."

"Right."

Priscilla couldn't help but think of what Gerald had told her yesterday about Beau having a key to the garage. Though she couldn't picture him stealing the convertible, his demeanor lately made her think something was up.

Eliza carried on, oblivious to Priscilla's ponderings. "Not that a lot of people are renovating their homes during the winter. Once things warm up I'm sure he'll work something out."

They finished their scones and made small talk while waiting to see if Candy would join them. The shop owner finally stopped by their table to refill their coffee cups. This time she took the extra seat. "Whew. Happy to be off my feet. We've been so busy today."

Eliza nodded. "I can see that. Business is booming."

"You can say that again." Candy grinned. "It's a mixed bag, I can assure you. I'm happy to have the customers but exhausted at the end of each day. And I'm overwhelmed every time I think about how this is affecting our wedding day. There's been no time to make plans, because I'm so focused on the business. I don't think Beau will wait forever." Her expression shifted to one of concern.

"Everything okay?" Priscilla asked.

"Yeah." Candy's gaze turned to Beau. "He's tired, that's all. And getting a little discouraged, even. With all the weddings swirling around me, I'm more focused on everyone else rather than myself. One couple asked me to do a chocolate wedding cake. I mean, who does that? I'm guessing Gail will be next. Don't you think? Heaven only knows what flavors they'll want." She paused for breath. "Which reminds me, we'll be talking about flavors for Rachel's cake pretty soon, Priscilla."

"Yes, it's still rather surreal."

"So, you're going to jump from planning one wedding to another, are you?"

"Well, I…"

"I'm sure you'll be ready for a rest before long. I know I will be." Candy stretched her back. "But, in spite of my exhaustion, I wouldn't let anyone else make Rachel's cake."

"Are you sure, Candy? Seems like you're swamped."

"I am, but we really need the income." She shrugged. "Anyway, let's finalize our plans for this wedding on Saturday. You getting excited, Eliza?"

"Sure am."

"I'm so glad you've been an easy-breezy bride. Thank you for that."

"Oh, you're welcome." Eliza beamed. "It's just a party for friends and loved ones to celebrate with us. No point in getting too fancy-schmancy. Simple white wedding cake will do."

"Perfect. I can handle that."

"Of course, I do like a bit of piping, as we discussed last time," Eliza added.

"Of course."

"And perhaps a filling. Strawberry?"

"It's the go-to for modern brides."

"Oh, and I remember now that Carson mentioned a groom's cake. That's a thing in the south, right? He's from Florida, you know. Can you make a cake that looks like a car? Maybe a convertible?"

"Seriously?" Candy's eyes widened, and Priscilla could read the panic in her expression.

Eliza laughed. "No, not seriously. I'm just kidding. I wouldn't throw that on you at the last minute, Candy. But if you want to bring a sheet cake in some sort of different flavor, he'll be delighted."

"Okay, so one white wedding cake with strawberry filling and piping and one chocolate groom's cake."

"Pretty sure he'll shoot for red velvet. That's his favorite." Eliza and Candy spent a few minutes discussing the cakes while Candy took copious notes.

Afterward, Eliza took care of paying for the cakes and thanked Candy in advance for her work. They arranged for the time the cakes would be delivered to the B&B on Saturday, then Candy rose to take care of her customers.

"Sorry, ladies, but Valentine's is the busiest day of the year."

"That's okay. Priscilla and I need to talk about my wedding dress alterations."

"We do?"

"Sure. Remember? Today at five? We're supposed to meet up with Amber to make sure the dress is perfect?"

"Oh, right. Today at five. Alterations. I knew that." Priscilla reached into her oversized bag and pulled out a folder she'd been carrying around for days.

"What's that?" Candy said as she happened back by.

"It's my folder with all the wedding details inside."

"She's very organized," Eliza explained. "You should see. Priscilla has things outlined in spreadsheet form."

"Like what?" Candy asked.

Priscilla shrugged. "Oh, the names and addresses of the vendors—the caterers, florist, photographer, musicians, alterations lady, and so on. And the seating chart for guests."

"You've got a seating chart?" Candy slung the dishcloth she'd been holding over her shoulder.

"Of course. The dining room at the Bluffs isn't that big and we've got sixty guests coming. If I don't make a plan, we'll never fit them all in."

"Impressive. What else is in there?" Candy acted as if she wanted to steal the folder away from her but then laughed.

"Swatches of fabric from the bridesmaids' dresses, color samples from the florist, even a photo of the centerpieces."

"She's on the ball," Eliza explained. "And she's got a full layout of how the evening will go, right down to the minute."

"Wow, you really are good at this, Priscilla." Candy gave her an admiring look.

"The only reason I have everything planned out to the minute is so the bride and groom can ride off into the sunset at the appropriate time, that's all. If I don't keep an eye on that, they will get busy visiting with guests and won't leave until after the sun goes down."

"And riding off into the sunset is the most important part." Eliza's grin was bright enough to light the room. "No one will want to miss that."

"Right." Priscilla swallowed hard, knowing this wasn't the time or place to share about the missing car.

"I think it's nice that you have someone to help." Candy looked Eliza's way. "I'm so scatterbrained. When I get married I'm probably going to lose Beau's ring or knock over the cake or something dreadful like that. I'm going to need a friend to step up and take the pressure off."

"Priscilla's always been that sort of friend." Eliza said.

"Then I'll hire you too," Candy said. "If we can just set a date." She bounded from her chair and headed off across the room to wait on another customer. Priscilla lost herself to her thoughts for a moment.

"You okay over there, Priscilla?" Eliza's words brought her back to attention.

"Well, actually..." Priscilla glanced at her watch. Did she have time to tell Eliza about the missing car before Gail arrived at eleven? "Eliza, I really need to tell you—"

"Oh, look who it is." Her friend pointed to the door and Priscilla watched as Sally entered the shop. Eliza raised her hand. "Sally, join us. Over here!" She waved and seconds later Sally was standing next to their table. The conversation about the car would have to take place later.

Eliza gestured for her to sit in the chair Candy had just occupied. Afterward, she faced the woman with a smile. "I'm glad you ventured in today, Sally. I've been wondering if you might like to stay for my wedding."

"Really?" Sally looked surprised at first, but after a few seconds her lips curled up in a smile. "Are you sure? I already feel like I'm butting in by taking up a room at the B&B. In fact, I've been looking at heading back to the mainland to get out of everyone's hair."

"Don't you dare." Eliza gave her a scolding look. "I want you to stay put."

"Thank you."

"Listen..." Eliza rested her hand on Sally's arm. "You couldn't possibly know this, but Carson's mom doesn't really warm up to just anyone. In fact, she's pretty cold to most people."

"That's weird. She seems really taken with me."

"She is. And I've been so glad to see it. So, any friend of Nancy's is a friend of mine. I think it will make her happy to see you on the guest list. What do you say?"

"I...I guess so, Eliza. But, again, I don't want to intrude."

"You won't. Now relax. Take a few days off and join the group. I think you'll have a wonderful time."

"I have, already." She offered a warm smile. "Though I find it funny that the one woman who can't seem to get along with others thinks I'm a peach."

"You've won her over, and I'd like to keep her happy."

"Then I accept. Happy to be added to the guest list."

"Perfect. Now, one important question: Chicken or beef?"

"What?"

"At the reception. We have to let the caterer know ASAP so she can make enough food. Chicken or beef?"

"Ah." Sally appeared to be thinking. "What chicken dish, specifically?"

"Chicken Alfredo."

"Then beef all the way. Unless chicken is cheaper. Then make it chicken."

"Beef it is." Eliza winked. "And welcome to the family, Sally. We're happy to have you on board."

Priscilla couldn't help but wonder if Eliza would still feel this way if Sally happened to be a car thief and not just an unexpected wedding guest.

CHAPTER ELEVEN

Just a few minutes after Sally's arrival at the bakery, Eliza had to leave to meet up with Carson. The ladies said their goodbyes, but Priscilla remained at the table with Sally and finished off her coffee and scone. When she was sure the coast was clear, Priscilla finally felt free to speak her mind.

"Can I ask a question, Sally?"

"Sure." Sally took a swig of coffee. "What's up?"

Priscilla put her cup down and gave the woman a pensive look. "Why are you still here?"

Sally's cheeks blazed red. "You mean here, on the island?"

"Yes. I know, it's none of my business, but I thought you lived on the mainland."

"I do, in a suburb outside of Boston."

"So, do you have family here or something?"

"No. No family here. Just . . ." The expression on Sally's face shifted from embarrassment to pain. "Just taking care of some personal matters."

Hmm. Personal matters that included a stolen 1954 Bel Air convertible, perhaps?

Sally paled and suddenly looked a bit shaky. "Is everything okay, Priscilla? You've got me sweating, and I know it's not warm in here. Have I done something? Said something? You think I'm butting in on Eliza's wedding? If so, I'll go."

Priscilla shook her head, suddenly feeling bad for making the woman so uncomfortable. "No, and I'm sorry if I've put you on the spot. I have something to tell you, Sally. Something awful."

"Oh dear." Sally put her cup down. "What is it?"

"The car? The Bel Air?"

"Best car I ever transported, I tell ya. Great restoration, and talk about a smooth ride. The whole trip down from Boston was like a vacation."

"It's missing."

"Wh-what?" Sally looked genuinely shocked. Her big green eyes bugged and she bumped her coffee cup with the back of her hand, sloshing coffee all over the tablecloth. Either her acting skills were stellar, or she was genuinely stunned. "When? How?"

"Gerald went out to his garage yesterday morning, and the car was missing."

"I don't understand. Are you telling me someone stole the Bel Air after I delivered it?"

"Yes, that's what I'm telling you."

Tears brimmed her lashes. "Oh, Priscilla, this is awful. Have you gone to the police? Checked the ferry?"

"Yes, to all of the above. To the best of our knowledge, the car hasn't left the island."

Sally attempted to clean up the spilled coffee with her napkin, but it was futile. "This is awful. How did Eliza take it?"

Priscilla couldn't take her eyes off of Sally's hands, which hadn't stopped trembling since the Bel Air came up in conversation. "To be honest, we haven't told her yet. I'm afraid it would wreck her."

Sally dropped the napkin and leaned forward. "But you have to tell her. Right? I mean, the wedding is day after tomorrow."

"Right. I plan to. I'm just waiting for the right moment to open up."

"She'll be devastated." Sally looked genuinely concerned. "I've never seen anyone that excited for a vehicle's delivery, and I've done this for years. She's been living for the day she can give that car to her new husband." Sally pinched her eyes shut and shook her head. "Trying to imagine what she's going to go through when you tell her. This is absolutely awful."

"Yes." Priscilla continued to watch Sally's responses, wondering if she would see anything that appeared fake or contrived. So far, the woman looked truly anguished over this news.

"No one else knew that car was headed to the island, so I can't imagine how the news spread to a would-be thief. Unless someone was following us online," Sally said.

"Online?"

"Yes. The world of classic cars is intense. And huge. And people talk, especially those who have reason to want the cars for themselves."

"You're saying someone planned all of this in advance?"

"That would be my guess. Whoever did this probably tailed me all the way from Boston."

"That's a horrifying thought." Priscilla shivered, just thinking about it. "You really think that's a possibility?"

"I'd be willing to bet money on it."

"Well, don't do that. Eliza's already out a ton of money. I'd hate to see a second friend go bust over this car."

Sally pushed her chair back and stood. "That does it. I'm definitely staying."

"What do you mean?"

"I'm staying until we find that car. That's all there is to it. Maybe not at the B&B. I don't want to be in the way. But I'm staying on the island to help you. I won't leave until that car is in Eliza's possession."

"That's very kind of you."

"I'm just heartbroken, and I know she will be too. Eliza is smitten—not just with the vehicle but with the man she purchased it for. I'm going to stay put on this island until I've helped figure out who has stolen the car from her, and why."

"How are your sleuthing skills?" Priscilla put her elbows on the table and leaned forward. "I'd love to hear your thoughts on whodunit."

"I'm in the car transportation business. I'm not a sleuth."

"Your being in the car transportation business could be a big help. What do you know about Tony Romano?"

"Tony?" Sally plopped back down in the chair. "You suspect Tony?"

"Just a thought. He's on the island. I saw him at a local Realtor's office yesterday." Then again, Sally already knew he'd been there, didn't she?

"Yes, I know he's here." Sally's cheeks flushed pink. "He's looking at buying property to open a new shop. He told me all about it a couple of weeks ago." Her eyes clouded over. "Priscilla, if you saw Tony going into the Realtor's office yesterday, then you saw me too."

"Yes." Priscilla shifted her gaze to the table.

"Oh dear." Sally's cheeks flamed pink. "Well, now I really feel like a fool."

"What do you mean?"

"I...well..." Sally ran her fingers along the damp tablecloth, not meeting Priscilla's eyes. "I've been single for a long time, Priscilla."

"I see." Only, she didn't really see what this had to do with anything. And didn't she just have this exact conversation with Eliza?

Sally glanced up. "It would be impossible to calculate how many cans of tuna fish I've eaten by myself. Or how many loaves of bread have gone stale because I only ate a couple of slices. Do you know what it feels like to throw away ninety percent of a loaf of bread?"

"You can freeze bread, you know," Beau said as he walked by. "We do that a lot around here."

Sally shrugged. "It's just not the same." She turned her attention to Priscilla once again. "I've spent years wearing socks to bed at night so my feet don't get cold."

"Sorry, but I'm not sure what that has to do with our discussion," Priscilla said. "You've lost me somewhere along the way."

"Just saying two can stay warmer than one. Only, I've never had two. I've always had one."

"It's not necessarily better with a husband in the bed," Priscilla informed her. "Gary always hated it when my ice-cold feet came anywhere near him, so I still had to wear socks."

"You should invest in an electric blanket," Candy suggested as she walked by with a plate of muffins for the crowd at a nearby table. "Or one of those warm stones you place at the foot of the bed. I hear they work really well."

Sally smacked herself on the forehead. "I don't think anyone is getting the point. I've been alone for a long time. I'm tired of washing dishes by hand because there are never enough to start a load in the dishwasher. I'm done with sitting in a restaurant by myself. That's so awkward."

"You could take a book," Candy suggested as she passed back by. "Lots of folks come in here with books. I have a hard time getting rid of them, in fact. They order one scone and stay all day using my internet."

"It's not the same." Sally leaned back in her chair. "Being alone is just so ... hard."

"I know what that feels like," Priscilla said. "And I've been to plenty of restaurants alone since my husband died, Sally. Truth is, many of us here have gone through seasons of being single."

"Seasons, sure. But don't you see? I'm forty-eight years old and I've never been married. I'll never have children. I'll never be a grandmother. I'll never..." She broke down crying.

Candy plopped down in the empty chair and slung her arm over Sally's shoulder. "Honey, many of us know what that feels like too. But God always finds ways of filling in the gaps. Where we see lack, He sees provision. Just promise me you won't give up." She pulled back her arm and stuck out her hand. "I'm Candy, by the way. I own this place. Didn't mean to horn in on your conversation, but I've got bionic ears. I've conquered the art of hearing above the crowd."

"Sally Jenson." The teary-eyed woman shook Candy's hand.

"Nice to meet you, Sally Jenson. I'd better get back to the kitchen now." Candy rose and worked her way through the crowd.

Sally looked at Priscilla and sighed. "I guess none of this is making sense to you."

"Oh, I think I'm starting to get the picture."

"I've had my sights on Tony for years." Sally lowered her voice and leaned forward. "I felt sure he was God's man for me. I've done everything except put a sign around my neck that says, 'Notice me!' But he doesn't. He's too wrapped up in that business of his. He's completely preoccupied, especially now that he's opening up a new shop. I thought I was going to lose it when he told me he was moving to Martha's Vineyard. It's been hard enough to hold his attention in Boston, where I'm on my own turf. I'm completely out of my element with the rich set."

"You might be surprised at how many of us on the island are just average people."

"Well, don't tell Tony that. He's counting on the ones with money to frequent his shop."

"But Sally, I didn't know about Tony's new shop. I was only keeping an eye on him because I thought maybe he had something to do with the disappearance of Eliza's car."

"You thought Tony was a thief?"

"Well, the idea crossed my mind, yes. But I haven't been able to piece together any evidence to that end."

"Trust me, you won't find any evidence, no matter how deep you dig. Tony Romano is as straight as an arrow. He's an amazing guy with the most unbelievable story. His wife died a few years back. She had leukemia. Tony raised their two boys by himself, got them all the way through their teen years and into good colleges. He's a stellar dad and a caring community member. So, the fact that someone would suspect him of anything makes me...cringe."

"Would it make you feel any better if I told you I suspected you as well?" Priscilla offered a forced smile.

"Well, terrific."

"Hey, you kept hanging around the island after the car went missing, and you were the last person to be seen driving it. We knew you had a key. You could've made a copy."

"You don't know me at all." Sally leaned back in her chair. "If I needed a sign that I should leave, I just got it."

"Oh, don't leave!" Candy's voice rang out. "At noon we're doing a big giveaway. The winner gets a giant heart-shaped cookie."

"Just what I need on Valentine's Day, a giant cookie I can eat all by myself." Sally went off about her singleness once again, her voice growing more and more animated.

Priscilla reached over and patted her hand. "Please, Sally, calm down for a minute."

"How can I calm down? You think I'm a car thief. You think the man I love is a car thief."

Priscilla sighed and leaned back in her chair.

"You think she's a car thief, Priscilla?" Candy placed a scone on Sally's plate. "Here you go, honey. A little sugar will iron those wrinkles out of your forehead."

"I'm a car thief who's old enough to have wrinkles." Sally picked up the scone and took a bite.

Candy looked flabbergasted by Sally's response to her words. "No, that's not what I meant. I meant worry lines. You have worry lines."

"I'm an old thief with worry lines." Sally took another bite of the scone.

Candy slunk away.

A couple of minutes later, Sally's color returned to normal. She took a few more bites of her scone and sighed. "Priscilla, I'm sorry. Please forgive my emotional outburst. I'm completely out of my element here. And I'm so embarrassed. I stuck around, hoping Tony would take notice of me, and when he didn't, I felt like a fool. Now look what I've done. I've made an even bigger fool of myself."

Priscilla turned her attention to the door of the bakery as the bell rang. "Oh my."

"What?" Sally turned and flinched as she saw Tony Romano walking into the shop. "No! You have to get me out of here, Priscilla. He can't see me like this. Is there a back door?"

"Don't be silly. You're just having coffee and Valentine treats with a new friend. Why would it matter if he runs into you here?"

"He'll think I'm following him. He doesn't know I'm still on the island."

"You got here first."

"I look awful."

"Your eyes are a little red, but other than that, you look like a million bucks."

Sally pulled out a compact and checked her appearance, then groaned. "There's no fixing this."

"Then don't try. Just look at this as an opportunity to say hello to an old friend who happens to be wandering into the same bakery where you're enjoying a scone with a new friend."

"A friend who thinks I stole a car. Oh, and that I'm old." She paused. "Are you sure there's no other way out?"

"Don't run, Sally. Face him with a smile. That's a life lesson my mother shared with me. When in doubt, nod and smile. It throws people off every time."

"Nod and smile." Sally's head bobbed up and down, and she pulled her lips back in a wide grimace. "Okay, okay."

Tony headed straight for the counter. A couple of minutes later, coffee cup and Danish plate in hand, he turned to look for a table.

"Invite him to join us, Sally," Priscilla said. "We've got an extra chair."

"No. I can't."

"Too late. He's looking right at you. Say something."

Sally looked as if she might be ill. She raised her hand and gestured for Tony to join them.

He walked to their table and sat down. "Sally, I had no idea you were still on the island. Didn't you deliver the Bel Air day before yesterday?"

"Yes." She smiled. "I decided to stick around and spend time with new friends. Do you know Priscilla Grant?"

He extended his hand. "Not yet. I heard all about you from Eliza, but I don't believe we ever met in person." He turned his attention to Sally. "I can't get over running into you here."

"I'm actually sticking around for the wedding," Sally explained. "I've been getting to know the bride's family. We're all staying at the same B&B."

He looked at her appreciatively. "Well, if anyone's easy to get to know, it's you, Sally."

"Th-thanks."

Tony went on to sing Sally's praises, and her face turned bright red. "Sally and I go way back," he told Priscilla. "We're old friends. She's brought me a ton of business over the years, and I'm grateful." He turned to face Sally. "Have I ever told you how grateful I am?"

"A few times." A shy smile followed on her end.

"Why did you say you're still on the island?" he asked.

"Oh, just getting some R&R and hanging out with friends. You?"

He smiled. "I've got some business to attend to here." He glanced at his watch. "Oh, speaking of which, I guess I'd better get on the road. I've got a meeting in an hour, and I'm not sure how to get there."

"If you have the address, maybe I can help you," Priscilla said.

He shook his head and reached for his coffee cup. "Nah, that's okay. I've got GPS in my car. I'll find it." He rose and gave the ladies a nod. "Great to meet you, Mrs. Grant. Always good to see you, Sally."

"Y-you too." Sally looked a bit nauseous. Either these two were hiding something or she truly was a nervous wreck in his presence.

He gave them a little wave and turned toward the door.

Sally dropped her head onto the table. "Ugh. He called me old too."

"He called you a friend."

"He called me an old friend."

Priscilla laughed. "I can't believe that's all you got out of that conversation. I really think you need to relax, Sally. The point is, the two of you are comfortable together."

"Do I look comfortable? And if he really wanted to spend time with me, why take off like that?"

"He said he had a meeting."

"Right. A meeting." Sally shook her head. "Not that it's any of my business. It's not. I'm a buttinsky." She paused. "Do you think he has a girlfriend on the island? That's a possibility."

"Sally, you need to calm down."

"I should. And if I'm staying for a wedding, then I need to be looking for something to wear."

A ruckus at the door caught Priscilla's attention. She glanced up to discover Gail and Uncle Hugh waving.

"Hey, Priscilla! Ready to go?" her uncle called out. "Let's shake this place."

Priscilla turned back to her new friend. "I have the perfect solution for your dress dilemma. Come with us. We're headed to my favorite dress shop in Edgartown."

"Dress shop?"

"Yes. After we make a quick stop to talk to Marvin Freemont."

"Marvin Freemont, president of the Vineyard Classics Car Club?" Sally's eyes widened, and she sprang to her feet. "I'm in, Priscilla. I'm in."

CHAPTER TWELVE

The trip to Edgartown was great fun. Gail took care of the driving, and Uncle Hugh sat in the back seat with Sally. They appeared to hit it off right away. From her spot in the passenger seat, Priscilla kept her eyes peeled.

"Where did you say this Freemont guy works again, Gail?"

"His office is in that little strip mall a ways down the street from the dress shop. It's next to the indoor pavilion where the car show is going to take place."

"He won't think it's weird, us just showing up like this to ask a bunch of questions about cars?" Priscilla wrung her hands. For some reason this whole thing made her feel a little unnerved.

"He's a car guy, Priscilla," Uncle Hugh said. "Those fellas are always happy to talk cars."

"Trust me," Sally chimed in. "I can keep him going for hours on end if you like. If I know anything, it's cars. And just for the record, I've read up on this guy. He's one of the richest men on the island."

"Really?" Gail seemed surprised by this news. "Must've escaped my notice."

"He gets a lot of press because of the cars. He's said to own more than any other person in the state."

Uncle Hugh let out a whistle. "Guess it's true he's loaded, then."

They arrived in Edgartown, and Gail drove straight to the strip mall.

"I recognize this parking lot," Uncle Hugh said. "Pretty sure they've held their summertime car shows outdoors, right here. Of course, with my memory, who can tell?"

Priscilla glanced back at him. "I didn't realize you were into classics, Uncle Hugh."

"What are you talking about? I am a classic." He laughed long and hard.

"To be honest, I don't understand the fascination with classic cars," said Gail.

"Remember how you felt the first time you drove a new car?" Sally asked. "Remember how it made you feel?"

Gail nodded. "Sure, felt great."

"Now add nostalgia to that. Picture yourself driving a car that turns heads, one that people talk about for all the right reasons. Those classics are eye-catchers. Some would say eye candy. They make people smile. They remind folks of simpler times."

Uncle Hugh seemed to lose himself to his thoughts. "When I see a classic car, I think 1950s soda shop, malts, cheeseburgers, and guys on surfboards."

"You never went surfing, Dad," Gail said.

"Just saying, it's the era I knew so well as a teenager. Gosh, I'm suddenly feeling very old. Haven't thought about soda shops in ages. Rock and Roll music playing on the jukebox, hot, salty french fries, and double-dating with Kimmy Ellison and a couple of friends. You're really taking me back in time."

"Yep, and all because we're talking about a classic car." Sally's voice had an excited lilt to it. "I just love how a car can change your perspective on everything."

Gail parked the car, and they got out.

"Which office is his, Gail?" Priscilla asked.

Her cousin glanced at the paper in her hand. "1301B." She squinted against the sunlight and then pointed at the second office. "Must be that one."

They walked to the entrance, and Uncle Hugh held the door for the ladies. Priscilla walked up to an overly made-up woman at the front desk and smiled. "Hello. We're wondering if Marvin Freemont is in today."

"Marvin?" The woman shook her head and pursed her brightly painted lips. "Not this morning. He's swamped with last-minute stuff for the show. Pretty sure he's at the mechanics' warehouse right now. That's where you find him half the time, anyway."

"Okay, thanks." Priscilla paused. "I was wondering if he knew anything about a 1954 Bel Air convertible."

"Why?" The woman looked her squarely in the eye, suddenly very interested. "You trying to sell one?"

"No." She shook her head. "It's not that."

"Well, if you ever do have one to sell, you know who to see. And if you want to leave your phone number, I'll let Marvin know you were here. I'm not saying he'll call back today. In fact, if I know him, he won't be able to think clearly enough to make any calls until after Saturday's show."

"Right." Priscilla scribbled down her contact information and thanked the woman for her time. Then she turned toward the door with the others directly behind her. At that very moment, the door swung open and a man stepped inside.

The woman behind the desk rose. "Marvin, perfect timing. These folks are here to see you."

"Really?" He looked at them. "How can I help you?"

"I, well…" Priscilla couldn't seem to get the words out. The man standing before her was tall and handsome, in a very prestigious sort of way. He had a certain air about him, one that spoke of money. She'd met many wealthy islanders, of course, but this one seemed different somehow. Perhaps it had something to do with his thick gray mustache or his silver televangelist hair with its wavy comb-over.

"Come into my office, please." He flashed a smile so bright, Priscilla could almost swear she saw a shimmer radiating off his white teeth. "How can I help?"

She couldn't get past the seersucker suit to respond. What sort of twenty-first-century multi-millionaire wore a suit from yesteryear? Still, she followed the man to a spacious office at the end of the hallway, her cousin, uncle, and friend tagging along behind.

"We were just hoping to ask you a few questions about a car that's gone missing," Priscilla said.

"One of my cars?" His brow wrinkled at once.

"No. It's a newly renovated Bel Air convertible. Gorgeous. Just transported to the island a couple of days ago."

His eyes widened. "Sounds like a real beauty. I've been trying to locate a car like that for ages but haven't had much success. Do you have a picture of the one that's missing?"

Sally pulled her phone from her purse and opened a photo of the car. "Check this out."

His eyes widened. "Wow. I like my cars like I like my women." He gave Priscilla a wink.

"Old?" Uncle Hugh offered.

"No. I was going in a completely different direction, but never mind. Let's just say I like cars in tip-top working condition, exterior completely remodeled, just like this Bel Air. No dents. No dings."

"So, you like your women to have plastic surgery? To look remodeled?" Uncle Hugh tried again.

Marvin laughed and pointed to Uncle Hugh. "I like you. You've got a great sense of humor. And I was just kidding, anyway."

"Sure you were," Hugh muttered. "Well, don't be expecting me to get this face lifted anytime soon. Marigold likes these wrinkles. Says they make me look seasoned."

Sally showed Marvin another photo and shifted the conversation back to the car. "Stunning vehicle. A real neck-snapper. Classic 235 CID Inline 6-cylinder. 136 hp. Powerglide automatic transmission. 3.9L 235 CID punched out to a '40 over piston."

"How many miles?" Marvin asked.

"When I dropped it off on Tuesday we were looking at 13,548. It runs like a dream. Smooth as silk."

"Sounds pretty close to perfect," Marvin said.

She nodded. "Yep. And the restoration on this baby was impeccable. Top of the line vinyl upholstery, inside and out. Excellent bodywork. Whitewall Coker tires. The works."

"Man." He dropped into his seat. "I'd love to take a look at that one."

"So would we," Priscilla said. "It's gone missing, as I said."

"Any clues?" he asked.

She shook her head, and Marvin clucked his tongue. "That's a real pity. When you stumble across a classic like that, you need to guard it with your life. There are some real lowlifes out there who would do anything to get their hands on a vehicle like that."

Sally and Marvin lit into a lengthy conversation about the vehicle's vinyl upholstery. He let out more than one whistle of admiration as she scrolled through the various photos.

When they finished, he leaned back in his chair. "Do me a favor, folks. If you do locate this car, be sure to register it for this weekend's show. A beauty like this deserves to be seen."

He handed them some materials about the show and then walked them to the front door. They said their goodbyes and headed back to the car.

"What did you think of Marvin Freemont?" Gail asked when everyone was settled, and she slipped her car into Reverse.

"I thought he was a showboat," Uncle Hugh said from the back seat. "Big talker."

Priscilla shrugged. "Seemed pretty knowledgeable about cars."

Gail shrugged. "I'm not sure why, but he struck me as a little odd. Over the top, maybe."

"He knows his stuff," Sally said. "That's for sure. And you can't deny he's one handsome fellow."

"Really? In that suit?" Uncle Hugh laughed. "If I'd known seersucker was in, I'd have pulled my old wardrobe out of mothballs."

This got a laugh out of everyone.

"I didn't care much for him," Uncle Hugh said. "Found him almost as annoying as Victor Fox. Can you imagine those two in the same room at the same time?" He slapped his knee and cackled. "I'd be hard-pressed to tell you which one annoyed me more."

"Did you pick up on what he was trying to say back there?" Gail asked. "All that stuff about plastic surgery?"

"Yes." Priscilla nodded. "He likes fast cars and fast women. And he likes both to be in tip-top shape, ready to be shown off to the world."

"With shiny hubcaps," Uncle Hugh threw in.

"And whitewall tires," Sally added.

"His love of all things perfect might explain the woman at the front desk," Uncle Hugh said. "She looked about half his age."

"Lots of older men date younger gals, Dad," Gail said.

"Oh? You think they're a couple? I just thought she was eye candy." He rolled his eyes.

"For sure, that wasn't her nose," Sally observed. "She's had a nose job. And a few other tweaks too, but I'm too much of a lady to point out which body parts."

"How do you know all that, just from looking?" Uncle Hugh asked.

"I worked for a plastic surgeon years ago. I can spot a fake nose a mile away. And it's getting easier and easier for me to know when a woman's lip liner is permanent."

"That woman's lip color wasn't from a tube?" Uncle Hugh's eyes widened.

"Nope. Tattooed liner all the way. And the eyeliner was tattooed as well."

"Well, for Pete's sake." Uncle Hugh sounded deflated. "If I ever get a hankerin' to tattoo my lips, please stop me. I'd hate to think I might get stuck for all eternity with a color that didn't suit me."

"I'll try not to let that happen, Dad," Gail said, grinning.

"I have a tattoo." Sally lifted her wrist to show off a tiny dove. "I'll never get this taken off. I got it in memory of my sister, who passed away over twenty-five years ago."

"I'm so sorry, Sally," Gail said. "How did she die?"

"Jacquie was killed in a car accident. She'd only had her license a few months. She went to a football game at the high school and never came back."

"Oh, wow." Priscilla gave her new friend a sympathetic look. "I'm so sorry, Sally."

"Me too. Nothing has been the same since she left. I was twenty-two, and she was seventeen. She was my only sibling, and we were really close."

"I'm surprised you ended up working with cars."

"Well, you know what they say—conquer your fears. For the first couple of years after she died I was scared to get behind the wheel. But at some point, I made up my mind to get past that. I dug my heels in and started working with cars, then ended up at the transport company, driving them. I've been all over the country, delivering cars as far away as California."

"All classics?" Uncle Hugh asked.

"Nope. You'd be surprised at how many people leave vehicles behind when they move. But mostly, folks buy cars online from people they've never met and I deliver them. It's good too, because I can usually tell whether or not the car is a lemon. By the time I pull up in the new owner's driveway, I've got a list of all the things they need to have looked at."

Priscilla gave her an admiring gaze. "I'm sure the owners love you."

"I wouldn't go that far, but they appreciate me. I take what I do very seriously. That's why I love the cars Tony works on. He really is in the transformation business. My first flip was a car I named Lancelot."

"Lancelot?" Uncle Hugh asked.

"Yes, sorry. I forgot to mention that I always name the cars too."

"Funny. I used to name my cars when I was young." Priscilla chuckled. "My first vehicle was a handed-down work truck from my dad. Pretty sure I named him Fred."

"Fred?" Sally raised her brows.

"Yeah. I never had much of an imagination, I guess. But Fred was good to me. Well, until that fateful day when he left me stranded on the side of the road with a busted radiator hose."

"That might not have been Fred's fault. Something as simple as a hose is usually the owner's responsibility." Sally shrugged. "Falls under routine maintenance."

"I never treated Fred right, I guess." Priscilla smiled. "He was my first vehicle, and I didn't know how to take care of him."

Gail eased her car into the parking lot at the Perfect Fit. "Sally, if you're looking for a great dress for Eliza and Carson's wedding, this is the place."

Uncle Hugh groaned and leaned back against the seat. "I'll be the one in the car taking a nap while you gals shop."

"That'll be just fine with me." Gail turned off the car. "Ready to do some shopping, ladies?"

Priscilla nodded. "Sure am."

"Just don't ask me to tattoo my lips and I'll be fine." Sally laughed and the ladies climbed out of the car, ready to get this shopping trip underway.

CHAPTER THIRTEEN

Y ou're going to love this shop, Sally," Priscilla said as they walked into The Perfect Fit.

"It's really quaint, at least from the outside. Just don't expect me to doll up too much, okay? I want to be able to recognize myself at the wedding."

"I promise, but don't be surprised if Trudy tries to get you to buy makeup between now and then. She sells beauty products."

"Trudy? Who's Trudy?"

Priscilla laughed. "Oh, that's right. You haven't met the whole family yet. Well, let's deal with the dress first, shall we? There will plenty of time left to talk about the rest of the cousins when we're done."

"I'm shaking in my boots just thinking about it."

As they made their way into the shop, Priscilla noticed Claire at the register. She turned to face Sally and whispered, "Let me introduce you to the groom's daughter."

"Sure." Sally shrugged. "Sounds good."

Priscilla waved at the young woman behind the desk. "Claire, how are you feeling?"

"Better and better with each passing day." A smile turned up the edges of her lips. "Finding out about my dad, meeting him in person, the surgery. The Lupus is in remission now." She beamed with obvious delight as she took a few steps in Priscilla's direction.

"I'm so happy for you." Priscilla hugged her young friend.

"At least for now." Claire shrugged. "I know it's something I'll deal with my whole life, but I'm glad, at least for now, to have a reprieve. And I have my dad to thank for it. If he hadn't come, if the kidney hadn't been a match..." Her words drifted off. "Anyway, it's a miracle that he's involved, and not just because he physically saved my life. The whole thing has given me a story— a testimony, I guess you'd call it—that I wouldn't change for anything."

"He's blessed to have you, honey. We all are." Priscilla gave her a tight squeeze. "Now, I want to introduce you to someone. This is Sally Jenson. She's from Boston and will be a guest at your dad's wedding. She's in the market for a new dress."

"Sally Jenson?" Claire's face lit into a broad smile. "Oh, my goodness. I just heard all about you from my grandmother. She's smitten with you."

"Really?" Sally grinned. "I thought she was a lot of fun too."

Claire's mouth fell open. "Wow. Well, to be fair, I haven't known my grandmother very long—I guess that's a story for another day—but I've never heard anyone refer to her as fun before. That's a first. You must bring out the best in her."

"I've only known Sally a short time," Priscilla said, "but she does see the best in people."

"That's very generous," Sally said.

"Sally, how did you and Eliza meet, anyway?" Claire asked.

"We're recent friends. See, I delivered..." Sally's eyes widened, and her words faded off. Priscilla swallowed hard and hoped she hadn't given away too much already.

"Delivered...what?" Claire asked.

"A wedding gift. I arrived on the island with a gift for the happy couple. And when I took the time to get to know Eliza, I realized she was one of the finest people I'd ever met. We became friends just like that."

"Awesome news. So, what sort of dress are you looking for? Tea-length? Something in a jewel tone, maybe? This is a Valentine's wedding, so anything jewel-toned will work, I think."

"Anything but flowers." Sally grimaced. "Sorry, but I've never been a fan of floral prints. These broad shoulders of mine look ridiculous with flowers plastered all over them."

"Then don't come to visit us in the spring or summer. The whole shop is filled with flowery dresses." Claire waved at her. "Follow me. I have some new items in that just might interest you. How do you feel about forest green?"

"Sounds doable."

"With your beautiful skin tone, I think it would be just the ticket."

Priscilla looked on as Claire drew Sally into an easy conversation. Before long they were talking about cars, their voices rising and falling in animated fashion. Go figure.

"Check out those two." Gail nodded in the direction of the two chatting women. "They seem like a good match."

"Thick as thieves," Priscilla concurred. "Would you believe they're talking about cars?"

"Really?" Gail looked perplexed by this notion. "Claire is a car girl?"

"Guess the apple doesn't fall far from the tree. From what I just overheard, her dad is buying a classic from her birthday year. He's having it restored then giving it to her as a birthday gift."

Gail smiled. "Aw, I didn't know she had a birthday coming up."

"She doesn't. But remember, he missed a lot of birthdays during her growing up years. I think he's trying to make up for it with one swell gift now."

"Sweet." Gail lowered her voice. "Let's just hope that car doesn't go missing."

"Trust me, after he finds out about this, he'll be watching it like a hawk. I think we're all going to keep a closer eye on our cars now." Priscilla paused. "Not that I would mind too much if someone took off with mine. It's been giving me fits for the past couple of months."

"A woman should always put safety first. Maybe it's time for a new car, Priscilla."

She shrugged. "I don't know about that. Maybe Sally could help me pick out a new car when the time comes."

Creases formed between Gail's eyes. "When things slow down, you're really going to tell me how you and Sally ended up being friends. Wasn't she your top suspect just yesterday? Are you sure she didn't take off with that car?"

Priscilla shrugged. "I have no idea, to be honest. She's won me over on so many levels. Maybe my discernment is down because I haven't been getting enough sleep."

"I doubt that. Maybe she's just really a nice gal who happened to be staying on the island for a few days for personal reasons."

"She explained all of that to me before you and Uncle Hugh got to the bakery this morning. I'll fill you in later."

Gail nodded.

While they waited, Priscilla turned her attention back to some of the things Marvin had said in their brief conversation. Had he left clues, perhaps?

Before she could give that too much thought, Sally walked into a dressing room with a couple of gowns. A few minutes later she emerged wearing a dark green tea-length dress that suited her perfectly.

Priscilla whistled. "Wow, Sally, you look like you're ready for—"

"The prom?"

"No way," Gail chimed in. "Much less froufrou than that. Definitely wedding-worthy."

"You think it's okay? Really? Because I've never spent this kind of money on a fancy dress before."

"Oh, did I forget to mention it's forty percent off?" Claire called out from the register. "We're running a Valentine's Day special."

Sally threw her hands up in the air and shouted, "Sold to the highest bidder! I'll take it. It's perfect."

She went back into the changing room, and Gail stepped into the spot next to Priscilla. "I can't wait until later, Priscilla. Tell me what you've learned about you-know-who." She pointed to the dressing room.

Priscilla lowered her voice and took a few steps toward the front of the shop. She gestured for Gail to join her. "I saw Sally tailing Tony Romano yesterday, the guy who restored the Bel Air."

"Tony Romano? Isn't he from Boston?"

"Yes. He's on the island."

"No way."

"Yes. I saw him at a Realtor's office. I was hiding in the bathroom."

Gail looked flabbergasted by this news. "You were hiding in a bathroom at a Realtor's office? How did I miss all of this?"

"Happened just after lunch. Well, after the part where I went to Victor's car lot. And definitely after I almost ran over him. Anyway, I was hiding in the ladies' room—"

"Your stories are getting crazier every day."

"And there she was, tailing Tony Romano. I wasn't sure why until she and I talked this morning at the bakery. She turned red in the face and had trouble completing a sensible sentence. To me, she looked like a woman enamored."

"Are you telling me Sally Jenson has the hots for Tony Romano?"

"Yes." Priscilla nodded. "She's staying on the island because he's here."

"Does that mean she's not a suspect anymore?"

"I didn't say that."

"Well, I'm glad, because I thought it was mighty strange that she was with you at the bakery and even stranger when you invited her along for this shopping trip."

The two women stopped talking the minute Sally walked out of the changing room with the dress slung over her arm.

She came to them and held the dress up. "I can't believe I'm doing this!" A girlish giggle followed, and she turned toward the register.

"You going to take it?" Claire asked as Sally set the dress down on the counter in front of her.

"You betcha. I can't believe it was that easy."

"That's why we call this place The Perfect Fit," Claire responded. "Happens more often than you know." She rang up Sally's purchase then put the dress in a bag. "Guess I'll see you Saturday at Dad's wedding."

"Guess so." Sally paused. "Oh, and for the record, I think your dad's getting a great wife."

"Thank you. I'm pretty fond of Eliza, myself."

They turned to leave but Priscilla snapped to attention. She turned back around. "Oh, Claire, I almost forgot the main reason I was stopping by the shop today."

"It wasn't just so I could make a sale?" Claire pretended to pout.

"Well, that too, but I wanted to talk to you about the décor for the dining room at the Bluffs. I worked on the centerpieces and took a bunch of photos. Just want to make sure they match the votives you bought." She pulled up the pictures on her phone, and before long she and Claire were deep in conversation.

"I'm so glad Eliza didn't want to go too far with the Valentine's wedding theme," Claire said as they wrapped up their discussion.

Priscilla tucked her phone back into her purse. "What do you mean?"

"Well, I went to a Valentine wedding once where the brides-maids all wore dark red dresses."

"Nothing wrong with that."

"And pink fur jackets."

"Ew." This response came from Sally, who shifted her bag from one hand to the other.

"Exactly." Claire fussed with several empty hangers. "And the cake was heart-shaped. In fact, even the hors d'oeuvres were heart-shaped, if I recall."

Gail wrinkled her nose. "Overkill, if you ask me."

"Some people know how to take a theme and run with it." Claire walked to a dress rack and started organizing the dresses. "I'm just giving you these notes for future use, Priscilla, should you ever coordinate another Valentine wedding."

"I'm not a wedding planner, Claire. This stint will be behind me soon."

"Well, once word gets around, you might be," Gail chimed in. "That's kind of how Candy got started with the bakery, you know. One day she was baking scones out of her own kitchen and bring-ing them to Bible study, the next she had a thriving business. Things like this happen, you know."

"Not to me," Priscilla argued. "Trust me, I'm too old to start a new business. I'm perfectly happy playing the role of—"

"Sleuth?" Gail asked.

"No. I mean, I'm not an official sleuth. I'm not an official...anything. And I'm perfectly okay with that."

"Got it. But, if you ever do coordinate another Valentine wedding, just promise me you won't do heart-shaped petit fours."

"Good grief, Gail. Stop."

Her cousin laughed. "Couldn't help myself, sorry."

Sally turned her attention to a rack with earrings and matching necklaces. She thumbed through them. "I went to a Valentine's wedding once where the whole room was done up in red and pink with cupids hanging from the light fixtures and ceiling fans. It was particularly interesting when they turned on the fans during the dancing. You've never seen so many cupids flying in circles in your life."

Priscilla laughed at the image that presented.

Sally held up a necklace-earring combo. "What do you think of these with my new dress?"

"Perfect," Priscilla responded. "But, seriously, you ladies don't really think I'd encourage Eliza to go in that direction, do you? I mean, she picked this weekend, at least in part, because it worked with everyone's busy schedules. And besides, Valentine's Day is today, two full days before the wedding. More of a happy coincidence than a mandate for Cupid to show up with his bow and arrow."

"I kind of feel like Cupid has already shown up, don't you?" Gail's lips turned up in a smile. "Eliza and Carson. Rachel and A.J.

Candy and Beau. Before long, Tommy and I might just run off together and tie the knot. Or you and Gerald."

"Wait...what?" Priscilla hardly knew what to say.

Gail put her hands up. "Sorry, I misspoke. I'm just trying to convey the message that half the island's either in love or tying the knot. That's all. Cupid is doing his work, spinning around the room on a ceiling fan. Maybe he's getting to all of us."

"I blame the Romance Channel." Sally carried the jewelry pieces to the counter and set them down. "They play all of those romance movies round the clock during the Valentine season. Gives people ideas."

"What's all this about romance movies?" Uncle Hugh's voice rang out. "And why are you gals still shopping? I thought you were just going to take a minute."

Priscilla turned to face her uncle. "We came in to tie up loose ends with Claire about her father's wedding."

"Your father's getting married?" Uncle Hugh extended his hand. "Congratulations." He leaned over and whispered in Priscilla's ear. "Who is this gal, again? I can't remember."

"I'm Claire. My mother and I own this dress shop. My father is Carson Fletcher. He's getting married to Eliza Jamison on Saturday."

"Uh-huh." Uncle Hugh's brow wrinkled. "So, let me get this straight. You work with your mother. And your father is getting married. To someone else who isn't your mother."

"Yes, it's a very long story. Maybe I can fill you in at the wedding."

"Nope. I'll be too busy kicking my heels up with my sweetie. You know Marigold Townsend?"

"Of course! She's a regular customer and was one of the first people on the guest list."

"It's good to be regular. I take fiber every day, myself." Uncle Hugh chuckled. "Now, where's the bathroom? I can't stand here all day talking."

Claire pointed him in the right direction and then took care of ringing Sally up again. Minutes later, Uncle Hugh emerged and took Priscilla by the arm. "Come look at this hat, Priscilla."

"Hat?" She didn't realize The Perfect Fit sold hats, but followed her uncle anyway. When he got her alone in the far corner of the room, he leaned in close as if he had a big secret to share. "Need to talk to you about something privately, Priscilla. Don't worry, I'll keep it short. I'm old."

"Oh, well, I—"

I've decided to pop the question. I'm asking Marigold to marry me."

"Uncle Hugh, that's wonderful news!" Priscilla lowered her voice when she noticed the other ladies were looking her way. "I'm thrilled for you both."

"Thanks. Just putting a bug in your ear before letting anyone else know because we'll need one of those coordinator things."

"Oh, I'm no wedding coordinator, Uncle Hugh."

"Could'a fooled me. Gail says you're doing a fine job with Eliza's wedding plans, and I hear you're helping your daughter as well. So, I figure you're the best person for the job. Now, look here,

Priscilla. I need to come up with some special way to pop the question. I was hoping you and I could meet to talk about my options."

"We're in countdown mode for Eliza and Carson's wedding, Uncle Hugh. If you can wait until after Saturday..."

He paused and released a sigh. "Well, I've waited this long. I don't suppose another couple o' days'll kill me." He laughed. "Maybe I should've worded that differently. At any rate, I'll be thinking about the proposal."

"That's a good idea."

"You think too." He patted her on the back. "Thanks for agreeing to help, Priscilla. You're a peach. Or, should I say pear? You're pretty good at pairing folks up, now aren't you?" He doubled over with laughter and eventually started coughing. This must've alarmed Gail, who rushed their way.

"Everything okay over here?" she asked.

"Yep, everything's okay." Priscilla fought the temptation to take a little bow and say, "Priscilla Grant, wedding planner extraordinaire, at your service!"

CHAPTER FOURTEEN

I promised you a walk, Jake, and a walk you shall have." Priscilla reached for the leash and clipped it to the dog's collar. "Now, I'm sorry this took so long, but I've been very busy. If you had any idea what I've been through the past few days you would under-stand. I dare say you would even forgive me."

Jake's tail wagged in enthusiastic response. Priscilla walked to the front door and opened it to discover Trudy standing on the other side.

"Hey, I was just about to knock." She grinned. "Taking Jake for a walk?"

"Yep. I owe him. Want to come?"

Her cousin's nose wrinkled. "I guess it wouldn't kill me to walk a bit. How far are you going?"

Priscilla shrugged. "Let's just see where the road takes us." She laughed. "Hey, isn't that another one of Victor Fox's cheesy slogans?"

"Probably." Trudy reached behind Priscilla and closed the front door.

Together, they walked down the road toward the Beekman home. Priscilla spent much of the time bringing Trudy up to speed on her investigation.

"Okay, I can't tell a lie, Priscilla," Trudy said after a few minutes. "Gail called and told me you took Sally Jenson with you to Edgartown this morning."

"That's why you came by, to see if I'd lost my mind?"

"Well, she was your number one suspect twenty-four hours ago."

"And is still on the list. But the more time I spend with her, the more I think she's just a lonely woman who has a crush on Tony Romano."

"So, talk to me about Tony. Why is he here? Out of the blue? Don't you think that's a little suspicious, what with the car missing?"

"Yes, but Sally seems to think he's innocent."

"And we all know we can trust Sally's judgment." Trudy stopped walking and gave Priscilla a pensive stare. "Look, Priscilla, everyone knows you're exhausted. People are tugging at you right and left."

"Yes."

"And maybe your judgment is a little impaired right now. Have you thought about that? You know how they tell you not to make any big life-changing decisions when you're grieving someone? Well, maybe the same thing is true when you're planning a wedding. Maybe you need to give yourself a window of time. No sleuthing until after this wedding. Or maybe even Rachel's. You know what I mean?"

"Trudy, I didn't go looking for this mystery. And trust me, I'm hoping the police figure this one out on their own. The very last thing I need to be doing right now is solving a crime." She paused and gazed out over the water. It usually calmed her, but not this time.

Priscilla turned and headed back toward the house, hoping Trudy would change the direction of the conversation. Thankfully, she dove into a discussion about the latest beauty products she was hawking.

When they got back to the house, Jake lay down on the living room rug, panting.

"I think we sufficiently wore him out," Trudy said.

"That was the plan. He needed the exercise. I did too, for that matter."

Priscilla invited Trudy to stay for lunch. "It's not much," she said. "But I've got some of those yummy rolls from the bakery, and they make great sandwiches. I picked up turkey from the grocery store a couple of days ago. And Swiss cheese."

"Sounds great."

Priscilla led the way into the kitchen, where she put together sandwiches. "You want chips too? I've got baked potato chips."

"Perfect."

They settled down at the breakfast table to eat, and Trudy continued the discussion about her new makeup products. After a while, she stopped. "I'm boring you."

"No you're not." Priscilla nibbled on a potato chip. "What makes you say that?"

"You're just unusually quiet."

"Am I?"

"You seem tired."

"I am. I mean, I slept well last night, but overall, I'm just exhausted. I don't mean to ignore you. Fill me in on what I've missed in town while distracted with this wedding."

"Hmm. Mildred updated the Revolutionary War display at the museum. Moths were eating through the costumes from the old display."

"Oh my."

"Yes. And Beau Ortmann has been in a rough mood the last few times I saw him at the bakery. Not sure what's up with him."

"Rough financial season, I guess."

Trudy shrugged. "Other than that, the only news is about Victor Fox."

"Victor? What about him?"

"Oh, he's on a campaign to sell one hundred cars in the next one hundred days. Something like that. His commercials wear me out."

"Me too." Priscilla took another bite of her sandwich.

Trudy used her napkin to wipe the crumbs from her lips. "Speaking of Victor, whatever became of Betty? Any clue?"

"I hear from her on occasion," Priscilla said. "Their divorce is final now."

"Figured as much."

"From what I understand, her daughter and son-in-law built a sweet little guesthouse on the back of their property and Betty has decorated it in all her favorite colors."

Trudy put her napkin in her lap. "I'm sure it feels good to finally have the freedom to make choices without Victor's iron fist coming down on her."

Priscilla guarded her response. "Yes. But I think Victor's changed, so I hate to keep categorizing him as the angry man he once was. Gerald said that he's come a long way. I'd like to think that's true. And, from what I saw at the car dealership yesterday, he seems different."

"What were you doing at the car dealership? Trading in your car?"

"To be honest, I went there looking for the Bel Air. I noticed he's selling classics now. Didn't see it, but I did take note of the prettiest dark blue SUV on his lot. It really caught my eye."

"You should buy it, Priscilla. Didn't you tell me your SUV almost stalled on you recently?"

"Yes, in Edgartown, right in front of Victor's place."

"Might want to check to see if there are any recalls on that vehicle." Trudy brushed her hands on her slacks. "We're too old to be stranded on the side of the road, particularly in the middle of the winter."

"Recalls? On my SUV?"

"Yep." Trudy nodded. "Happened to me once. I bought a new car and had all sorts of trouble with it. Turned out it'd been recalled for a problem with the fuel tank."

"Oh my goodness. I never thought about that."

"Better check into it. In my case, I took it back and forth to the dealership more times than I could count but they never got it working right." She paused. "A reliable car is important, Priscilla, so I'm glad to hear you're looking at one. Though I hate the idea of anyone giving that Victor Fox a penny. I still don't trust the man."

Priscilla shrugged. "Well, I didn't commit to anything. He doesn't even know I'm interested." As she spoke the words, Priscilla had to wonder—was she interested in a new vehicle?

"I love the idea of an SUV," Trudy said. "Tall enough to give you a good view, but not way up there." This led to a funny story about how she'd recently gone for a ride in a friend's new truck, one she had trouble getting in and out of. After a few minutes of chatter, she pushed her chair back and made an announcement. "We should do it."

"Do what?" Priscilla asked.

"Swing by Victor's lot and look at that SUV you keep talking about."

"I only brought it up once."

"Maybe I'll change my mind about you buying from Victor once I see the vehicle."

"It's two o'clock, Trudy. I have to meet Eliza at five at the alterations place and then Gerald is picking me up for dinner at seven."

"That's perfect. That gives us just enough time. And don't worry, Priscilla. We'll take my car. If Victor sees the shape yours is in, he'll decide to cheat you on its trade-in value."

"But I..." Priscilla gave up. She grabbed her purse and followed her cousin through the living room and out the front door. Minutes later she found herself in the passenger seat of Trudy's car, listening to a crazy love song on the radio. Trudy sang along at the top of her lungs. When they turned into Victor's car lot, Trudy pulled into a parking spot and shut the car off.

"Just let me do the talking, Priscilla."

"What? I'm not ready to talk to anyone about a new car, Trudy. I'm not at that point yet."

"Then what are we doing here?" Her cousin opened her door and stepped out.

Priscilla opened the passenger door and reached for her purse before getting out. "We're here because you thought it was a good idea."

"Still do. Show me this car you've got your eye on."

Priscilla's gaze ran up and down the various rows. "It must be in a different spot from yesterday."

"Someone must've taken it out for a test drive. You don't want them to buy it out from under you, do you, Priscilla?"

"Honestly, Trudy, I don't really care at this point. I'm in no hurry to—" Her gaze landed on the glistening blue SUV, shimmering under the afternoon sun. "Oh." She couldn't help but smile. It was even prettier than yesterday.

"Is that it?" Trudy pointed and took off in the direction of the car. "It's a dream."

The next fifteen minutes were spent listening to Trudy try to talk a salesman down on the price of the vehicle. The poor guy finally gave up and headed back inside.

"Well, that was grueling," Priscilla said. "And embarrassing."

"Why? They always overcharge on used cars. And they're accustomed to haggling, trust me. Dan taught me how, years ago."

They headed back toward Trudy's car, which was parked near the warehouse. Priscilla happened to catch a glimpse through the door. "Oh, look. They've got more cars in there."

"Yeah, probably not ready for the lot yet. But they will be."

"Just makes me wonder..." Priscilla squinted against the sunlight and tried to see through the small opening into the darkened warehouse.

"You're thinking the Bel Air might be in there?" Trudy asked.

"Maybe."

Trudy took a couple of steps toward the warehouse door. "I say we go in and find out for ourselves."

"What? No way." Priscilla shook her head.

"We're going in, Priscilla. Just follow me. And if anyone asks any questions, let me answer."

Priscilla followed Trudy through the narrow opening into the shadowy interior of the warehouse. "I can't believe we're doing this. I can't even see anything, it's so dark. How are we going to tell one car from another in here?"

Trudy pulled out her phone and turned on the flashlight. "There you go." She pointed the light at the first of many cars. The whole place looked like a giant trash heap. Pieces of the vehicles were strewn all over the place.

"Do you think maybe these cars are stolen or something?" Trudy asked. "Maybe he steals them and sells the parts?"

"Could be. But I suspect these are just the older cars that folks trade in. Probably only good for auctioning off or selling for parts."

Trudy pointed the light at the floor. "Watch your step, Priscilla. We don't need to end up with any broken bones."

"I'm being as careful as an old lady who's crawling around in a warehouse in the dark can be. Ouch!" Priscilla let out a cry as she bumped her leg into something sharp.

"Are you okay?"

"Yes. I just ran into a broken bumper."

"Well, be more careful. And keep it down, will you? Someone could hear us."

They made their way from row to row, Trudy's flashlight finally growing dim. Priscilla thought she saw something familiar a few rows down but couldn't be sure.

"Look, Trudy. Right over there. Looks like a classic. Definitely a convertible." She reached for her phone and turned on its flashlight. "Never mind. It's a newer model. Cream-colored. And it's not a convertible. The top's just been pulled off for some reason."

Off in the distance she heard voices. Two men, it sounded like.

"He paid you how much?" the first guy asked.

"More than I'll make in a couple months working here, but it's under the rug."

"Is the car here?"

"No, are you kidding? No way would I keep the car here. You think I want the police raiding this place?"

"Then where?"

"Someplace safe. That's all I'm saying. Someplace very safe."

Through the narrow opening, she caught a glimpse of the two men. Neither looked familiar. One was older, and very tall. The other one was shorter and had a round midsection.

At that moment, a large overhead light flipped on and Priscilla's breath caught in her throat as she saw Victor Fox standing directly in front of them.

"Ladies? Do you mind if I ask what you're doing in my warehouse?"

"I, well..." Priscilla squeezed her eyes shut. She didn't want to lie, so the truth would have to do. "Looking for a car."

"I have over two hundred excellent cars on my lot you could look at."

"Right." Priscilla turned off the flashlight on her phone. "I've seen those. I was actually looking for something...else."

The worry lines on his forehead deepened. "If you have a specific make or model in mind, why didn't you just come to me? Why go sneaking around in my warehouse?"

"Well, you see Victor, it's like this—"

"This warehouse is off-limits."

"And why, exactly, is it off-limits?" Trudy asked. "What are you hiding?"

"Hiding?" He looked genuinely perplexed by this notion. Then his eyes narrowed. "Oh, I get it. You think I've got a stolen car in here, don't you? That classic one that's gone missing. I already told you, Priscilla. I haven't seen it." His face fell, and he looked away. "I've been working hard to regain people's trust. I see now it's going to take a lot more time."

Priscilla felt terrible. "I'm sorry, Victor. But there's only two days left until the wedding, and I'm desperate to find that car."

"Well, I don't have it. And don't think I didn't notice you looking at that gorgeous dark blue SUV on my lot yesterday. And again today."

"O-oh, you noticed that? Well, I—"

"Of course I noticed. Who wouldn't notice someone oohing and aahing over a great vehicle like that. It's only got twenty-two thousand miles on it, by the way, and is in tip-top shape. We just lowered the price on it this morning. You should take advantage of my Valentine's Special, good for the next six hours. We close at nine."

"Right. I saw it, but was looking for something a little smaller." There. That wasn't a lie. She had been thinking of getting a smaller vehicle, something to save on gas. "And I'm afraid it's the wrong time for me to be looking for a car right now."

"Here at Victor's it's never the wrong time to look for a car. And you never have to worry about the car's condition—I've got the best mechanics on the island."

"You do?"

"Yeah. Bruce and Brady Hawthorne. Top guys in their field, and brothers, no less. I wouldn't trust anyone else with my vehicles."

"Well, that's good."

"When you buy that SUV—and I know you will—we'll throw in a full two-year warranty. My guys will fix any problems that might come up during that time period. When you drive away in a Victor Fox car, you're driving away a winner."

Okay, so this guy really was a politician at heart.

"That's comforting." She took a few steps toward the ware-house door, Trudy following on her heels. "Thanks for your time, Victor. I wish I could stick around for a visit, but I have to meet Eliza for her final fitting."

"Right. Eliza. She's getting married this weekend."

"Yes, and I'm in a hurry to get to her. Maybe we'll talk cars later. How would that be?"

"Fine, Priscilla." He waved as she walked quickly toward Trudy's car. "And remember, here at Victor's Pre-Owned Cars, you'll walk home with a fistful of dollars!"

Right now she didn't care anything about walking away with money in her pocket. She just wanted to get out of here, and the sooner, the better.

CHAPTER FIFTEEN

Priscilla made it to Amber's Alterations at five minutes till five. She buzzed inside, spent about half an hour chitchatting with Amber and Eliza about the dress, and then headed home to get ready for her Valentine's date with Gerald. By the time he arrived, she was dressed in her favorite dark blue dress and had even donned an appropriate amount of makeup and jewelry. Trudy would be proud.

When Gerald came in, he gave her an admiring look. "I'll be the envy of all the other fellas at the steak house."

"Thank you, kind sir." She bowed.

Jake rose from his spot on the rug and ambled their direction. Gerald reached down and scratched the pup behind the ears. "Seeing Jake makes me miss Sammy even more."

Priscilla gave him a sympathetic look. "I'm so sorry, Gerald."

His expression grew more serious. "It's the weirdest thing. It used to drive me crazy when she barked at the neighbor's cat. Now I miss it. And remember how I used to complain about her slobbering? I even miss that."

"Aw, I'm sorry, Gerald."

"It's okay. I guess it's true what they say—you don't know what you've got till it's gone."

"Right. I definitely understand that."

"I guess you do, sorry. I didn't mean to create such a somber mood. Just saying I'm glad Jake is still here. I enjoy his company." Gerald rubbed the dog's ears once again and before long Jake had rolled over onto his back, begging for a belly rub. "You're a good boy, aren't you?" Gerald rubbed the spoiled pooch's belly.

When he finally stopped, the dog rose and sauntered over to Priscilla, as if looking for more attention. She petted him on the head and sighed. "To think, when I first got to the island I wasn't so sure if Jake and I were a good match. Now I can't imagine my life without him." She clamped a hand over her mouth. "Oh, I'm sorry, Gerald. This probably isn't making you feel any better."

"Nah, you're just giving voice to what I'm feeling. My house seems...empty."

"Have you thought about getting another dog?"

He shrugged. "I'm sure I will someday, but for now I'll just live vicariously through you." He pointed at Jake. "I'll swing by from time to time and get my slobbery dog kisses here."

Priscilla smiled. "Be my guest. And if you're really feeling down in the dumps, feel free to bathe him too. And take him for a good, long walk. And clip his nails. Those are a pain to cut."

Gerald laughed and put his hands up in the air. "Okay, okay. I'll do my best to pitch in and help with Jake's care, as long as you agree to give me joint custody."

"Joint custody, eh?"

"I'm just kidding." Gerald offered her a smile so warm it caused her to blush. "But I do appreciate you letting me spend time with him. It's comfortable here." He gave her a pensive look. "And not just because of the dog."

Priscilla wasn't sure what to say. Having Gerald around was getting more comfortable every day.

Her cell phone rang. She picked it up and saw Eliza's name on the screen.

Priscilla started the call with a cheerful, "Hey, everything okay?"

"Yep. Just calling about the convertible."

Priscilla's heart skipped a beat. "Oh? What about it?"

"I stopped by Gerald's place a few minutes ago, but he wasn't home. I had this great idea to put my suitcase—already packed—into the trunk. You know? Then I'm ready to go when we pull away. It'll take care of one last thing to do on the wedding day. But Gerald wasn't home, and I felt uneasy going into his garage without him there. Besides, he probably keeps it locked."

Priscilla suddenly felt a little light-headed. "Oh, right. He's here, actually. We were just going out to dinner."

"Aw, that's sweet." Eliza paused. "Well, I suppose I can put my suitcase in the trunk tomorrow. No rush. I still have time. I think maybe I'm just getting anxious."

"I understand." Boy, she understood all right. If they didn't locate that car, and quick, the suitcase would have no place to go. For that matter, neither would the bride and groom. If not for the fact that Priscilla and Gerald were headed out to a romantic dinner, she would spill the beans about the car. But to do so right now would spoil their evening together.

Priscilla ended the call and turned to face Gerald. "Looks like we'd better get back on the trail, my friend. If we don't find that car soon, this story won't end with a driving-off-into-the-sunset scene at all."

"And we all know that every good story has to end like that," he said. "Heaven forbid we should ever know what happens after the sunset."

"Right." She gave the dog one last pat then reached for her purse. "Let's hit the road, Jack."

Gerald grinned. "Great. You could write ad copy for Victor."

"Ugh. Victor. Remind me to tell you later about my latest visit to his lot."

"Will it spoil our evening?"

"Maybe. The story can wait till tomorrow, I guess."

Gerald placed his hand on her back as they walked out to his car. The drive to Edgartown was pleasant. He made small talk and eventually asked about Rachel and A.J.'s wedding. Before she knew it, they had arrived at Fleming's Steakhouse.

"Whoa. Crowded parking lot."

"Even worse than I was afraid it might be," Gerald said. "But don't worry. I have a reservation for seven thirty, and we just need a table for two. Shouldn't be too long of a wait."

At the very moment he parked the car, Priscilla's cell phone rang. She answered when she saw Uncle Hugh's number.

"Priscilla, I had some ideas about this proposal. Thought I'd run them by you."

"I'm so sorry, Uncle Hugh, but Gerald and I just got to Fleming's in Edgartown for our Valentine's date."

"Oh, I see."

"I know you're wanting my input but I'm just not sure I'm the right person, at least not if you need ideas in a hurry. Until this wedding is behind me, I'm swamped. And even then, I have Rachel's wedding. You know?"

"Priscilla, I just can't do this on my own. But if I wait too long, well…I'm old."

"I know, you said that, Uncle Hugh. So, can you come up with a way to ask her on your own? You're creative. And you know Marigold better than anyone else, certainly better than I do. Remember, I'm the newest family member on the island."

"This is true. Though I do appreciate your creative streak. And I understand you're very organized."

"You don't have to be organized to propose, Uncle Hugh. You just have to summon up the courage."

"On the contrary. If I get this wrong, she'll never forgive me. What if I go to all the trouble and bomb? Then what?"

"You love her. She loves you. You won't bomb. There's no way she'll turn you down."

"So you're telling me that if Mr. Right came along and offered you a proposal, say, with an Italian opera singer in the background, that would blow you away?"

"I can't picture any man hiring an opera singer, sorry."

"See there? My latest and greatest idea just got washed out to sea. Now I'm truly sunk."

"Why don't you just take her to dinner, get down on one knee, and say 'Will you marry me?'"

"The one knee thing is problematic. And I don't know that I'm the 'propose in a restaurant' sort. She might get embarrassed. She might choke on a chicken wing."

"You're overthinking this, Uncle Hugh. Just take her for a walk down by the water's edge and ask her there."

"In February? It's freezing out there. She'll catch pneumonia. And I'm not sure my cardiologist will release me to walk more than a couple of blocks yet, anyway."

"I'm sorry I haven't been more helpful. I think my creativity is just zapped."

"Well, when you get around to unzapping it, let me know. In the meantime, I'll keep working on ideas." He paused. "Say, instead of the water's edge, what if I propose to her on the ferry? That's romantic, right? Of course, I'm probably not healthy enough to face all that wind right now, but it might be worth it if she says yes. What do you think?"

Priscilla struggled to find the right answer for that one.

"I can tell from your silence it's a dud. Don't want my big moment to be a dud. Get some rest, Priscilla. And let me know if the Lord downloads any ideas in dream form tonight."

"I will, Uncle Hugh."

She couldn't help but laugh as she ended the call.

Gerald looked her way, his brow creased. "That sounded interesting."

"Oh, it was. Uncle Hugh has been after me to help him come up with ideas. He wants to propose to Marigold."

"Why doesn't he just invite her out to dinner and ask her?" Gerald asked. "Isn't that the normal way to handle things?"

"I tried that, but he wasn't sure he could pull it off. You don't want to hear his excuses, though. Kind of kooky."

"Poor guy."

"Yeah. And time is not in his favor. He wants a quick proposal and even faster wedding."

"No doubt."

Gerald got out of the car and came around to her side to open the door. Priscilla loved that he always insisted on doing that. It made her feel special. When she got out of the vehicle, her gaze shifted down the street to where she and the others had met up with Marvin Freemont earlier today. She would have to tell Gerald about that over dinner. Not that talking about classic cars was particularly romantic, but he wouldn't mind.

They walked inside the restaurant, and Priscilla found herself captivated by the beautiful décor and wonderful aroma. She paused and sniffed the air. "Mmm. Good choice, Gerald."

"You haven't even tasted the food yet."

"Don't have to. I can tell already this was a good choice. And they don't make you wear a bib, like at the last place you took me to."

"Hey, it kept your clothes clean."

It took a few minutes to be seated, but before long Priscilla was drinking a glass of iced tea and waiting for her steak to be brought to the table. Gerald seemed to be enjoying himself. He appeared very relaxed tonight. Well, until she brought up the missing car.

"I just felt so guilty when Eliza called earlier."

"You have to tell her, Scilla."

"I know. It's so strange. I've tried a couple of different times, but something always interrupts us. And I couldn't tell her when she called a little while ago. It would ruin her Valentine's evening. It's as if she's not supposed to know yet."

He shrugged and took a bite of his salad.

"I'm just so stumped by this whole thing." Priscilla took a fork and pulled the tomatoes out of her salad. She put them in Gerald's bowl. "Cars don't just disappear."

"Right." He bit into one of her tomatoes.

"Let's think this through. We have to figure out how the car got off the island."

"If, in fact, it is off the island," Gerald countered. "There's really nothing to lead us to believe it's on the mainland."

"I know. But just on the off chance, I say we explore every avenue."

"There are only two avenues—the ferry or an airplane. We know there's been no record of the car leaving by ferry, so that leaves the airport. I made a call this afternoon and there's no record of the car being transported off the island by plane."

"Legally, you mean. Anyone could've loaded that car on a flight in the wee hours of the morning."

"All the flights are monitored, Priscilla."

"So, we take a closer look at the flights that left in the middle of the night. That's all I'm saying. And one other option is possible. There are shipping companies that send things back and forth on their boats all the time. They could transport the car across the Sound that way, right?"

"True," Gerald mused. "I hadn't thought of that. I'll get in touch with my boss at the station and check out the shipping companies to see if anyone has a record of the car leaving. But I still say that vehicle is safe and sound, here on the island."

Priscilla nodded. "I hope you're right."

"Hey, I do have one very important thing to tell you. Almost forgot."

"What's that?" she asked.

"Remember how I told you that Beau Ortmann has a key to my garage?"

"Yes."

"Apparently, he returned it months ago. He left it on my kitchen counter in the little dish where I keep loose change."

"So, he's out as a possible suspect."

"Not that he was a real suspect in the first place. I never saw him as a car thief. Only as a poor guy who might never get married because his fiancée is so busy."

"Man. Wish we could do something about that."

"He says he's working on a plan," Gerald said. "Guess we'll just have to wait and see."

"Guess so. But I'm glad to hear he didn't have a key. I couldn't imagine Beau as a thief." She paused a moment and then chuckled. "Boy, aren't we a romantic pair."

Gerald looked up from his salad. "What do you mean?"

"Here we are, at a candlelight dinner on Valentine's night, and all we can talk about is the latest whodunit." Priscilla reached across the table and took his hand. "Sorry. I guess it just comes with the territory when you ask me out. Are you disappointed?"

"Nope." He gave her hand a squeeze. "Never thought I'd find a woman who shared my passion for the law. I'm proud of you, Scilla."

"Thank you. I've often wondered why God uses me to figure some of these things out."

"Sleuthing, you mean?"

She shrugged. "Still can't get used to that label. But, yes. Why me? I'm just a simple farm wife from Kansas."

"Far from that," Gerald responded. "If you want the truth, I think God gave you an extra dose of discernment. You're a people reader. You notice things, and not just with suspects. You're a caring, loving person, Scilla."

"Thank you." His flattering words caused her cheeks to warm.

"Don't thank me. Thank the One who made you that way. I'm always so amazed at how He uses you. You're the first one to notice when someone is hurting. The first to offer a kind word or a hug. Take Eliza, for instance. After Victor lost his position as selectman and she was without a job, who swept in and befriended her? You did. And remember Betty, how you stepped up to make sure she was okay? You even took Jake in, no questions asked, when he needed a home."

"I wouldn't say 'no questions asked.'"

"Point is, you figured it out. That's what I love about you. You don't give up."

Did he really just use the word love?

Before she could ponder it further, the waiter arrived with their food. The smell of the sizzling steak made her even hungrier than before.

As she took her first bite, Gerald moved on to another topic altogether, the weather. Still, Priscilla couldn't stop thinking about his flattering words. He noticed that she noticed. He cared that she cared—about others, even her dog. In other words, Gerald was paying attention to the things that mattered to her. That suddenly made Priscilla feel very, very good.

Everything about the evening was perfect…until Marvin Freemont walked in with his beautiful young receptionist. Priscilla watched as he pulled out the woman's chair and gestured for her to sit.

"I don't believe it," she muttered. "Casanova."

"What? Casanova?" Gerald turned and squinted as he looked Marvin's way. "Oh, you mean that guy? You know him?"

"Yeah. Marvin Freemont. I told you about him, right? Runs the car club. Something about the guy just hits me the wrong way. He's too…perfect."

"Hey, isn't that what you women want all us guys to be?" Gerald quirked a brow.

"Of course not." She looked Marvin's way again. This time he noticed her and gave a little wave. "Oh, great. He saw me."

"So what, Scilla? He won't come this way. He can tell you're with someone."

"Right." She chewed her lip. "And maybe I'm wrong about him. I hope I'm wrong. Maybe that's his wife. Maybe they've been married twenty-five years and have two-point-five kids and live in a house with a picket fence."

"I don't believe I've seen this side of you before."

She leaned back in her chair. "I'm sorry, Gerald. I don't know what's wrong with me. Somewhere between the wedding and the MIA Bel Air, I'm getting a little cranky."

"Let's agree to set our crankiness aside and enjoy the rest of the evening, shall we?"

"Okay." Still, something about the man bothered her. Priscilla couldn't be sure if it was his smooth-talking ways or his odd suits. He did remind her of Victor Fox in many ways—a schmoozer who always wanted to one-up everyone else. Not that she needed to be thinking about Victor Fox tonight. Or Marvin Freemont. She'd better focus on the fella right in front of her, the one with the wrinkled brow.

The rest of the meal was enjoyable. Priscilla got a kick out of the soloist who traveled the room singing a cappella love songs, though she felt her cheeks grow warm as the singer crooned "It Had to be You" at their table. When the meal came to an end, she and Gerald walked hand in hand to the car. He had just opened her door when someone called her name.

"Hey, Priscilla. How's it going?"

She turned around to discover that Eliza and Carson had pulled into the parking spot next to them.

"Oh, hey. It's going great. We just finished dinner."

"Ironic." Eliza laughed. "You just can't shake me, can you? We didn't have plans to go out tonight, but our families insisted we have one last dinner alone. In fact, my cousin and her husband gave us their reservation. Isn't that sweet?"

"It is Valentine's Day, after all," Carson added. He shook Gerald's hand and gave Priscilla a smile. "I hear you've been working hard on our behalf."

She shrugged. "It's been my pleasure."

"Just a couple more days and you'll get to step away from all this craziness." He chuckled, then turned to face Eliza. "Honey, did you tell her who called this afternoon?"

"No, I haven't had a chance yet." Eliza faced Priscilla. "The craziest thing has happened."

Priscilla's heart skipped a beat. "Oh? What's that?"

"Well, I got a call from a reporter at the *Gazette*. They want to do a piece on us. About the wedding. And the cars."

"Cars?" Priscilla fought to catch her breath. "Do you mean . . ."

"Hey, honey, could you go on inside and make sure our table is ready?" Eliza gave Carson a tender kiss on the cheek. "I'll be right in. Just thought of something I need to tell Priscilla. Wedding stuff. You understand."

"Sure." Carson headed to the front door of the restaurant, and Gerald had the good sense to get into his car. This left Priscilla and Eliza alone.

"The reporter doesn't know anything about the convertible, thank goodness. But he heard through the grapevine that Carson and I are both car enthusiasts and thought it would be a good idea to run an interview, a human-interest piece, I guess you'd call it."

"Ah. When?"

"Tomorrow morning at nine. The story is going to run in the Saturday morning edition, just before the wedding—and the car show, of course. Can you come to the interview with us? I think I'd be less nervous if you were there."

"Oh, I—"

"Carson thinks I'm silly for being nervous. Of course, he has no idea about the Bel Air. I'm terrified I might let something slip. If you're there, you can signal me if I start to go astray."

"Well, I guess I could join you, but I hope it doesn't take long. My to-do list is still pretty full."

"Right. The timing is awkward, I know. I've got a lot on my list too. I know you're probably swamped, Priscilla, but I'd love for you to come."

"I'll be there."

They hugged, and Eliza headed toward the restaurant. Priscilla got into the passenger's side of Gerald's car, leaned her head back against the seat, and groaned loudly. "I'm such a coward."

"You have to tell her."

"I know. I will. But I can't do it now. It will wreck her one last date with Carson before the wedding. And besides, don't you think there's some chance we'll find the car before..." Her words faded away. "Never mind. You're right. I'll tell her first thing in the morning."

"Before the interview?"

"Before the interview. I promise." She spoke the words aloud... and meant them.

CHAPTER SIXTEEN

Priscilla finally decided to bite the bullet when she returned home that night. She waited a couple of hours to give Eliza time to return from her night out with Carson. At ten forty-five she picked up the phone and punched in Eliza's number, then waited for her friend to answer.

"Oh, Priscilla!" Eliza answered with an enthusiastic squeal. "I'm so glad you called! I just heard from Anna. She's offered to cover the cost of the linens as her wedding gift to me. Isn't that amazing? That sweet woman has really come through for me." She sighed. "Oh, everything is going to be perfect, just like I planned."

"Maybe not quite perfect." Priscilla sat down on the sofa and braced herself for the inevitable.

"What happened?"

"It's about your car."

"Which one?" Eliza suddenly sounded concerned.

"The new one. The convertible."

"Oh, are you wondering what time to have it at the ceremony? I'd say after five because Carson will already be inside the B&B then. But be sure to tell Gerald to hide it down the street until after the ceremony. In a safe place, of course. Not next to a curb where it might get bumped. And please don't worry about my suitcase. I'll just put it in when we leave."

"Actually, what I have to tell you—"

"And not too far away from the B&B because Gerald—or someone—will have to go and fetch it at the appropriate moment. I'm thinking just after the final dance. The deejay will make an announcement that the guests can follow us outside, blowing bubbles as we leave. We'll get to the door, and...bam!"

"N-no c-car," Priscilla managed.

"Yes, car. Silly." Eliza giggled. "You trying to give me a scare or something?"

"I'm trying to tell you something, Eliza. The Bel Air is missing."

Eliza gasped. "What? Is this some kind of joke?"

"No. I wish it was. When Gerald went out to check on the car yesterday morning, the garage was empty."

"E-empty?" Eliza choked out the word. "This isn't possible. It's a nightmare. Please tell me I'm dreaming. Pinch me."

"I would pinch you but it wouldn't change anything, Eliza. The car has been missing since yesterday morning. We contacted the police and checked the ferry schedule to make sure no one has left the island with it, but nothing has turned up. There are no leads whatsoever."

Eliza's voice grew shrill. "Oh, no! It's got to be Sally Jenson. That's why she's been hovering so close to me, why she wouldn't leave the B&B, even when we needed the room. She's behind this, isn't she?"

"I'm pretty sure she's not, but she was high on my suspect list until yesterday."

"I don't get it. I don't. No one else knew where the car was, right?"

"Only a couple of people. And I don't know how someone would have managed to slip away with the vehicle in the middle of the night without Gerald hearing. He feels awful, by the way."

"You don't think Gerald..." Eliza's words trailed off. "No, never mind. Stupid question. He's no thief."

"He works for the Coast Guard. Pretty sure he's one of the good guys."

"I thought everyone involved was a good guy, but it looks like I was wrong." Eliza's voice broke, and Priscilla felt sure she was crying. "I don't believe it. All that money. All those phone calls to Romano's. All that time to make sure every detail was right. And all of it, for this? So someone could pull the rug out from under me at the very last m-minute?" Her words were broken up by sobs. "This was the f-finest gift I've ever given anyone, Priscilla. The very finest."

"I know."

"And to a man who means the world to me."

"I know."

For a moment, neither of them spoke. Eliza finally broke the silence. "So, now what?"

Priscilla didn't know what to say but tried to muster up a few words of confidence. "I'm so sorry this happened. Trust me when I say we won't give up."

"Who is 'we'? Who all knows?"

"The cousins. And, I'm sorry about that. Trudy just happened to be on the phone with me when Gerald walked into my house yesterday morning to let me know the car had gone missing."

"Let me guess. She told Joan, and Joan told Gail."

"Something like that. But their hearts were in the right place, I can assure you. Everyone just wants to see you and Carson drive off into the sunset tomorrow night in that convertible. Trust me, we've looked everywhere, from Edgartown to the Steamship Authority to Tisbury."

"With no luck?"

"Sadly, no."

"Priscilla, why didn't you just tell me the minute the car went missing?"

She released a slow breath. "Because, Eliza, I didn't want you to panic. And I wanted to have time to search for it. I never gave up on the idea that it might be found in time for your big day."

"But there are no leads."

"Not yet. I did have one question, though. Can you remind me how you found that car on the internet? Refresh my memory."

"Oh, it's a site where lots of people sell classic cars."

"Was there any interest from other buyers?"

"Yes, it got kind of ugly, in fact. Went into a bidding war. The guy bidding against me was relentless. If I could ever figure out who he was, I'd give him a piece of my mind. Made my life miserable. I ended up spending a lot more than I'd planned, but I won in the end."

"Why do you suppose he wanted that particular car?"

"No idea. Unless he was a dealer, just picking it up for a buyer. Sometimes the dealers do that—they buy low and sell high to someone else. Happens all the time, in fact."

"People like Victor Fox?" Priscilla didn't mean to say those words aloud.

"I suppose that's possible but it doesn't seem likely." Eliza grew silent. "What does it matter, anyway? The point is, my car has gone missing. There's not going to be a 'driving off into the sunset' moment."

"Unless a miracle occurs. And I do happen to believe in miracles, Eliza, and I'm praying. I haven't stopped."

Eliza released a long breath and for a minute, Priscilla thought she might burst into tears once more, or lash out in anger. Instead, Eliza surprised her by coming back with a calm response. "The car is insured."

"I figured it was."

"So, if it doesn't turn up, the money won't be lost. I'll miss sharing the experience with Carson, of course, but he doesn't even know about it, so he won't be disappointed."

"When are you going to tell him?"

"Is our honeymoon too late?" Eliza gave a dry laugh.

"I wouldn't blame you. Get him off the island so he doesn't go crazy looking for it like Gerald and I have over the past couple of days. The police checked footage from the ferry. Trudy and I even went through Victor Fox's warehouse stock to make sure he hadn't absconded with it."

"Victor's not the nicest man on the planet, but I can't picture him stealing a car, even out of spite. Who else have you been looking at?"

"Well, Tony Romano, of course. His business has been going through some changes. I can tell you about that later. Oh, and Sally, of course."

"Sally." Eliza's voice grew tense. "I have to wonder if that's why she's still on the island, because she's hiding my car somewhere."

"If you had asked me yesterday I would've given you a resounding yes. It's looking more doubtful now. She seems to be in your corner." From across the room, Jake started whining.

"Who else could it be, then?"

Priscilla took a few steps toward the dog and put her finger to her lips, hoping he would take the hint. "I've got my eye on someone else but have no proof he was involved."

"Who?"

"Marvin Freemont."

"Ugh. That guy's such a jerk."

"You know him?"

"Of course. I'm a member of the Vineyard Classic Car Club, remember? He approached me a few months back about buying my Corvette. He made a ridiculously low offer. I turned him down, of course, but he wouldn't stop nagging me. I finally had to sic Carson on him. The guy just wouldn't take no for an answer." She paused. "Can we go back to Tony Romano?"

"Sure."

"Have you researched him thoroughly?"

"Not really. I know he's looking at setting up shop here, or at least I think so." Priscilla sat down on the sofa, and Jake walked over to her. He continued to whine.

"That's weird. In all the times I talked to him, he never mentioned opening a restoration business on the island."

"I know. I thought it was strange too." Priscilla reached over to pat Jake on the head, hoping he would stop whining. It worked immediately. Well, until he jumped on the sofa. She decided not to scold him until she ended the call with Eliza.

"Listen, let's just get through this interview in the morning," Eliza said after a moment. "I'll do my best not to let on that anything is bothering me. That way Carson won't be troubled by this. But you have to stick with me, Priscilla. Closer than ever, I mean. I'm really going to need you now."

"I know, and I'll be there."

"Tomorrow morning, nine o'clock."

"Yes," Priscilla said. "And don't give up, Eliza. We'll pray and see what happens."

"Okay." She didn't sound very enthusiastic, but at least she wasn't crying any longer.

Priscilla ended the call, reached over to hug the dog, and immediately burst into tears.

CHAPTER SEVENTEEN

Priscilla arrived at the *Vineyard Gazette* a full fifteen minutes ahead of Eliza and Carson. When they walked in, she couldn't help but notice that Eliza's eyes were puffy. The reporter, a fellow named Daniel, greeted them with a handshake and a smile, then led them to a conference room at the far end of the hall.

"You'll have to forgive the way I look," Eliza said as she took a seat at the table. "I'm afraid I'm not feeling very well this morning."

"Poor thing woke up with cold symptoms." Carson leaned over and gave his bride-to-be a kiss on the cheek, then took the seat to her right.

"I'm so sorry, Eliza," Priscilla said, taking the seat to Eliza's left. She felt a wave of guilt wash over her when she saw how haggard her friend looked. She should have told Eliza sooner. This was too much for her to bear just hours before her wedding. And now an interview, on top of everything else? Maybe they could just beg off. Cancel.

"Hopefully this article will give you a boost." Daniel sat across from them. "I'll try to make this as painless as possible and get through my questions quickly." He flipped open his notepad. "I appreciate you meeting with me. I know you're both under the gun right now, so this won't take long."

"We're grateful for the interview request," Carson responded. "Quite an honor." He rested his hands on the edge of the conference table and then pulled them back down again. Priscilla wondered if he might be nervous. Not that she blamed him. She'd probably be sweating if someone asked to interview her.

"I'll be recording our Q&A, if that's all right with everyone." Daniel fussed with his little recording device and set it on the table. "Let's start with the cars, shall we?"

Eliza flinched.

"Have you ever analyzed where this passion for classic cars comes from?" Daniel looked directly at Eliza.

She seemed to relax a bit. "Oh, that's easy. My dad was a car guy. He was always tinkering with one car or another. He didn't have a lot of money—not saying I have tons, either—but he always knew how to buy low and flip a car for a profit."

"He didn't keep them for personal use?"

A smile tipped up the edges of her lips. "He kept a couple, but he was more interested in the transformation process. Once the vehicle was restored to its former splendor, he wanted to see it loved and used by someone who would genuinely appreciate all the work he'd done. Someone who could afford to take care of it, keep it clean and in good working order, that sort of thing.

"Makes perfect sense to me." Daniel set his tablet down on the table and glanced at it before looking at Carson. "What about you, Mr. Fletcher? Why classic cars?"

Carson paused and appeared to be thinking. "My story is the opposite. I grew up with no father at all. My mom has since remarried, but for years I didn't even have a stepdad. It was just Mom and me. Anyway, an older guy in our neighborhood—Titus—used to work on cars in his driveway, and I couldn't help stopping by to ask questions. He was kind enough to answer. Before long, I was under the hood, learning from the master, and wishing I had a vehicle of my own to tinker with."

"How old were you when you bought your first car?"

Carson's face lit in a delightful smile. "Nineteen. It was a piece of junk. No other way to describe it. 1964 Ford Galaxie. But it was mine. All mine. And I worked on that hunk of junk between college classes, late into the night, until it resembled an actual car."

"I'm sure you were very proud of it."

"Sure was. And it just kind of went on from there. That's the thing about car enthusiasts. We're always thinking about the next car, the next project."

"Sounds like my wife and her interior decorating." The reporter laughed. "I can't tell you how many times I've walked into the living room to find it a different color. She even reupholstered the sofa herself." He glanced back down at his tablet." How many cars have you flipped over the years?"

Carson shifted his gaze to the table. "Well, I did a few, but then life intervened. I got wrapped up in a lifestyle I'm not proud of. Kind of lost my way for a while. But all of that has turned around now."

"Glad to hear about the turnaround." Daniel flipped the page of his notepad. "But why do people go crazy over classic cars?

Doesn't make much sense to me to buy something old and run down when you can get the latest, greatest technology."

"Not everything is about technology," Eliza said. "Though the engines in these older vehicles are something to see. Real beauties. People buy classic cars because of the way it makes them feel behind the wheel."

"How does it feel?" Daniel asked.

"Like you've zipped back in time." Eliza took on a dreamy-eyed expression. "Like you're seventeen years old, cruising down the boulevard in your hometown, pulling into the drive-in for an ice-cream cone or soda."

"I didn't have a car when I was seventeen," Daniel said. "But I do understand that feeling. I got the same sense of nostalgia when I was surfing, like you don't have a care in the world."

"I was a child of the seventies," Priscilla chimed in. "I remember driving around in my dad's old Pontiac Ventura. Wasn't quite as romantic as you're describing."

Eliza smiled at her. "Well, like I said, it's all about how the car makes you feel. I have a particular memory of going out with a boy during my senior year. His dad owned a couple of classic cars, including a Corvette. We loved to go cruising."

"And parking?" Carson's brow quirked.

"Heavens, it's been so long, I barely remember his name, let alone whether or not we went to Chatsworth Hill."

"Oh, is that what they called it?" The reporter smiled. "Chatsworth Hill?"

She nodded and grinned once more.

"So, let me get this straight," Daniel said. "You have fond memories of a boy who drove a Corvette, so you ended up buying one for yourself later on?"

"This has nothing to do with the boy from high school," Eliza said. "The important part of the story is the car."

"Sounds like he's smack-dab in the middle of the story." Carson turned to face her. "But maybe that's a different article altogether."

They all laughed, and the mood in the room lightened. For the first time all morning, Priscilla found herself feeling at ease.

"The truth is, I inherited my car when my brother passed away two years ago," Eliza explained to Daniel. "So it's extra special to me. When I'm in that car, I'm thinking about him, not a boy from high school, trust me."

"I'm so sorry to hear about your loss. I'm sure you miss him a lot."

Eliza's eyes flooded with tears. "Very much. But the car is a constant reminder of the things he loved."

"And the things you love." Daniel glanced back down at his notes. "Speaking of which, will your wedding have a classic theme? And by classic, I mean old-timey."

"Yes. Our goal is to take people back to a simpler time."

Daniel chuckled. "So, not like my friend's daughter's wedding last month, where the bride and groom said their vows while bungee jumping."

"Absolutely not." Eliza grinned. "That's definitely not for me. I'm pretty plain Jane."

Carson reached over and squeezed her hand. "No, you're not, honey. You're beautiful."

Her cheeks turned crimson. "Oh, I just mean I'm not into the exotic or unusual."

"Except when it comes to cars." Carson quirked a brow. "She likes her cars like she likes her men. Older, but with life left in 'em."

Eliza laughed. "I guess you could say that. Not that you're old, Carson."

Daniel glanced at his notes then directed a question at Carson. "If you could have any car on the planet, what would it be?"

"Oh, that's easy," Carson responded. "A 1954 Bel Air convertible."

Priscilla's breath caught in her throat. She watched in amazement as Eliza kept her cool.

"Why a Bel Air?" the interviewer asked.

"Nothing says Nifty Fifties like the Bel Air convertible." Carson's eyes glistened as he spoke with great zeal. "And I just love the way it's shaped. Was there ever a finer car?"

"Any particular color?"

Carson nodded. "Surf green. Definitely."

Eliza's eyes filled with tears.

"I see this is affecting you, Ms. Jamison. Are you fond of that same make and model?"

"Very much so. To own one would be a dream."

"Well, here's to dreaming, then. Maybe sometime in the future I can have the two of you back to discuss that new Bel Air you're buying. How about that?"

Carson nodded. "If that ever happens, you'll be the first to know."

The reporter referred to his notes once again. "Let's see here. What else did I want to ask you?" A pause followed. "Oh, yes. Are you both members of the Vineyard Classics Car Club? I did a piece on them a couple of months back."

"I've been a member for a few years," Eliza said. "But I'm not as committed as I used to be. I've been busy."

"And I'm new to the island, myself," Carson added. "Maybe it's something I'll look into after we're married."

"It's a large club with about seventy members and over a hundred cars represented," Daniel explained. "You would be among like-minded people, that's for sure. Of course, you have to have a real passion for cars to sit through the hours of conversations about carburetors, pistons, and so on. Not really my bag, but you'd love it. I went to their car show last fall and was duly impressed. You haven't lived until you've seen that many cars in such bright colors with their hoods popped. It's quite a sight."

"I've been to a lot of shows, just not here on the island," Carson said. "In fact, I headed up a club in Florida for many years."

"Then you really need to get to know Marvin Freemont." For a moment, Daniel's eyes seemed to cloud over and he frowned.

"You okay?" Priscilla asked.

"Yeah." Beads of sweat popped out on his forehead. "Just had a flashback to the interview I did with that guy a couple years ago. He's a little...aggressive." A forced smile followed. "Hey, off the record—maybe you should take over the group, Carson. I know a lot of their members would be grateful for someone as kind as you."

"No, thanks. I'm going to have my hands full over the next few months." Carson's eyes widened and his cheeks blazed red. "That's not at all what I meant to say. I mean, I'm going to be busy, being a newlywed and all, but I definitely didn't mean to imply…"

Eliza started laughing and couldn't seem to get control of herself. Priscilla hoped all of this wouldn't end up on the front page of the paper. What a fiasco that would be.

On the other hand, it would make everyone laugh. Nothing wrong with laughter. The more she thought about it, the more tickled she got. Before long, she was belly laughing too.

Daniel glanced up at the clock on the wall. "I guess it's time to wrap things up. I've got plenty of material."

"Boy, have you ever." Carson's face remained bright red.

"I won't use any of that," Daniel said. "Wouldn't do that to you. It'll be a fun, upbeat piece celebrating your upcoming wedding and the cars. That's all."

"Promise?" Eliza gave him a pleading look.

"Absolutely." He pushed his chair back and rose. "But it is a shame that your wedding falls on the same day as the car show at the Edgartown pavilion. I know you'll be sorry to miss it this year."

A hint of a smile tugged at Eliza's lips. "I'd say our plans are infinitely better."

The interview came to an end, and Carson had to leave to run by his office. Eliza opted to stay with Priscilla, who guessed this decision had more to do with the missing car than wedding plans.

They walked out to Priscilla's car together, and she made apologies before her friend climbed in the passenger side.

"I apologize in advance for my car."

"Doesn't look messy to me."

"It's not running well. Sputters a little."

True to her word, the vehicle fought to start. She finally managed to get it going and put the car into Reverse but kept her foot on the brake. "So, where are we going?"

"Something's been bothering me ever since we spoke last night. Other than the obvious, I mean." Eliza chewed her lip.

"What's that?"

"I'd like to learn more about Tony Romano and that business of his. Have any of his former customers filed complaints? Have cars gone missing? That sort of thing."

"You don't have to drive to Boston for that." Priscilla eased the car out of the parking spot. "We just need a computer, that's all."

"Can't go to my place. It's overrun with family."

"We're right across the street from the museum. Mildred lets me use her computer all the time."

A couple of minutes later they entered the museum to discover Mildred dressed in Revolutionary War attire to promote the new display. She agreed to let the ladies use her computer, so Priscilla led the way into the office with Eliza following behind.

Priscilla took a seat and flipped on the computer. "If folks have filed complaints against Romano's, we'll find them." She did a general search using the name of the business along with the word *reviews*, then pressed the search button and waited. Only a couple of less-than-stellar responses came up.

Priscilla skimmed the first one, then pointed at the screen. "This guy says that Tony took longer to get his car done than first projected, but it sounds like the car was in really bad shape."

"What about that one?" Eliza pointed to a second one.

Priscilla clicked the link and a story opened up. "Oh, wow. Well, this family accuses him of shoddy work." She glanced up from the computer. "We can't say that about him. The work he did on your car was amazing. You were delighted."

"Check the BBB, then. If there are any serious complaints, you'll likely find them there."

Priscilla typed in the words *Better Business Bureau* and entered the site seconds later. She found the search box and typed in *Romano's Restorations*, then waited to see what would happen.

"Look at that, will you?" Eliza pointed to the screen. "They have an A+ rating. No complaints filed against them at all." She paused and appeared to be thinking. "Actually, I'm pretty sure I did this same research before I ever chose Romano's. That's how I ended up with them in the first place."

Priscilla nodded. "I'm not really surprised by that. As I said, his quality of work is excellent. And he finished the job on time. Should we read some of the reviews?"

"There are dozens of them, so let's just pick a few."

Priscilla scrolled to the first review, which highlighted Tony's excellent workmanship. She released a sigh then closed the BBB site. "I think we can safely say Tony has a pretty good track record. He hasn't stolen any cars from customers."

"Until now, perhaps. It's always the innocent-looking ones that prove to be the most dangerous, Priscilla. I'm sure you've figured that out the hard way."

"Of course. I'm just saying his track record is good, his work is stellar, and his reviews are great."

"All of those things do point to an innocent man, but I still plan to keep my eyes wide open." Eliza released a loud sigh. "Not that I need to be focusing on this right now. I'd much rather be planning my wedding."

"Of course."

Eliza's eyes clouded over. "And I can't stop thinking about Sally getting so buddy-buddy with all of us, including my future mother-in-law. I still can't shake the feeling that she had something to do with my car's disappearance. It's just too coincidental. She was the last person to drive it. It would've been easy for her to have a copy of the key made."

"We don't have any evidence of that, at least not yet."

Eliza's eyes brimmed with tears as she looked away from the computer. "All we have is a missing car—a very beautiful, valuable car— and one potential suspect who's cozying up to the family. Call it friendship. Call it whatever you like. I call it suspicious. Very suspicious."

Priscilla nodded, a thousand questions running through her mind at once. Had they all been taken in by the smooth-talking Sally Jenson? She wouldn't rest until she got the answer to that very question.

CHAPTER EIGHTEEN

Priscilla spent the rest of the morning making calls. Around eleven she found herself completely exhausted. With nothing else on her agenda until the evening's rehearsal, she decided to sneak in a nap. She slipped back into her PJs and tumbled into bed. Jake looked over at her, clearly confused.

A phone call from Gerald woke Priscilla up about thirty minutes later. She tried not to sound groggy as she answered. "Hello?"

"Priscilla, I've been thinking."

"That's a dangerous activity." Her movement in the bed alerted Jake, who showed up next to her, tail wagging. "Thinking about what?"

"About your question the other day regarding the airport. We know the car didn't leave the island by ferry, but how do we know for sure it wasn't flown out?"

"Right." She stifled a yawn. "I thought we covered this."

"Not in detail."

"Is there a way to check?"

"Sure. I've been doing a ton of research online. Most people who transport by air are wealthy. Either that, or they're in a hurry. It's an expensive process. But the more I think about this, the more confused I get. Doesn't make sense to me that someone would steal a car, even a valuable car, then spend a ton of money to ship it out. How would a dealer make any money that way? You know?"

Priscilla glanced down at Jake, who continued to wag his tail. "Unless they were stealing it because they already had a buyer in place who was willing to pay for air transport. Someone who the car means more to than the dealer. I'm guessing that happens a lot."

"Ah. Hadn't thought of that."

"I mean, it's totally conceivable that someone stole the car because someone else is paying them to." Priscilla pushed back the covers and swung her legs over the side of the bed.

"True." He paused. "I wish I didn't have to work today. I'd make a quick run to the airport if I had the time. Just ask a few questions. Of course, I'm not exactly sure who we need to talk to yet, but likely one of the companies that does freight and shipping."

"Right." She stood and patted Jake on the head. "Well, thanks for stirring my curiosity, Gerald. I might do a little research myself."

"Okay. Just be careful. We don't need a repeat of that warehouse incident."

"I will."

"Oh, and Scilla?"

"Yeah?"

"I won't rest until I help you find that car. I can't stop feeling like this is my fault."

His words stopped her cold. "It's not, Gerald. I should never have asked you to store that car in the first place. It's my fault for asking."

He shook his head. "I've lived in my home for years, and I've never had so much as a piece of mail stolen from my mailbox. I take in a car for a friend and it goes missing within hours? I just find that too strange."

"It is strange, but that doesn't make it your fault."

"I wish I hadn't ignored that nudge to go outside and check on the car that night. Instead, I went back to sleep. I keep telling myself that if I'd gone out there, this would've ended differently."

"Right. You might've been shot. Or kidnapped. Or who knows what else. I, for one, am glad you didn't go out there, Gerald. I'd rather lose a car than someone I care about."

"Someone you care about?"

"Of course. You know I care about you. If anything ever happened to you…" Her words drifted off and for the first time in their short-lived relationship she felt the familiar pangs of partnership with this amazing man. "I don't know what I would do."

"That might be the finest compliment you've paid me yet, Scilla. And thank you."

"For what?"

"For boosting my self-confidence and easing my guilty conscience. I'm still sorry the car went missing on my watch, but I am glad it's just a car. Of course, I'd be hard-pressed to tell that to those guys in Edgartown. Pretty sure some of them have requested to be buried in their vehicles. That's how strongly they feel about them."

"Who would want to be buried in a car?"

He laughed. "You don't know these car guys, Scilla. They're an interesting lot. They eat, sleep, and breathe the cars they love. The whole thing is really a 'who can outdo the other' sort of thing. Trust me when I say their competitive spirit is strong."

"Oh? Trying to outdo one another?"

"More like outshine one another. Notice how everything about the cars is always perfect? The engines are so clean you could eat off them. Everything is bright. Attention-grabbing. That's the goal, to draw the most oohs and aahs from onlookers. The more people covet your vehicle, the better."

"Gee, after having one stolen right out from under me, I don't think I ever want anyone to covet my vehicle again."

"Hey, speaking of your vehicle, I've been meaning to talk to you about your car. I know you've been worried about it."

"Trudy told me to check to see if there's a recall on it, but I haven't had time."

"Funny you should mention that. I had the same thought, so I did some checking online and there is a recall on it."

"No way. Now I feel like a goober for not even thinking of that. Well, thank goodness, right? I'm sure it'll be an easy fix."

"Maybe. I'm a little worried because the recall is for an engine issue. I was surprised to find several articles from owners, and none of them were good."

Priscilla's hopes dashed. "You're kidding."

"I wish I was. From what I could gather, the issue has to do with metal debris in the crankshaft."

"I have no idea what that means but it doesn't sound good."

"It's not. It can lead to engine damage, stalls, and other problems. Point is, this issue greatly increases your chances of being in a crash, Priscilla."

"Whoa." She suddenly felt a little dizzy. "Really?"

"Here's what concerns me—several of the comments I read led me to believe that those who took their vehicles back to the dealership didn't see much of a resolution to the problem."

"You're saying even if I take it back in and have the work done, it might continue to stall?"

"We have no way of knowing, of course, but it's possible."

"I hate that this is so complicated. And if I ever needed a working vehicle, it's now. How am I going to help Rachel with the wedding if I can't get from one place to another?" She paused to think through the situation with less emotion. "I'll probably just take it back to the dealership and let them work their magic. Maybe it'll take?"

"Maybe. I hope." Gerald didn't sound convinced.

"Gary always taught me to hang on to a car until the bitter end. Besides, I can't bear the idea of car payments."

"What if you found something at a really good price? Could you pay cash?"

Priscilla thought about it. "Maybe. I loved that SUV on Victor's lot, but it was a good five thousand dollars above what I could handle in cash."

"Even with his Valentine's special?" Gerald laughed. "He didn't offer you the deal of the century?"

"Pretty sure his idea of a deal and mine are worlds apart." She paused. "Anyway, I don't need to be thinking of myself right now. I need to stay focused on Eliza."

"That's my girl, always thinking of others."

Had he really just called her his girl?

They ended their call, and she dressed and took Jake for a walk. Thank goodness all the last-minute details for tomorrow's wedding were finally done. After the walk, she turned on her computer and took a seat. A bit of digging led her to Vineyard Air Cargo, a local company that shipped large items on and off the island. From what she could tell, they had an office near the airport.

"This might call for a quick trip, Jakey," she said to the dog. And she knew just who to invite along for the ride. She punched in Trudy's number and waited for her cousin to pick up.

Trudy answered with a cheerful, "Good morning!"

"Good morning to you too. Hey, how would you like to take a little trip to the airport?"

"Are you flying me to the Caribbean for that long-hoped-for vacation?" Trudy asked. "If so, I'm in."

"Nah. Just driving to the airport to do a bit of snooping. Wondering if the convertible was flown off the island."

"Well, that sounds like fun too." Trudy laughed. "Come and get me." She paused, and her tone shifted. "Never mind. I just remembered the last time I rode in your car. I'll come and get you."

"Okay, okay."

Priscilla checked the weather app on her phone and was sad to see that colder temps were predicted. She shivered just thinking about it, and reached for her coat.

Exactly ten minutes later, Trudy arrived. Thirty minutes after that they pulled up to the airport in the center of the island.

"We're looking for Vineyard Air Cargo," Priscilla explained as Trudy eased into a lane on the right. "They ship vehicles and other large items from island to island, and to and from the mainland."

It took some doing, but they finally located the offices for the air cargo company in question. Priscilla took the lead, introducing herself and Trudy. The woman at the front desk had them take a seat while she called her boss to tell him he had visitors.

A man with salt-and-pepper hair came to the reception area and greeted them with a handshake and a smile. "I'm Liam Kirkland, CEO of Vineyard Air. Please, join me in my office, Mrs. Grant. Mrs. Galvin."

They followed the well-dressed fellow into a small office with large picture windows looking out onto the tarmac.

"Wow, great view." Priscilla walked straight to a window and looked out at the planes in various sizes.

"The best on the island. I get to watch flights go in and out all day long."

"Then you were probably watching a few weeks back when my husband and I left for Florida," Trudy said. "It was so nice to get away from this cold weather for a while."

"No doubt." Mr. Kirkland offered Trudy a warm smile.

He gestured to the chairs opposite his desk, and Priscilla took a seat. Trudy settled into the spot next to her.

Mr. Kirkland sat in his leather chair and rested his hands on the oversized desk. "So, I understand you have a question about car transport."

"Yes." Priscilla and Trudy spoke in unison.

"You can take it from here, Priscilla," Trudy said and shifted her colorful purse from one side of her lap to the other.

Priscilla turned to face Mr. Kirkland. "You have planes, I assume, that transport vehicles in and out?"

He shrugged. "A few, but most people transport cars to the island via ferry. It's far less costly. Air transport for vehicles is cost prohibitive for most."

"For those with the money to purchase luxury vehicles, I doubt this would be an issue," Trudy interjected.

"Right." He nodded. "Many of the well-to-do transport by air."

Priscilla leaned forward in her chair. "What if a person wanted to get a car off of the island, let's say... quietly. Could that be done by plane? Without others noticing, I mean?"

"Well, I daresay the pilot would notice. And the person who drives the car onto the plane. And anyone who happened to have this particular view." He gestured to the windows.

"Ah." She paused to think through her next question. "So, if a customer came to you on the sly and wanted to ship a car, say, late at night, would that be doable?"

Wrinkles filled his brow. "It would be extremely unusual. We generally stick to daytime flights."

"Have you ever shipped classic cars?"

"Sure. The Vineyard has one of the largest classic car clubs in the state, maybe in the country. Lots of expensive vehicles come and go from the island, but most by ferry, and very few under the cover of darkness." He paused and gave her a curious look.

"These are very specific questions, Mrs. Grant. Do you have reason to believe someone brought such a vehicle onto the island?"

"More likely someone took a car off the island. All very hush-hush. And please, call me Priscilla."

"Priscilla." He gave her a curious look. "I can assure you, no one—at least not over the past week or two—has transported a vehicle off of the island via plane. At least, not one of our planes."

"Are you sure?" She gazed directly into his eyes.

"Of course I'm sure. I have detailed information about what sort of cargo is on every flight in and out. Nothing gets by me."

"Could I see that information, please?"

"It's private. Classified."

"Classified? Ooh. Sounds so...FBI-ish." Trudy giggled.

The man leaned forward and put his elbows on the desk. "I'm telling you, no cars have gone in or out in the last two weeks. Isn't my word good enough?"

Priscilla felt her heart skip a beat. "Sure, but I was just hoping you'd show me—"

"If you have any more questions, I would suggest you go to the police. They might be able to help you." His jaw tightened.

"I've upset you. I didn't mean to." Priscilla exchanged glances with Trudy.

Mr. Kirkland shook his head and rose from his seat. "I'm not upset. Just perplexed that such an accusation has been brought against Vineyard Air Cargo. We run a tight ship, Mrs. Grant. Nothing gets by our security team."

"Oh, I wasn't accusing. Just probing. One never knows until one asks." She forced a smile. "If you know what I mean."

Mr. Kirkland walked to the door and opened it, a clear sign that he was ready for them to leave. Priscilla rose and walked to the door with Trudy following closely behind.

"Thanks for your help." She extended her hand and Mr. Kirkland shook it. "Enjoy your view."

He rushed them out the door and Trudy turned to face her, eyes widening. "Wow. I got the same feeling I had when I went out on a date with Bobby Sanderson in eighth grade. He couldn't get rid of me fast enough."

"It was awkward, wasn't it?"

"Bobby, or this guy?"

"Both." Priscilla waved to the woman behind the desk and headed to the door.

Once they reached the parking lot, she turned to face Trudy. "He was very defensive. Didn't you think?"

"Very." Trudy fished around in her purse, finally coming up with her keys. "Do you think he's hiding something?"

"Either that, or he was genuinely offended that I supposedly accused him of allowing a car to be transported illegally."

"You didn't make a personal accusation, so I don't know why he reacted like that. So strange."

Priscilla thought about Mr. Kirkland all the way back to Tisbury. If everything was on the up-and-up why was the man so irritated by her questions?

"Priscilla, have you eaten?" Trudy's question interrupted her thoughts. "If not, let's hit that quaint little place in Edgartown we went to last month. Remember?"

"The diner? Sure."

As they pulled away from the airport, Priscilla's cell phone rang. She answered it to Eliza's boisterous voice. "Just twenty-four hours until the wedding. Well, technically twenty-six. But the countdown has begun!"

"Someone is very excited, I see."

"I sure am. I'm getting married tomorrow! And tonight's going to be such a blast, celebrating with the wedding party and family. And you, of course." She paused. "Just wanted to let you know I've been making some calls to other classics owners to see if I can track down the car. So far I've come up empty."

"Still working on it on this end too. Trudy and I are right now leaving the airport. We just had a chat with the president of Vineyard Air Cargo to see if anyone has transported the car off the island by plane."

"He said no?"

"He said no." Priscilla did her best not to sigh aloud.

"Funny you should mention Vineyard Air Cargo," Eliza said. "There's an article in the paper about them."

"What? Really?"

"Yeah. I'm not surprised you didn't see it. You've been a little busy. I wouldn't have noticed it myself, but my in-laws pointed it out. The company is under investigation."

"No way."

"Yeah. Something about mismanagement, maybe? Wasting funds. That sort of thing. Who knows what else."

"That might explain Kirkland's defensive tone today," Priscilla observed.

From the driver's seat, Trudy shot her a curious look. She would have to explain after ending the call.

"I thought that fella was hiding something." Trudy started talking about how the man's body language had clued her in to the fact that he was up to no good, but Priscilla tried to remain focused on the phone call.

"The article said the company is going to be cleaned up from the inside out, whatever that means." Eliza sighed. "Anyway, thanks for checking it out, just in case."

"Of course. We're just trying to narrow the field."

"But probably not in time for the big day." Another pause followed on Eliza's end, then her voice shifted back to its happy tone. "I can't believe I'm saying this, Priscilla, but I'll just have to get over it. It's just a car. As my mama was prone to say, 'It's a non-eternal.'"

"Great way to look at it," Priscilla said. "I really admire you, Eliza. You've got a good attitude."

"I have a great husband-to-be. We're going to have a stellar wedding. Only a handful of people even knew about the whole 'driving off into the sunset in the new car' thing, anyway. Carson won't be disappointed, because he never knew. And there will still be a sunset. That hasn't changed."

"True. But you'll have to tell him, eventually."

"I will. It cost a lot of money to purchase and restore that car, money from my inheritance, no less." She sighed. "But the vehicle was insured. If it's not returned, I can always file a claim."

"Kind of a shame it didn't disappear while it was under the care of the restoration company. Then Gerald wouldn't feel so guilty."

"I don't blame Gerald. He was great to offer his garage. This isn't his fault."

"He feels to blame, though. I can tell."

"Let's not talk about the car anymore, Priscilla, unless it magically reappears." Eliza released a happy sigh. "I'm about to become Mrs. Carson Fletcher. His world will be my world. His daughter, my daughter. I can't wait."

"Only the best for you, my friend," Priscilla said. "If anyone deserves the best, you do."

"Thank you, Priscilla." Eliza paused. "Hey, I almost forgot to tell you that the car show is up and running."

"So soon?"

"Well, not officially. They start in the morning. But there's always a gathering of the owners the day before. They meet in the pavilion, eat way too much food, and get caught up on who's bought what. Basically, a show-off time."

"Any sign of a surf-green Bel Air?"

"No idea."

"Trudy and I are going to lunch in Edgartown. We'll swing by and take a peek."

"You're so sweet, Priscilla. Thank you for taking the time to do that."

"Happy to be of service," she said, and ended the call.

CHAPTER NINETEEN

About ten minutes into her lunch with Trudy, Priscilla's cell phone rang. Her heart skipped a beat when she saw the name on the screen. "Uncle Hugh, you okay?"

"Sure. Are you busy?"

"Oh, well, I—"

"Remember that little something-something I wanted to talk to you about? You were going to help me come up with a plan?"

"Right, but after Eliza and Carson's wedding, remember? I'm so scatterbrained right now, I'm sure I'm the last person to give sensible advice."

"Okay. Gotcha."

He sounded sad as the call ended, but Priscilla couldn't think of any solution to that problem. She certainly wasn't up for helping with a proposal right now, not with everything whirling around her.

As Trudy and Priscilla drove through Edgartown after finishing their lunch at the diner, Priscilla noticed the parking lot in front of Marvin Freemont's office.

"Look, Trudy. Banners."

"Yeah, just like Victor's place. Ugh. Not the greatest memory in the world."

Priscilla pointed at Marvin in the parking lot talking to a group of men. "According to Eliza, they're already setting up for tomorrow's car show. Should be pretty exciting. If I wasn't coordinating a wedding, I'd stop by to look at the cars."

"Looks like some of the contestants have already arrived but haven't parked inside the pavilion yet." Trudy pulled her car over to the curb and put it in Park. She pointed at one of the classic cars. "Man, I love that powder-puff pink convertible. It's gorgeous. And did you see that baby-blue sports car? Yummy. Reminds me of my childhood. One of my neighbors had an older-model sports car like that." She paused. "Well, not exactly like that, but close." She paused again. "Okay, not even close. It was orange and really ugly. But it was a sports car. Or maybe a muscle car. Is that the same thing?"

"You're funny, Trudy. But they're not contestants. It's not a contest."

"It's not?" Trudy looked perplexed. "I thought they won ribbons for the best car. Stuff like that."

"Oh, maybe." Priscilla kept a watchful gaze on Marvin, who didn't seem to notice her. He was too busy talking to the group of men and pointing to various places around the lot.

Trudy sighed. "Can you even imagine driving something like that?"

"I can." Priscilla smiled. She paused a moment and gave the pink car a closer look. To own such a vehicle would be pure bliss. Well, except for the maintenance. And the insurance. And the risk of having such a gorgeous vehicle stolen.

Trudy glanced her way. "What do you say, Priscilla? Do we have a few extra minutes to look at the cars?"

Priscilla glanced at the clock on the dash. "Sure. As long as we get back to Misty Harbor by three thirty. I have some things to do before the wedding rehearsal tonight. And I need to pick up some clothes from the dry cleaners."

They got out of the car and walked onto the parking lot. Trudy headed straight for the pink convertible. Priscilla couldn't help but be impressed when she saw it up close. The owner of the vehicle walked their way and started sharing several stories about the car. Priscilla didn't understand half of what he said about the beautiful classic's motor and so on but nodded and smiled while he spoke. The longer he went on about the car, the colder she got. She pulled her coat tighter and wished she'd thought to wear gloves.

"Do they have these car shows a lot?" Trudy asked.

"Two or three times a year," he explained. "Mostly it's the same cars, same owners. But every now and again you see something new and special come in." He paused and pointed at an incoming vehicle. "Like that. Don't think I've ever seen that one before."

Priscilla snapped her head around to see a deep-purple Jaguar pull into the parking spot next to them. She watched in amazement as a woman—probably in her seventies—hopped out and popped the hood.

"Never would've guessed it," Trudy said. "I could picture that woman in a sedan, not a hot rod."

"It's fun to try to match the owners to the cars," the man said. "Sometimes I make a game of it. I've gotten pretty good, but that one threw even me."

From across the parking lot, Marvin Freemont looked their way. Priscilla couldn't help but notice that his eyes narrowed as his gaze landed on her. Uh-oh.

"You okay, Priscilla?" Trudy asked.

"Yeah. Don't look now, but there's a man walking toward us. I met him yesterday. He—"

Trudy turned and watched Marvin approach, then whispered, "Ooh, I like him. He's easy on the eyes."

"Trudy! You're married."

"That doesn't mean I'm blind."

Priscilla shook her head and leaned in close to whisper, "Before you get too attached, I met this man and he's—" She couldn't finish the sentence before Marvin drew near.

"Mrs. Grant, we meet again." Marvin extended his hand. "To what do I owe the pleasure?"

She tentatively shook his hand. "My cousin Trudy and I just had lunch at the diner, and she was intrigued by one of the cars."

"Stop by tomorrow," Marvin said. "When was the last time you saw a bunch of guys—and gals—stand around a popped car hood, examining a car's motor? And have you ever known anyone who paid as much attention to brushing dust off their tires as these guys? They polish these cars until they shine."

"They're like kids in a candy store, sounds like." Trudy glanced over her shoulder at the pink caddy.

"Or women in a jewelry store," Marvin said. "Even then, the women aren't gathered around drooling like this."

"I can't take my eyes off that pink convertible," Trudy said.

"Gorgeous car. It's a 1962 Cadillac Coupe de Ville."

"Yes, I know. He told us all about it." Trudy practically swooned as she glanced at the car once again. "I didn't understand half of what he was talking about, but I sure would like to pack that baby up and take her home with me."

"Wish I'd known. Just sold it to him for a mere hundred and forty-two thousand."

"Wh-what? Who would pay that kind of money for a car?"

"The new owner, obviously. And pretty much anyone else who shows cars of this quality. There's a lot of money to be made in flipping cars, Ms...." His gaze narrowed as he looked Trudy's way. "I don't believe I got your name."

"Galvin. Trudy Galvin." Trudy's eyelashes fluttered.

"Ms. Galvin." Marvin kissed the back of her hand.

Trudy pulled her hand away but couldn't stop staring at the man. "It's *Mrs.* Galvin."

Priscilla decided an intervention was in order. "You were saying, Mr. Freemont? There's money to be made?" She shoved her hands in her coat pockets, her fingers turning numb from the cold.

"And spent." He grinned. "Folks with a fascination for these old cars will turn themselves inside out to get what they want. You might be surprised at the lengths they go to."

She might not be surprised, actually.

"And I would've paid more if they'd asked it."

Priscilla turned when she heard the car owner's voice behind her. "Really?"

"Really." The man offered a genuine smile. "Cars are my passion. Same with everyone else you'll meet at tomorrow's show."

"Not everyone has a lot of money to spend," Marvin added. "Some of our members buy the cars in rough shape and do the restorations on the cheap. I guess I'm more of a snob. Give me an excellent restoration any day. There are few companies out there that do quality work, and I only use the ones I trust to produce the best outcome." He gestured to a couple of mechanics looking under the hood of a vehicle. "My guys are the best."

Hmm. Something about the pair looked familiar. She had seen them before, and recently. Suddenly Priscilla was struck with an idea. "I'll be right back. Need to talk to those guys about something."

"What guys?" Trudy asked.

Priscilla pointed to the mechanics, one very tall and slim, the other short with a rounded belly. "Right over there. My car's been giving me problems, right? Maybe I need to see a mechanic. And not just any mechanic."

"What do you mean?"

"I've got someone special in mind." She walked over to the duo and called the brothers by name. "Brady and Bruce Hawthorne?"

The tall one glanced her way. "Yeah?"

"Hey, I heard about you from . . . a mutual friend."

"Oh? Who's that?"

"Victor Fox. You know him?"

"Yeah, I work for Victor. What do you need?"

"I need a good mechanic. My car's been giving me problems. I thought maybe you could look at it."

"Ah." He turned his attention back to the motor. "Look, I'm really busy right now. Picking up some extra work from Marvin too. Maybe next month, when things slow down?"

"Extra work?" She gestured to the cars lined up on display. "One of these?"

"Nah, something else. Anyway, I'm too busy. You need a regular mechanic. I'm not regular."

"Do you do body work too?" Priscilla asked.

"Nah. Just mechanical. Marvin's got other guys for that at his warehouse." He pointed to a large metal building behind the pavilion.

"I know other people in the business." Priscilla put her hand over her eyes to shield them from the glare of the overhead sun. "A friend in Boston. Tony Romano."

Was it just her imagination, or did the mechanic flinch?

"I know him. He's worked on quite a few of Marvin's cars, but I think they fell out or something. How do you know Tony?"

Priscilla tried to play it cool. "Oh, me and Tony, we go way back." Well, they did, relatively speaking.

"I see. Interesting. You're a car person?"

"Oh, I'm not. I . . ." She decided not to say anything else. Not that she could speak without her teeth chattering, anyway.

The mechanic turned his attention to an incoming sports car, and Trudy tugged on Priscilla's arm. "What was all that about?" she whispered. "Why did you tell him you know Tony Romano?"

"Just seeing his reaction. Seemed strange to me."

"Me too. Do you think they're working together? Do you think they had an evil plan to steal the car from Gerald's garage?" Trudy's voice grew more animated. "Something about Marvin Freemont just sends shivers down my spine."

"You're shivering because it's twenty-eight degrees out here."

"True. Still, I'm not sure what it is about the guy. Did you see the way he kissed my hand?" She glanced down at her hand and sighed. "Either he's the world's most gentlemanly gentleman or he's a fraud. What say you, Priscilla? Are you getting tired of talking about all of this? Just wish this car stuff was behind you?"

"I say..." Priscilla watched as a car with *Romano's Restorations* on the side pulled into the parking lot. "I say it ain't over till it's over." She had a feeling this investigation was far from over.

CHAPTER TWENTY

Friday evening's wedding rehearsal came off without a hitch. The dinner that followed was great fun, and gave Priscilla an opportunity to meet the families. She couldn't help but notice how well Sally Jenson fit in with the others. Was the woman hovering close because of a possible link to the disappearance of the Bel Air, or did she simply want to be a friend to Eliza? If such a thing could be ascertained by observing, Priscilla would have to say it was the latter.

After the dinner, she pulled Sally aside to ask a few questions.

"Everything okay, Priscilla?"

"Yes. Well, no. I mean, we still haven't located the car, but something very strange happened today."

"What's that?"

"I saw Tony Romano pull into the parking lot at the pavilion in Edgartown where the car show is being held."

"Oh, I know all about that. A lot of those guys are his friends."

"Including Marvin Freemont, club president?"

"No." Sally shook her head. "You've got that wrong. Tony used to work for Marvin. He restored several cars for him. But Marvin ripped him off on more than one occasion and even tried to involve him in some shady stuff. Tony wasn't having it."

"Yet, there he was, driving up to the event like he fit right in."

"I'm telling you, he does fit in with those guys. Marvin has tried to ruin Tony's reputation with the group members, but the ones who really know him, trust him."

"So, let me ask you this. If Marvin said that some of the guys flip their cars 'on the cheap' what does that mean?"

She frowned. "He would tell you that using guys like Tony is 'on the cheap.' For Marvin, bigger money equals better quality. He's got local guys—mechanics and bodywork guys—who do quality work and charge a ton for it. Tony charges plenty for his work, but he doesn't take advantage of people that way."

"Okay. Thanks for clearing that up."

"You're welcome. And by the way, I went by the lot today. Got to hang out with Tony and a couple old friends we've known for years. It was a blast."

"I'm glad."

"I'd heard rumors that he was moving here to the island. Setting up a new shop. So, when I saw him in Misty Harbor the other day, it stopped me in my tracks. I knew the rumors must be true." Her cheeks flushed. "Remember, I'm the one who followed him into a Realtor's office." Sally released a sigh. "It's shameful, I know. And all the time I was tailing him I tried to think up a story I could tell him if he saw me. Of course, he knew I was on the island to deliver the car, but coming up with an excuse for why I'd suddenly turned up at a Realtor's office? That would've taken some effort." She paused. "Not that I could've pulled off a lie, anyway. Even as a kid I couldn't lie without giving myself away."

"Are you upset that he's thinking about moving here?"

"Maybe a little." Sally shrugged. "Tony and I have worked alongside each other for years. We have a history. If he moves away…" Her eyes brimmed with tears. "Anyway, he's definitely looking at setting up shop on the island, and I have to get over that."

"It's never easy when a friend moves," Priscilla said. "My best friend back in Kansas would attest to that. We haven't seen each other in ages. But there's always the internet. And cell phones. Staying in touch is easier these days than ever before."

"Not sure he would miss me enough to want to stay in touch." Sally shrugged. "I guess that's what's really upsetting me."

"I'm sorry."

"Me too. But guess what? When I saw him today at the car show I told him I was staying for the wedding, and he asked if I needed a date." Sally's cheeks flamed pink. "I couldn't tell if he was flirting so the other guys would notice or if he actually meant it."

"Who asked you out on a date?" Eliza's voice sounded from behind them. "Tony Romano?"

Sally put her hands to her cheeks, as if to cover the crimson color that remained. "Yes, but I told him no, of course."

"Why would you do that?" Eliza put her hands on her hips. "Seriously?"

"Well, I'm already butting in," Sally said. "It's not my place to invite one more."

"Even if it's the guy you've been pining after for years?" Eliza swatted her on the arm. "Get on the phone right now. Call him, girl."

"What?"

"Call him. Invite him to the wedding." She paused and concern clouded her eyes. "But if Carson notices him at the wedding and asks who he is, don't mention the convertible."

"Of course not."

"I haven't given up on that Bel Air," Eliza said. "I won't, until the sun sets at 5:17 tomorrow evening." She smiled and returned to her guests.

After the dinner ended and the speeches were given, Priscilla invited the women of the wedding party and her cousins to meet up at her house for a makeshift bachelorette party. They settled in a short while later with their hot cocoa and stash of cookies and candies.

"Ladies, I don't know how to thank you," Eliza said as the party got underway. "You've been the best friends I could have asked for."

"You're easy to love, Eliza." Priscilla gave her a warm hug.

"I'm not so sure about that. All those years I worked for Victor Fox, I kept to myself. Didn't have many friends. Just took care of my mama and stayed busy. It's been refreshing to experience life with girlfriends. You've opened up a whole new world to me."

"More like a Pandora's Box," Trudy said, laughing.

After a moment, the room grew silent.

"Well, aren't we just the world's craziest party animals?" Anna lifted a bag of candy in the air. "Chocolate, anyone?"

"Ooh, you said the magic word!" Eliza reached into the bowl and pulled out a piece of candy.

"Don't go too crazy with those," Joan cautioned. "Chocolate has caffeine in it. You don't want to be up all night."

"I don't?" This caused Eliza to double over with laughter. When she came up for air, she said, "Sorry, ladies. No idea what's wrong with me. I think I must be giddy or something."

"Probably just exhaustion," Joan said. "Lack of sleep will do that to a person. All the more reason not to have caffeine this late at night."

Eliza popped a chocolate into her mouth, as if in defiance, and then giggled.

"You're such a rebel." Trudy reached for the bag and ate one as well.

"What do women our age do at bachelorette parties, anyway?" Gail asked as she settled onto the sofa.

"Nap?" Joan suggested.

"Talk about beauty products?" Trudy lifted her cosmetics bag. "I think it would be fun to do makeovers."

"I've had enough makeovers for a while," Priscilla said.

This garnered a frown from Trudy, who set her bag down and plopped onto the sofa next to Gail.

"I'm dying to know about your honeymoon," Gail said. "Where are you guys going, Eliza?"

"To Florida. That's where Carson's from."

"Oh, right. Where in Florida?"

"We're going to make the rounds, starting in Miami, then hitting several other famous beaches."

"In February?"

"Well, it's a lot warmer in Florida, remember. And we plan to get on a cruise ship in Ft. Lauderdale and head to the Eastern Caribbean for a week—the Bahamas, St. Thomas, St. Martin, and so on. It's going to be amazing."

"I'm so jealous, especially after the weather we've had this year. I'm done with cold spells." Gail shivered. "Can you pack me in your suitcase?"

"That might be awkward, Gail," Joan said.

"Still, the idea of the tropics sounds amazing right about now."

"I say we talk about men." Sally giggled and then clamped a hand over her mouth.

"Do you have a special guy, Sally?" Claire asked.

"Oh, I...well, no." She paused. "Priscilla heard my story at the bakery the other day. I don't want to bore her with it again. But I highly suspect there won't be any knights on white horses in my life story. And that's okay. I've reconciled myself to that fact."

"It's not a fact," Eliza said. "You never know what God might do. I'm proof of that. He could swing wide the door, and a man could come riding in on a white horse."

"Or in a classic car," Trudy added. "That would be more up your alley."

"Not that we're trying to set you up with anyone," Joan said.

"I can think of one man I'd like to set her up with." Trudy giggled. "Just met him. His name is Marvin Freemont, and he runs the car club."

A shiver went down Priscilla's spine at the mention of the man's name.

"He's one handsome devil, isn't he?" Trudy went on. "And he knows a lot about cars, Sally. You've gotta love that about him."

"Not really my type," Sally countered. "Nice and all, but a little too prissy for me. I like men who are a little rough around the edges."

Priscilla turned to face Claire. Time to get the spotlight off of Sally. "What about you, Claire? Do you have visions of a knight on a white horse?"

"I guess I'm like Sally. I've reconciled myself to the fact that no man is going to want to take on someone like me."

"Someone like you?" Sally gave her a curious look. "What do you mean? You're gorgeous."

Claire shrugged. "Health issues. Lupus. Kidney transplant. It's a lot. You know?"

"Well, sure, but when you find the right man, none of that will matter. He'll be willing to scale mountains, leap tall buildings, and all that. That's what love does, it takes on anything."

"You've been reading too many romance novels, Sally."

"Maybe." The woman shrugged. "Don't take my word for it, anyway. I'm single."

Priscilla's heart went out to Claire. She turned to face her, emotion lacing her words. "Claire, I don't know if I've told you this, but I'm so proud of you."

"Me?" The young woman looked genuinely perplexed. "Why?"

"You've been through so much. Lupus. And then finding out about your dad the way you did, welcoming him into your life..." Her words faded off.

"Of course I welcomed him! He came bearing the gift of life. Who else would offer someone a kidney?" Claire grinned. "Besides, I'm learning where I get some of my strange quirks from. I've never shared this with my mom, but I've always had a thing for cars."

"No way."

"Yep. From the time I was a kid, I've always been excited for the car show in Edgartown. I can't tell you how many hours I've spent walking up and down the rows of cars, examining the motors, talking to owners about pistons." She laughed. "Now I know why. I come by it honestly. But I'm not looking for a man. If it happens, it'll have to be the Lord's doing."

"That's what happened in my case." Eliza pointed to herself. "I've been single my whole life. I know nothing. Literally. Nothing. So, fill me in, ladies. What does my future as Mrs. Carson Fletcher look like? Inquiring minds want to know."

"Great idea." Priscilla walked to the end table and picked up a notepad and pen. "We'll give you our best advice and you can write everything down." She handed the pad and pen to Eliza.

Trudy rolled her eyes. "Well, first and foremost, I hope you own earplugs."

"Earplugs?" Eliza scribbled on the paper. "Why?"

"In case he snores. And he probably will. Never met a man in this age group who didn't snore like a buzz saw."

"I don't even want to know why you seem so sure of yourself on that one." Sally chuckled.

"My friends all complain that their husbands snore, silly. That's all."

"Look the other way when he's eating," Joan said. "Watching a man eat can be brutal."

"What?" Eliza scribbled on her paper. "Why?"

"The slurping. The open mouth. The crumbs. It's brutal, I tell you."

Eliza dismissed that with a wave of her hand. "I've been out to eat with Carson dozens of times. He's a very neat eater."

Joan narrowed her gaze. "In public, sure. But wait till you get him on the sofa on Super Bowl Sunday. Then it'll be chips crunching, crumbs falling everywhere."

"Oh, and socks," Trudy hollered out.

Eliza lifted her pen. "He's going to eat socks?"

"No. He's going to take them off and leave them in a pile on the floor. Ask me how I know. Right next to his shoes, which never make it into the closet onto the shoe rack."

"These are small things, ladies."

Trudy clucked her tongue. "Sure, they seem small at first. But when you're years into the marriage, you either reach a point where you lose your mind or you give up on ever changing him."

"What if I just give up on changing him before we ever get married? How would that be?" Eliza offered a faint smile. "I'm not interested in Carson being anyone—or anything—different from who he is."

"You say that now, but that's only because you haven't seen the mess he's going to make in the shower. If I had a nickel for every time I've had to scrub the shower after Dan gets through, I'd be a rich woman."

"You're not making marriage sound very appealing, ladies," Priscilla said. "Aren't we supposed to be encouraging her?"

"Oh, I wouldn't trade Dan in for anything in the world." Trudy's lips curled up in a smile. "Even if he does leave the cap off the toothpaste. And use every pot and pan in the house when he cooks."

The ladies all took a turn, going around the room with advice. After a while everyone started winding down. Priscilla went into the kitchen to boil water for tea. She was surprised when she heard Eliza's voice behind her.

"Priscilla, do you have a minute?"

"Oh, man. You're not going to give one of those friendship speeches that will make me cry, are you?" Priscilla asked.

"No, I've already spent half the day crying."

"You have? Why?"

"Well, first I cried because Mama isn't here to see me get married." Eliza's eyes flooded. "I hate that she passed away right before Carson and I got engaged."

"I hate it too. But I like to think she's looking down on you."

"Yes. And, of course, I'm sad about the car, but that's not really the issue that's troubling me, if you want the truth of it."

"What is it?"

"I'm not sure I can do this, Priscilla."

The teakettle whistled, and Priscilla turned off the stove. "Do what?"

"Get married." Eliza plopped down into a chair at the breakfast table.

Priscilla stared at her friend, unable to come up with anything logical to say. She finally managed, "You're just nervous, Eliza. It happens to all brides on their big day."

"Do they all feel like running for the hills? I'm seriously thinking I might be sick." She put her hand on her stomach. "Is that normal too, or is it just the chocolate?"

"Maybe a little of both." Priscilla chuckled. "On my wedding day, I actually got sick. And I couldn't stop worrying that I might faint once I got to the altar."

"Oh, no." Eliza shook her head. "I never thought about that."

"Well, don't start thinking about it now. And don't lock your knees."

"What?" Eliza's brow wrinkled.

"When you're standing in front of the pastor, don't lock your knees. Keep them slightly bent. That's the primary reason people faint."

"Good grief. Now I'll be worrying about that too." Eliza drummed her fingertips on the table. "I've never been the sort of person to stand up in front of a crowd. Weird, I know, since I worked for a politician for so long. Victor was always in the spotlight. I was just the shy secretary who blended into the background while he did his thing. The idea of being up in front of so many people is…intimidating."

"I remember feeling the same way at my wedding. If we could've eloped, I would have loved that. But there's something so special about having your loved ones all around you. You'll have very fond memories of your big day, honey."

"Unless I faint. Or get sick." Eliza released a slow breath. "Then I'll have a completely different set of memories."

"The key is to remain calm and to keep your focus on Carson. He's going to be so busy staring into your beautiful eyes that you won't have time to think about anything else. This is all about the two of you, Eliza."

"Right. So I don't need to panic over being up at the front of the room, the center of attention."

"Just enjoy it. That's all I'm saying."

"I'll try." She rose and put her hand on Priscilla's arm. "And just in case I haven't said it a thousand times, you're a great friend, Priscilla. I don't know anyone else who would've gone to so much trouble for someone they've only known a few months. I've been a handful, I know."

"A wonderful handful." Priscilla wrapped her arms around Eliza. "And by the way, I've been thinking a lot about something you said when you found out the car went missing."

"Oh? Which thing?"

"The non-eternal thing. It really struck me as a terrific way to view the stuff that comes in and out of our lives—and by stuff, I mean possessions, money, and so on. I've heard the expression all my life: You can't take it with you. And I know that's true. But in the moment, when I'm fretting over wanting a new car or the latest greatest smartphone or TV, it'll be great to look at that item and say, 'It's a non-eternal.'"

"You can't take it with you. Boy, that's sure and certain."

"Now, I think it's time you and your wedding party headed back to the B&B to get some sleep. You have a big day tomorrow."

"I do." A faint smile followed from Eliza.

They walked back into the living room, and Eliza made her announcement to the group. "It's getting late, ladies. I think I'd better get back and hit the hay."

Sally looked disappointed. "It's barely ten o'clock. I thought we were just getting started."

"I know." Eliza yawned. "But it's been a big day, and tomorrow's going to be even bigger." She said goodbye to the group and headed for the door with Anna and Sally behind her.

It didn't take long for the other ladies to follow suit. All but Trudy, who lingered in Priscilla's easy chair. "I would leave, but I'm so tired I don't know if I'll make it home."

"Should I call Dan to come and fetch you?" Priscilla offered.

"Nah." Trudy rose and yawned.

"Would you like another piece of chocolate for the road?" Priscilla offered. "Remember, chocolate has caffeine in it."

"I'd be up all night." Trudy extended her hand. "Okay, okay, I'll take it. And I guess I should go home." She unwrapped the candy and popped it into her mouth. "Hey, am I the only one who finds it odd that Sally Jenson is so buddy-buddy with Eliza?"

"You're not the only one, but I can't seem to fault her."

"Yet. There may still be a story we haven't uncovered." Trudy shrugged. "Guess I'm the only one who finds the whole thing rather strange. I've said all along that she's our number one suspect."

"But we can't seem to link her to the car's disappearance."

"Yet. But you've heard that old expression: keep your friends close, keep your enemies closer? That's what Sally is doing. She's keeping her enemies—or, in this case, the people she's ripped off—very, very close. Mark my words." Trudy rose and reached for her jacket. "Guess I'd better scoot out of here. I know we're expecting colder weather and I don't want to be out in it, if snow should come."

"Snow? You really think it'll come to that...again?"

"I don't know. After that huge nor'easter a few weeks back, I was hoping the bad weather was behind us. Maybe not."

"It has been unusually cold and snowy this winter," Priscilla agreed.

"I guess that's been a bit of a shock for you, Priscilla."

"Well, this is my second winter on the island. And it got cold in Kansas too. Trust me when I say the wind could blow across the farm hard enough to knock you down at times."

Trudy yawned as she slipped her jacket on. "It's not usually like this on the island. This has been a particularly cold winter for us."

"Figures." Priscilla chuckled. "I move here, and the weather changes."

"Honey, you moved here and everything changed." Trudy rested her hand on Priscilla's arm.

"What do you mean?"

"I mean, you've brought us all to life again. You showed up, and the whole energy of the island shifted."

"You make me sound like an earthquake, not a cousin. Have I really stirred things up that much?" Priscilla asked.

"Let's just say you've challenged the status quo. When has a woman—especially one so new to the island—ever gone around solving mysteries and showing up the police department? Everyone is talking about your knack for sleuthing."

A dark feeling came over Priscilla as she thought about the missing convertible. "If only it would kick in now."

CHAPTER TWENTY-ONE

O n the morning of the wedding Priscilla awoke with a headache. She stumbled out of bed, her thoughts in a whirl. The
to-do list before today's ceremony was a mile long, starting with
showering and getting dressed.

Less than an hour later, she carried the first load of centerpieces
out to her car. When she stepped outside of her front door the
headache disappeared. In fact, she felt like bursting into song.
What a beautiful day this had shaped up to be. The sun shone
brightly overhead, and though the weatherman had predicted a
dip in temperatures, the Lord had seen fit to provide warmer ones
instead.

Priscilla whispered a prayer of thanks as she loaded everything
in the car. Finally convinced she was ready to leave, she took
the wheel. The vehicle sputtered and spewed but finally started.
She backed out of the driveway and pulled onto the road. Then
she noticed the newspaper she'd run over. Oops.

Priscilla slipped the car into Park and got out to fetch the
paper. Before she pulled away, she opened it in search of the article
about Carson and Eliza. She found it on page four, along with a
lovely photo of the two of them. The headline "Classics Are Better
in Twos" made her smile.

Priscilla skimmed the article and couldn't help but admire the reporter's accuracy and excitement over the couple's big day. Still, reading the article made her heart ache as never before over the missing car. She paused, right then and there, to pray about it. "Lord, I don't have a clue where it is, but You do. Nothing escapes Your notice, Father. I ask You to shine Your searchlight on that vehicle and return it to its rightful owners. Please, Lord."

She put the car into gear and headed toward the B&B. Of course, she was hours early, but she needed to check on the dining room to make sure adequate tables had been set up, and on the courtyard, to make sure everything was in place for the outdoor ceremony. The wedding party would need food at noon and would begin dressing at one o'clock, just as the photographer arrived to take pictures of the process. Oh, and she needed to make sure Candy showed up with the cake at two. The florist should arrive at the same time.

There were a million other details to attend to, but Priscilla decided not to overthink things. There would be plenty of time to refer to her spreadsheet once she arrived at the B&B.

When she got there, Anna pulled her aside.

"The craziest thing has happened."

"What's that?"

"Eliza had a bit of a nervous breakdown this morning. Something about Carson liking mustard on his sandwiches instead of mayonnaise. Or maybe it had something to do with her fears he might take his socks off? I couldn't make any sense of it. Want to guess who got her calmed down? Sally."

"She's very levelheaded, that Sally."

"Glad you think so, because she's now a bridesmaid."

"What?"

"Yep. You heard me. Never mind the fact that her dress is different. She's in. I, for one, think it's a fabulous idea. She seems to be the only one who can keep Eliza calm. In fact, she's in the bride's room right now, helping her get ready."

"Wow."

"Yes, wow. The woman is a miracle worker. I don't know where she came from, but God bless her."

Priscilla shook her head. "I'm stymied. A week ago, we didn't even know this woman. Now she's everyone's best friend."

That turned out to be a good thing, at least for Priscilla. When she checked on the bridesmaids, Sally was at the center of the pack, taking photos on her phone and keeping the ladies energized while they put on makeup. She even helped out with the bride's hair.

"I've got skills!" she called out when Priscilla popped her head into the room. "Trudy gave me some makeup lessons. She's a classic." Sally clamped her hand over her mouth and then pulled it away. "Sorry," she said.

"She is a classic," Priscilla countered. "And those products of hers can restore just about any woman back to her former glory."

This got a laugh from everyone in the room.

Priscilla got a closer look at Sally and couldn't help but smile. Though all the other ladies in the room were fully made up, her face was bare.

"You're a great help to the others, Sally," Priscilla said.

"Yeah, about time to start on myself, I guess. Need to do something before that photographer arrives."

Sally checked her appearance in the mirror and groaned. "I'm a blank slate."

"Don't be so hard on yourself. I can't wait to see the transformation."

Sally released a sigh. "I love those transformation shows. Watching rooms transform from ugly to beautiful. Watching people get makeovers. It's so much fun. Maybe that's why I love car restoration so much. But when it comes to my own appearance..." She looked in the mirror once again. "I guess I've never really cared much about that. I'm so easygoing when it comes to clothes and hair styles."

"Want my opinion on that?" Priscilla asked.

"Sure."

"It's fun to put on makeup. It's also fun to get dressed up. But, girl...give me a day when I can just hang out in PJs anytime. Please don't tell Trudy I said this. She's of the opinion that a woman shouldn't check her mail unless her face is fully made up, and she's wearing the proper undergarments to smooth out every wrinkle. But me? I'm a farm girl all the way. Casual is just fine with me on ordinary days."

"Ah, but this is no ordinary day!" Trudy's voice sounded from behind them. "This is Eliza's wedding day and this caterpillar"— she pointed to Sally—"is about to be transformed into a butterfly. With the proper reinforcements." She held up a girdle.

"That's for me?" Sally looked terrified.

"Yep." Trudy gave the girdle a stretch. "Mesmerizing to think that this would also fit a supermodel."

"Well, good luck getting me into it," Sally said. "And just for the record, I'm pretty sure you'll have to cut me out of it."

"Nonsense. We'll get 'er done. And you'll be the talk of the town."

"Hopefully for all the right reasons."

Everyone who had stopped to listen to this exchange got back to work in preparation for the photographer's arrival. Priscilla was just about to leave the room when Eliza called her over.

"Hey, Priscilla, did you see the article in the paper?" She picked up a copy and waved it in the air.

"Sure did. He did a great job. The photo of the two of you is perfect. I love the way Carson is looking into your eyes."

Eliza gave the paper a closer look. "Aw, I'm going to have to frame this one. Hey, speaking of photos, what time did you say the photographer is set to arrive? We don't want to finish our hair and makeup until he gets here. That's kind of the point, to let him catch candid shots of us in the process."

"Not too candid," Claire said, and then laughed.

A local sandwich shop delivered a tray of cold cuts and rolls at noon, along with chips and soda. The ladies went crazy, devouring them in minutes.

One o'clock came and went but the photographer never showed. Priscilla made several phone calls but received no response. It turned out Anna had a great quality camera and was able to take several photos of the ladies finishing their hair and makeup.

Around one fifteen the men showed up, most still dressed in jeans and T-shirts and looking a little rough around the edges. Priscilla passed around cups of coffee and pointed them to the room where they would get ready. Tuxedos were already in place, hanging in the closet. After leaving them to their own devices, she noticed Candy in the dining room, stacking cake tiers.

"Hey, you're early. I thought you weren't coming till two." She glanced over at the red velvet sheet cake and smiled. "That turned out nice."

"Thanks. I know I'm early, but I'm always nervous there's going to be some last-minute catastrophe, so I show up early every time."

"Catastrophe? I've seen your work. It's amazing."

"Thanks." Candy worked at a frantic pace to set up the cake, her gaze never shifting to Priscilla. "Stacking the tiers always makes me nervous, Priscilla. Sorry. It's hard to talk and work at the same time, that's all."

"Of course. I'll leave you to it, then."

"Thanks."

Priscilla watched as Candy worked to level the various tiers and then trim them out with frosting from a piping bag. Anna joined her and snapped a few photos of Candy at work.

"Looks gorgeous," she said. "But then again, Candy's work is always impeccable."

"She's the best. That's for sure."

Anna took another photo, catching Candy's profile. "Can you even imagine what her own wedding cake is going to look like? It's probably going to be magazine-worthy. I mean, if I baked wedding cakes, I'd insist on doing my own. Wouldn't you?"

"I don't know. I guess it would be pretty tough to trust anyone else to handle something you know you could probably do better yourself."

"A wedding planner's work is never done." Anna snapped a photo of Priscilla, then showed it to her.

"Ugh. I look awful."

"Don't be silly. You look just like every other wedding planner I've ever photographed."

"Have I mentioned how relieved I am that you have that camera?"

"Anything else I can help with?"

"Yes, I just saw Tilly pull up with her team. Please go into the kitchen and make sure she has everything she needs. I'm going to check on the florist."

"It's not quite one thirty, Priscilla. Isn't he supposed to arrive around two?"

"Yes."

Anna put her hand on Priscilla's arm. "Rest easy. Breathe. In. Out. In. Out."

She did just as her friend suggested, then had a brief conversation with Tilly about the chicken Alfredo before trying the photographer once more. She hung up when she saw him enter the courtyard.

"I'm so sorry, Ms. Grant," the man said. "I got delayed."

"What happened, Kurt?"

"Ugh. Mr. Freemont hired me to do his event. A car show. I always photograph them."

"I know all about the car show. It would've been nice to know you'd double-booked yourself, though. We could have made other plans."

"I didn't, I promise. I had a ten o'clock gig with him and one o'clock here. It's never taken me more than two hours to shoot his show, but he had some vehicles off-lot that needed photographing as well."

"Off-lot?"

"Yeah, stuff in the warehouse." He shrugged. "Anyway, I'm sorry I'm late."

"Wait, this stuff in the warehouse . . . are we talking about cars he plans to put in the show?"

"No. Pretty sure one of the cars is already sold to his uncle— big-time collector on Nantucket. The others just came through restoration and needed to be photographed so he can list them online to sell."

"Ah. What sort of cars are we talking about?"

"I didn't know you were into classics, Ms. G."

"There are a lot of things about me that might surprise you. Tell me about the cars he had you photograph."

"Well, I'm not really into cars like all those guys at the pavilion, so I don't know the right names. There was a gold and white one with really cool leather interior, a cherry-red one with flames down the sides, and a cool convertible. Nice cars. That guy he uses to do the restorations is really good at what he does."

"Tony Romano?"

Kurt shook his head. "Nope. He uses a local company called Vintage Restoration. High-end place, all the way. He likes 'em because they come to his warehouse to do the work. Makes things easier. Never heard of Tony Romano before."

"I see."

"Did I hear someone say my name?"

Priscilla turned around the minute she heard the familiar voice. "T-Tony. You're here?"

"Yeah, is that okay? Sally invited me. Said the bride told her to."

"Yes, that's right. Good to see you again." She shook his hand.

"Thought I'd come early because she said they were short on people to help set up. I've got some experience with electrical, so I thought maybe I could offer assistance to the sound guy or something like that."

"That's very nice of you." Priscilla pointed the photographer in the direction of the bridal party, then pulled Tony aside. "I'm glad you're here, actually. I'm guessing you've heard from the police?"

"About the Bel Air going missing?" His expression tightened. "Yeah, I heard. Didn't exactly make my day."

"Didn't make ours, either."

"I slaved for weeks on that car. Some of my best work went into it."

"We're still trying to figure out who stole it."

"Trust me, I've been thinking about that too."

She relaxed, knowing at once that she could trust this man. "Can I ask you a question?"

"Sure."

"I'm not trying to get into your business, Tony, but I overheard you talking to someone in the Realtor's office a couple of days back…about money."

"Right. For the shop I'm opening."

"Yes. I know that now. But you told him that things back in Boston were tied up. What did you mean by that?"

"My dad passed away six months ago and the shop, which was in his name, is going through probate right now. Things will be settled in a couple of months, and I'll have the money I need to build a new shop here. It's what my dad would've wanted. He visited the Vineyard all the time as a kid because he'd restored so many of the cars for club members."

"Really? That's it?" She wanted to throw her arms around his neck and give him a big hug.

"Well, sure. What did you think I meant?"

"Oh, nothing." She felt her cheeks warm. "And please forgive me for being such a snoop. And by the way, welcome to the island. If I ever need body work done on my car, I'll know who to call."

"Thanks, but I only work on classics."

"Hey, according to some, I'm a classic." Gerald's voice sounded from behind her. "Are you talking about me behind my back again, Priscilla?"

She turned to face him and smiled when she saw how fine he looked in his tuxedo. "Heavens, no." But standing there, looking so handsome and sweet, he was certainly giving her plenty to think about.

CHAPTER TWENTY-TWO

The next few minutes buzzed by. The florist showed up at two and the process of handing out bouquets and boutonnieres began. The guests started coming down from their rooms at two thirty and Priscilla watched as they milled about, visiting. She checked her folder multiple times to make sure everything was happening in perfect order. Nothing could go wrong on this day. Well, nothing other than the obvious thing that had already gone wrong. But none of these people knew about that. They were carefree, easygoing, and ready to get this party underway.

At about twenty minutes before three, Priscilla's nerves got the better of her. She couldn't stop thinking about what the photographer had said. An odd scenario was building in her head, but she didn't have time to think it through right now.

Overwhelmed, she took a seat in one of the chairs and tried to steady her breathing.

Gerald sat next to her. "I see you, Scilla. You're the one everyone looks to, to fix things."

"Oh?"

"Sure. Problem with one of the cousins? Go to Priscilla. Issue with the caterers? Get Priscilla to fix it. People lean very heavily on you and I'm sure it's wearing you down, today of all days."

She released a long, slow breath, feeling the weight of his words.

"Do me a favor, okay?" He slipped an arm around her waist. "Just for once, lean on someone else. Don't be the rock for everyone in your world."

"You probably should've waited to give me this little speech until after six o'clock. I'm still in wedding planner mode at the minute. And Rachel's wedding is coming up next. Then I'm sure Candy will ask me to help with hers. Not to mention Uncle Hugh."

"Ah. Uncle Hugh. He pop the question yet?"

"No, but I'm sure he will, once I slow down long enough to help him come up with a plan. Point is, I'm going to have a lot on my plate over the next few months."

"Sure. You're the mother of the bride and friend to all. But do yourself a favor, Priscilla. Help Hugh find someone else who can help too. I happen to know that Janetta up at the church is dying to start a wedding planning business."

"She is?"

"Yep. She'd probably love to step in and help."

"I had no idea."

"Sometimes you take on so much that it doesn't give you time to slow down and realize there are other people out there who could be helping. I'm not saying you're not great at what you do. That's one of your problems, in fact. You're good at too many things." He pointed to the folder in her hands. "And organized too."

"Okay, now you're just being silly."

"No, I'm not. You're a great counselor, an amazing friend, good at organizing things, excellent at drawing conclusions, stellar at picking up on clues. You're a remarkable woman, Scilla." He pulled her closer. "I'm just a little worried that you'll end up burned out. Exhausted."

"I'm halfway to exhausted already." She leaned her head against his shoulder.

"Just don't get so drawn in to every situation that you miss what's right in front of you." He gazed at her with such tenderness that she had to wonder about his meaning. "And think of it this way—if you learn to let go, you'll be giving lots of other people opportunity to step out and try new things."

She shrugged.

"So, what do you say?"

"I say...I was never meant to be a full-time wedding planner. And I'll also say that I'm terrible at making centerpieces."

"No, you're not. They look great."

She held up her hands to show off the blisters on her fingertips. "Three words: Hot. Glue. Gun. I cannot be trusted with crafting projects, trust me."

"Not when you're operating on little to no sleep. That's your problem, kiddo." He gave her a kiss on the forehead. "Just promise me you'll think long and hard about every 'opportunity' that comes your way. Only say yes to the ones you're completely sure of."

"Okay, okay. I'll do that. I won't be guilted into anything. Unless a job that pays the big bucks rolls in. Then I won't be able to help myself." She stood. "Why am I sitting down? This wedding starts in just a few minutes. I need to check on the guys."

"I'll look in on Carson."

"That's great, but I have to make sure the boutonnieres are on properly and get the men lined up, just like we practiced."

"I can help with that too. I'm one of the groomsmen, remember?"

"Yes, and your boutonniere is on the wrong side." She fixed it and then bounded toward the room where the groom and his other groomsmen were waiting.

She got them lined up and took care of crooked boutonnieres, then gave Gerald some final instructions.

"It's going to be beautiful, Priscilla." Carson rested his hands on her shoulders. "You've worked hard, and we're all so grateful." He paused, and his eyes brimmed with tears. "Want to know what else I'm grateful for?"

"What's that, Carson?" She brushed some lint off of his jacket.

"I came to the island to meet my daughter and also ended up meeting the love of my life. Funny, how God works."

"More than a coincidence."

"I think it's wonderful how well she gets along with Claire. I couldn't have asked for more."

"Well, Claire is easy to get along with. And after all she's been through with the Lupus, she deserves folks to treat her well."

"Definitely. But I mean that Eliza barely knew Claire, and now they're getting along so well. Which is really nice, if you think about it, because Claire's mother is still very much a part of her life."

"Everything is working out perfectly."

"Yes, it certainly is."

Off in the distance the music changed, a cue to the wedding party to take their places.

"You know what to do?" she asked the guys. They all gave her a thumbs-up.

She bolted down the hall to the bride's room and found the ladies in a panic, looking for a missing bouquet. It was located behind a chair. Sally reached down to try to pick it up but let out a gasp. She looked Priscilla's way and cried out, "I can't breathe."

"What? Why? Are you having an asthma attack? Hyperventilating?"

"No." Sally's eyes widened. "It's this ridiculous girdle Trudy made me wear under my dress. It's so tight I can't catch my breath."

"Slip into the bathroom and pull it off."

Sally shook her head, her wild-eyed expression sharing her alarm at that idea. "Um, no. I can't. Trust me when I say it's going to take a team to get it off. I wasn't kidding when I said we would need scissors."

"Well, if it makes you feel any better, you look like a million bucks. And there's a certain guy out there who's probably not going to be able to take his eyes off of you."

"I hope he's a doctor, because that's what I'm going to need."

Priscilla couldn't help herself. She laughed out loud at that one.

"A couple of days ago you told us about your dove tattoo, Sally. It's beautiful. And I'm sure your sister was too."

"She was a peach." Sally's eyes clouded over. "You know, I don't know that I put it together until now, but Eliza reminds me of her. Same personality. Same generous spirit. Same kind heart. They even have the same laugh."

"I guess that's why you two have become friends so easily."

"Guess so. Which is weird, because I'm usually a loner. Don't really make friends like that."

"Eliza has a gift. And for the record, she's not the only woman in the room you've won over. You're a favorite, and it's easy to see why. You're an amazing woman, Sally, and a precious friend."

"Thank you."

A warm hug followed.

Minutes later, guests in their seats, music cued, and the gorgeous outdoor ceremony began. The weather, though chilly, was absolutely perfect.

As Eliza walked down the aisle, the strangest emotions crept over Priscilla. In a flash, in the blink of an eye, she saw herself and her husband, Gary. He stood at the front of the church—young. Handsome. Healthy. His tear-filled eyes landed on her as she slowly made her way down the aisle on her father's arm. Her heart thump-thumped with anticipation as joy bubbled to the surface.

Just as quickly, the memory ended. Priscilla blinked back tears and focused on Carson's expression as he watched his bride move toward him.

She wiped her eyes with the back of her hand. Before long they would be doing this again, but with a different bride and groom. It would be Rachel's turn.

This was not the day to think about that, however. Today, she needed to stick to the plans in the folder. Then, when everything came to an end, she would eat the largest slice of wedding cake Candy Lane would serve her.

CHAPTER TWENTY-THREE

The ceremony came off without a hitch—and right on schedule too. At exactly three thirty the guests were ushered into the dining room for the reception. The bride and groom made their entrance, along with the wedding party. Tilly scurried about with trays of salmon puffs, the perfect appetizer, while the guests milled about. Priscilla overlooked it all, checking in with every vendor as the event moved forward.

"And so it begins."

Priscilla turned as she heard Gerald's voice. "What?"

"Their marriage. Their happily ever after." He quirked a brow and then the most delightful smile lit his face. "Isn't that what they always call it in the movies and romance novels?"

"Yes. But, truthfully, most romance novels end at this point so the reader is left to wonder how—or if—that happily ever after actually pans out."

"Marriage isn't all a bed of roses." Creases formed between Gerald's brows. "There's a lot of bending back and forth. Not that I'm trying to be a downer at the wedding reception."

"That's what I told Eliza." Priscilla paused, overcome with memories of life with Gary. After a moment, she swallowed the lump in her throat to speak. "But it's worth it. Even the hard times are learning opportunities. I wouldn't be the woman I am today if not for my marriage to Gary."

Gerald reached for her hand and gave it a squeeze. "Then I just have one thing to say. God bless Gary." A little wink followed, and he pulled Priscilla's hand to his lips and kissed the back of it.

A shiver ran down Priscilla's spine as she looked into Gerald's eyes.

"This whole thing has me feeling a bit . . . reminiscent," she said.

"About your wedding day?"

"Mm-hmm." Priscilla nodded. "Things were pretty simple back in those days. Weddings weren't such a production."

"Clearly, you've never met my ex-wife." He laughed.

"Was she a fussy bride?"

"She knew what she wanted, and she got it. We'll just leave it at that."

"Back in our day weddings were easy-breezy. We had a cake and punch. We didn't have a band or dancing. And we used the church's fellowship hall, not a rented facility."

"Life was simple back in the olden days."

She fought the temptation to slug him on the arm. "Very funny."

"Truth is, it does make me hope again."

"Oh?" Priscilla faced him.

He gazed at her with such intensity her heart began to flutter. "Never thought I'd say that, after what I went through. But seeing the way Carson looked at Eliza as she walked up the aisle, well . . ."

His words drifted off. Gerald shook his head, as if awakening himself from his ponderings. "Anyway, it was a great wedding. And in case I haven't already said it, you did an amazing job setting all this up, Priscilla. I saw a side of you I hadn't seen before."

"Priscilla Grant, wedding planner." She took a bow, then straightened. "Trust me, I'm just kidding."

He shrugged. "You've got the goods, kid. Good thing too, with Rachel's wedding approaching. She's lucky to have you." He took hold of her hand. "Martha's Vineyard is lucky to have you."

Priscilla found herself overcome at his sudden display of affection. "Thank you, Gerald."

The magic spell was broken when Trudy approached, hands on her hips. "Did you see that Victor Fox is here? Now why in the world would they invite Victor?"

"He was her boss for many years, and—from everything I've been told—he's changed a lot."

"I can attest to that," Gerald added. "And for the record, Carson and Victor are both in the same AA group."

Trudy shook her head. "I still wouldn't have invited him. I've never trusted that guy, not ever. He's all glitz and glam, whether he's selling himself as a politician or selling used cars. What a showboat."

"Well, Carson, as I'm sure you know, is a recovering alcoholic. The addiction recovery group at church seemed like the perfect place for Victor, so I invited him. The two men hit it off and before you knew it—"

"Victor was getting an invite to the wedding."

"Yep."

Priscilla wanted to chime in, to say something positive about Victor for a change, but found herself distracted by a conversation going on to her right between Tony and Sally.

"You look beautiful this afternoon, Sally." Tony's words were thoughtful and sincere.

"Thank you." Her cheeks blazed crimson. "It took a village."

He smiled. "I highly doubt that."

She responded with a shy glance. "You might be surprised."

"The last time I saw you, you looked just as pretty."

"In a T-shirt and jeans with very little makeup on?" She looked genuinely stunned by this notion.

"Sure, why not? As many years as I've known you, that's the Sally I've known." He took hold of her hand and gazed at her with more intensity. "Not saying this isn't nice too, but some women just don't need to go overboard with the primping."

Sally gave him a wink. "Hey, when you've got it, you've got it."

The next thing Priscilla knew, Tony upset the seating chart by insisting that Sally sit next to him. This impulsive move made Priscilla scramble to rearrange a few things, but she didn't care, as long as the two were happy.

As she watched them taking their seats, a flood of emotions rushed over her. To think, these two had been suspects. Now it all seemed so silly.

Still, someone had stolen that car...but who?

Her gaze traveled to Victor, who had also opted to take a seat at a table he was not assigned to. The man had planted himself next to the groom, and they were deep in conversation. Priscilla watched all of this with curiosity.

"A penny for your thoughts."

She turned to face Gerald. "Oh, hey. I've been thinking about all those signs at Victor's car lot."

"What about them?"

"Some of them would make good life lessons. You know, the kinds of things you'd embroider on a sampler and hang on the wall."

"Like, 'Bring in a Lemon and Take out a Peach.'"

"Well, maybe not that one, but there are plenty of others. What about 'Don't Dream It, Drive It!'"

Gerald shrugged. "Maybe. I think he's just trying to be positive. Uplifting."

"I think he's trying to sell cars." Priscilla laughed. "But I can't really fault the man for being good at what he does. He was a good politician—much as it pains me to admit it—and he's a good used car salesman. I'm not sure the gap between the two is particularly large, which might've made the transition easier. Hype is hype, whether you're in a position of leadership or sitting behind the desk at Al's Used Car Lot."

"It's Victor's Used Car Lot."

"I know. I was just giving an example." She smiled. "I apologize for being so hard on him, Gerald. Sometimes I think I get caught up in what other people are saying—the gossip going around—and don't give people a chance. That's one of the things I admire most about you."

"That I gossip?"

"No, silly." She rested her hand on his arm. "That you see the good in people and stick with them while their potential is developed. You did it with Victor and you've done it with me too."

"You?" He laughed. "Would you seriously have me believe that you were anything less than perfect from the moment I met you?"

"Far from perfect. But you've stuck with me, through thick and thin." She reached for a salmon puff. "If I keep eating these, it's going to be more thick than thin."

He laughed again and slipped his arm over her shoulder. "I love that sense of humor, Scilla. I really do."

Gerald headed off to visit with someone else. Priscilla looked to her left to see that Gail had joined her. "Oh, hey."

"It's going great. You did a fantastic job."

"Well, I won't say everything is picture perfect, but the most important things are happening as they should."

"Any word on the car?"

"It's funny you should ask. I was just sitting here, thinking about that car. The photographer said something earlier that got me thinking."

"About what?"

"About who. Marvin Freemont."

She paused to think it through. The photos of the cars for sale. The one vehicle in the warehouse that already had a buyer. Marvin buying a car for his uncle—a "big-time collector"—in Nantucket. A "cool convertible." Priscilla's mind began to reel as the pieces came together. The car that had already been sold to Marvin Freemont's uncle...a convertible...was...Eliza's Bel Air. She felt sure of it.

"Gail, excuse me. I have to ask Tony something."

Priscilla rushed to Tony and tapped him on the shoulder. "Sorry to interrupt, but I have a quick question. Sally said you used to work for Marvin Freemont?"

"Sure, but don't even get me started on that guy or I'll give you an earful."

"I'm sure you could. But here's another question—do you happen to know if he has an uncle who collects classics?"

Tony nodded. "Big-time buyer. He's not on the Vineyard, though. I think he's on—"

"Nantucket."

"Right." Creases formed between Tony's brows. "How come?"

"Call it a hunch."

She sprinted back to Gail, now out of breath.

"Are you okay?" her cousin asked. "You look ill."

"I can't believe I'm saying this in the middle of Eliza's wedding reception, Gail, but I have to leave. I've got to go get that car."

"Wait...what? Two minutes ago, you didn't know where it was. Now you're ready to leave a wedding to track it down? Are you sure?"

"Pretty sure. Can you hold down the fort until I get back?"

"Priscilla, you can't just go marching into a strange man's shop and accuse him of stealing. Besides, it's evening. His office will be closed."

"I won't be alone. I'm calling the police. Now. And I'm not going to his office. I'm headed to the warehouse behind the office. Let's just hope and pray I make it in time."

"But you have to have proof. Remember? They told you that intuition wasn't enough. Just the facts, ma'am, and all that."

"I know two facts: we're down to two suspects—Victor Fox and Marvin Freemont. Both happen to employ the same mechanics. Something I overheard one of those mechanics say just hit me like a lightning bolt between the eyes. At the time, I thought they worked just for Victor, so I didn't link what he said to Marvin. Then the photographer confirmed something in our conversation earlier today. I can't believe I'm just now putting it together."

"When did you hear what the mechanic said?"

"A couple of days back when Trudy and I were scoping out Victor's warehouse."

"You guys sneaked into a warehouse on Victor's car lot?"

"Well, maybe. Okay, yes. We did. But if we hadn't been snooping, I wouldn't have overheard this guy in the first place." Anxiety gripped her and she turned to squeeze her cousin's hand, knowing what had to be done.

A sense of urgency prompted Priscilla to rush over to Eliza, who was posing for a photo with her in-laws. Time for one last chat. She approached her friend, pulled her away from the others, and said two words: "Marvin Freemont."

"What about him?"

"Remember you told me about the bidding war? Or, the near bidding war? When you found the Bel Air online."

"Right. But what about Marvin?"

"He was bidding against you."

"That was Marvin?"

"I'm convinced he was bidding because he already had a buyer—his uncle. He mentioned something in passing the other day about knowing someone who'd been looking for a Bel Air. Your wedding photographer helped me fill in the missing pieces. I gave him quite a talking to when he arrived late, but he explained that his tardiness had something to do with photographing cars in a warehouse behind Freemont's office. He described two cars that were looking for buyers and one car that was already sold. I'm convinced that sold car is your Bel Air."

"Priscilla, really? He stole it out from under me and then sold it?"

"If we're lucky, it's still there. I think Marvin was waiting until the wedding got underway to make a move—maybe ship it by plane." She paused. "I hate to tell you this, Eliza but I have to—"

"Leave. Go right now, Priscilla. And if you don't make it back in time for the cake cutting and toasts, don't fret. I'll put Anna in charge." She put her hand on Priscilla's arm. "I'll pray you stay safe. Take someone with you, promise? Maybe Gerald."

"He's part of the wedding party."

"Someone else, then. Don't go alone. And call the police."

"I'll do that on my way."

She rushed back into the kitchen to tell Anna she was leaving. The poor woman looked stunned. Then, as she headed toward the door, Priscilla almost ran into Tony and Sally, who were standing in the hallway talking.

She interrupted them. "I know where the car is. I've got to get to Edgartown."

Tony gaped at her. "Now?"

"Yes, right now. And I need you to drive, if you don't mind. My car is acting up."

He pulled keys from his pocket. Sally took one look at him and announced that she was going too. Before long, Gerald joined the group.

"We can't all leave," Priscilla argued. "They won't have any wedding guests left."

"Look around you, Priscilla." Gerald gestured to the room, filled with happy, talking people. "They'll never even know we're gone."

"Okay, then." A quick glance at her watch showed Priscilla that it was three fifty. If they left right now, they could make it to Edgartown, track down the car, and return to the wedding by four forty-five. If all went well. Oh, how she prayed all would go well.

CHAPTER TWENTY-FOUR

The quartet of sleuths piled into Tony's car and headed for Edgartown, moving as fast as the speed limit would allow.

"Fill us in, Priscilla," Sally said.

"It didn't take long to narrow down my list of suspects. You were out, Sally, once I realized your true reasons for being on the island."

At this announcement, Sally blushed.

"And Tony, you stayed on the list a little longer, but you're out now that I've heard about your plan to build a new shop here on the island."

"Thanks for believing me."

"You're welcome. Of course, I had my eye on another car enthusiast…"

"Victor?" Gerald said.

"Yes. But I've drawn the conclusion, based in part on Gerald's discernment, that Victor isn't the evil man he used to be. So, that left me with one person—Marvin Freemont."

"Wow, Priscilla." Sally shook her head. "I've had suspicions about him all along, but how did you figure it out?"

"I'll start with two words," Priscilla said. "Marvin's uncle."

Gerald looked at her. "His uncle?"

"I'm guessing his uncle has been looking for a 1954 Bel Air convertible for a long time, judging by how hard Marvin fought for it. But then Eliza outbid Marvin, which threw a kink into their plans." Priscilla leaned back against the seat, deep in thought. Oh, how she prayed Eliza's Bel Air was still on the island.

It seemed to take forever to get to Edgartown, but when they arrived at the pavilion the car show was wrapping up. Once inside, they walked straight up to Marvin Freemont, who was commanding attention from an audience of car enthusiasts. Something he said made them laugh. He held the crowd spellbound.

Until Priscilla approached.

He paled and checked his watch. "Aren't you supposed to be at a wedding or something?"

"You know I am."

"Thought it wasn't over until after five."

"Now, how would you know that? You really have done your homework, haven't you?" She pulled him away from the crowd. "The police are on their way. Where's the car, Marvin?"

"What car?"

She could hear the sirens off in the distance.

"The car you stole. Is it in the warehouse with the other two Kurt photographed this morning?"

His brow wrinkled, and he took a step back as the sirens grew louder. "I don't have any idea what you're talking about."

"The 1954 surf-green Bel Air convertible that you saw in our photographs the other day," Priscilla said. "That's what we're talking about."

"The one I worked so hard on," Tony added.

"The one I drove to the island," Sally chimed in.

"The one you stole from my garage." Gerald's jaw clenched.

"You're out of your mind." Marvin glared at all of them.

The sirens grew louder as the police cars approached.

"Three things you might want to know before the police pull in," Priscilla said. "We know you have a buyer for the Bel Air, we know you've been paying your mechanics under the rug, and your photographer has a big mouth."

"You've got no proof."

"Your photographer does, and he seems like a decent guy, so the police won't have any trouble getting what they want out of him. He took photos of your off-lot cars this morning, including shots of a vehicle you'd already sold. He came straight from your warehouse to the wedding I coordinated this afternoon."

Marvin slumped. Then, just as quickly, he squared his shoulders.

"You're too late. That car was here and gone. I tracked it from the minute it sold. Knew it was at Romano's. Knew it was transported to the island. Knew exactly where you were going to store it."

"You're very thorough," Tony said. "I'll give you that."

"You people think I don't know how to play this game?" Marvin's face turned red. "I had keys to that car before you did, Romano. And I'd scoped out your garage days in advance, O'Bannon."

Gerald looked him squarely in the eye. "In other words, you've got snitches. Tell it to the police."

"I'm guessing he's done this before," Sally said, with a hint of sarcasm in her voice.

"A few times," Tony added.

"Look, you've got no proof I ever touched that vehicle," Marvin said. He turned to watch as the police cars pulled in. "And that car is long gone, so good luck tracking it down."

Priscilla smiled sweetly at him. "It's not long gone. It's on the island."

"What makes you say that?"

"Because the Steamship Authority has been watching every ferry leaving the island since Wednesday. And they have footage of the day before that. The car didn't leave by ferry."

"There are other ways off the island."

"No, Marvin. That car is here. You've got it in hiding. You planned to transport it off the island by plane tonight to Nantucket, right about now, in fact. But you're too late."

"You don't know what you're talking about. Whoever took that car—and you'd better be careful who you accuse—has parceled it off for parts."

At that very moment, the first of two police cars pulled into the parking lot. Minutes later, the officers walked Marvin back to the warehouse where the three cars were discovered, in all their shiny splendor.

Priscilla breathed a huge sigh of relief when she saw that the Bel Air had not been damaged in any way. The gorgeous surf-green convertible took her breath away, just as it had when she clamped eyes on it the very first time. She could almost picture Carson behind the wheel, driving off into the sunset in this stunning vehicle.

Carson! Eliza!

Priscilla swallowed hard. They needed to get this car back to the wedding, and as soon as possible. It took a bit of wrangling, but Gerald convinced the officer that they could be trusted with it.

With minutes to spare, Sally took the wheel of the Bel Air and the team of sleuths headed back to the wedding for the big reveal.

CHAPTER TWENTY-FIVE

At four forty-six, Priscilla and the others arrived at the B&B with the Bel Air. Sally parked it in the driveway, near the door. As they entered the dining room, Priscilla made an executive decision not to tell Eliza. She would find out soon enough.

Nothing could spoil this evening, even the sight of children making a mess on the far side of the room. Anna approached Priscilla, clearly distraught. "We came back to a fiasco. Someone needs to man the chocolate fountain."

"I hired someone to man the chocolate fountain."

"Well, I believe she's stepped away to go to the ladies' room. Point is, there are approximately a dozen junior high-aged children playing in the chocolate, making a terrible mess. And you don't even want to know what they've done with the marshmallows. It's shocking, really."

"Okay, okay, I'm coming."

"No, let me." Gerald rose and brushed his hands along his pants. "I was a kid once. Pretty sure I can handle this."

Priscilla bit back a smile as she said, "Just don't eat all the marshmallows."

"I'll limit myself to three. Or possibly four. If they're still edible." He disappeared through the crowd.

"He's been coming to your rescue a lot lately, Priscilla," Sally observed.

"He's very gentlemanly, that's all." She saw Tony approaching Sally with his hand extended.

"I think someone is hoping you'll take a spin around the dance floor with him," Priscilla said with a grin.

Sally nodded. "I will. I just hope he knows how to do CPR when I pass out from lack of oxygen. This undergarment is killing me."

"You're funny, Sally." Priscilla patted her friend on the shoulder.

"Okay, pray for me. I'm going in. But I make no promises for how this story will end."

As Tony swept Sally into his arms and onto the dance floor, Priscilla could only imagine that Sally's story would end well.

The band played a familiar love song, one she hadn't heard in years. Gerald drew near and offered her his hand. "We don't have much time, but I want to take advantage of it."

"Of course."

He swept her out onto the dance floor for a romantic spin.

"You're quite the dancer, Gerald," she said after a moment.

"Thanks. I had to take lessons before my daughter got married. I'd like to think I learned a thing or two." He paused and gazed into her eyes. "Well? How did Eliza take the news?"

"I didn't tell her."

"You didn't?" He looked genuinely stunned by this.

"I thought maybe it would be best to surprise her. I can hardly wait, in fact."

"I hope there's a doctor in the house. She might just pass out."

"From happiness," Priscilla responded. "Nothing more."

"Look around you, Scilla."

"Hmm? What do you mean?" Priscilla looked around the room. She focused on the band playing a '50s R&B tune. Then her gaze traveled to what was left of the wedding cake. She shifted her position and caught a glimpse of the caterers hard at work, clearing plates from the table. Finally, she paused to watch the bride and groom taking a spin around the dance floor, their eyes firmly locked on each other. A wave of bittersweet joy washed over her in that moment.

"You arranged all of this, Scilla. It's a great kickoff to their happily ever after, and they have you to thank."

"If I hadn't done it, someone else would have."

"But the point is, no one else did. You took the time to care about even the tiniest details because that's the kind of person you are. You notice everything. You pay attention. That's what makes you a great sleuth and that's what makes you a terrific—"

"Please don't say wedding planner." She put her hand up.

He laughed. "I was going to say friend. You took excellent care of Eliza, not because you need to go into business as a wedding planner but because you took the time to get to know her and then mold her special day around the things she loves. She'll never forget her wedding day and I don't think she'll ever forget you, either." He took her hand and gave it a squeeze but never lost his rhythm in the process. "You're pretty unforgettable."

As if on cue, the band began to play the song "Unforgettable."

"Wow. Did you ask them to play that?" she asked.

"Hey, I notice the details too. That's what friends do, remember?"

"Right. That's what friends do." Only, as he swept her into his arms and across the dance floor, she had to conclude—they were more than just friends.

Priscilla's gaze shifted to Victor, who sat alone at a table watching the others dance.

"Do you think Victor will ever get married again?" she asked.

Gerald shrugged. "Not for a while, I hope. He's not ready for that anytime soon."

"Has he given up on the idea of winning Betty back?"

"I think it would take a miracle for her to ever trust him again after all he put her through. Right now, I'm more interested in making sure his walk with the Lord is solid, that he's making progress working on himself. We're meeting weekly, and he's seeing a counselor."

"You're a great friend, Gerald."

He shrugged. "I believe in second chances. I've been given a few of those, myself. Besides, you know what they say—healthy individuals make for healthy couples. No point in trying to pair him up with anyone until he's ready."

"Amen to that." She glanced around the room, a smile tipping the edges of her lips as she watched the various couples dance. "I'd say we have a lot of healthy couples in Misty Harbor, wouldn't you?"

He slipped his arm around her waist and pulled her close. "Mm-hmm. I would."

One of those couples made their presence known on the dance floor. Uncle Hugh was making quite a production out of dancing with Marigold.

"So, did you notice your uncle?" Gerald asked.

Priscilla's radar went up right away. "Do you think he's ill?"

"No, I'm referring to the way he's dancing with Marigold Townsend, like he's a kid or something."

"Oh, my. I hope his heart can take it."

"Pretty sure his heart is leading him all the way, if you know what I mean."

The music changed to a ballad and several of the couples left the floor. Gerald held Priscilla close. She didn't argue with him. This amazing night would end in a few minutes, and she wanted to soak up every bit of sweetness she could.

Unfortunately, their intimate moment was interrupted when Gail walked toward Priscilla, forehead wrinkled in concern. "I'm so sorry to interrupt your dance, but Priscilla, you've got to help me."

"Do what?" She paused and looked into her cousin's eyes.

"Drag Pop off the dance floor. Dancing is the last thing he needs to be doing after his heart attack."

"It's just a slow dance," Gerald observed. "And if you watch closely, you'll see his feet are barely shuffling. If he and Marigold moved any slower, I think we'd call what they're doing necking and not dancing."

"Well, necking's not exactly easy on the heart, either." Gail sighed. "Not that it's really my business. He's my father, not my child. And I've given him all the right advice over the past few weeks to be as healthy as he can."

"I'd say he's doing all he can to stay young at heart," Gerald said. "Maybe that's even better for his heart than all the other stuff put together. You know what I mean?"

"Yeah, maybe." They all stood in silence and watched Uncle Hugh ease his way around the dance floor, his arms wrapped around Marigold as if they were meant to be that way...forever.

"It's Valentine's weekend, Gail. Let them be." Priscilla smiled. "I think it's romantic, and if anyone deserves something good to happen, it's Uncle Hugh."

About halfway into the dance, the music came to an abrupt halt. The sound of a man's voice echoed across the room. Priscilla glanced up to see Uncle Hugh standing on the stage, microphone in hand.

"Sorry, folks!" he called out. "But if I could have your attention for a moment, please."

All the dancers froze in place.

"Any idea what he's up to?" Priscilla asked.

"Mm-hmm. I have my suspicions." Gerald turned to face the stage, slipping his arm around Priscilla's waist. "But let's see if he confirms them."

"Ladies and gentlemen, I have something to say, and this seemed like the best place to say it." Uncle Hugh paled, and for a moment Priscilla wondered if his heart might be acting up again.

"Do I need to call 911, Hugh?" one of the older fellas called out. "You're lookin' a little pale."

With the wave of a hand, Hugh dismissed any concerns. "Nope. Don't call anyone. I can assure you I'll be feeling much better in a minute, as long as things go my way."

The crowd stirred, and Priscilla watched as her uncle extended his hand toward a certain woman.

"Marigold Townsend, would you join me on stage?" he asked.

The precious woman accepted his outstretched hand and climbed the three steps to the stage. She looked half intrigued, half mortified. "What's all this about, Hugh?" she asked.

"Just have something on my mind, and I'd like to share it in front of those who know and love us best. There's a question I've been wanting to ask you for days." His gaze shifted to Priscilla. "I asked a certain niece of mine to help me come up with a plan, but she's been a little busy planning weddings. I even ran a few of my ideas by her, but they didn't cut the mustard."

Priscilla fought the temptation to respond. Instead, she stared in silence at Hugh and Marigold, whose cheeks flamed pink.

"You can do it, Hugh!" one of the men yelled out.

"Give me a minute and I'll try." He took Marigold's hand in his. "Finally decided I was overthinking it, just like Priscilla said. I don't need anyone's help." His voice quivered as he gazed into Marigold's eyes. "There's no one else on the planet who knows you like I do, Marigold, so why involve anyone but the two of us?"

"I'd say we're all pretty involved, Hugh," Carson called out.

This resulted in a reverberation of laughter around the room.

"Okay, okay. So, you're all involved. But I'd like to ask you to please just let me handle this next part on my own." Hugh reached into his pocket and came out with a tiny box. His gaze shifted to Marigold, who stood, mouth agape, staring at him. "Marigold, you deserve the best, and I'm far from the best. But you know that I love you with my whole heart." He placed a hand on his chest. "Which, according to the cardiologist, is in far better shape, now that I've had that surgery. I'd like to think I've got a few good years left in me, and I want to spend every one of them with you."

Marigold burst into tears and said, "Oh, Hugh!"

He popped open the box and took hold of her left hand. "Now, I know it's proper to get down on one knee, but you and I both know that if I made it down to the floor they really would have to call 911. These old knees of mine are in rough shape. But I hope you can see that, in my heart, I'm kneeling. Can you see it, Marigold?"

She nodded.

"Will you marry me, sweetie? After all these years? Will you?"

Marigold released a loud "Yes!" and the crowd erupted as Hugh placed the ring on her finger. Afterward, he placed a kiss on her that no one in Misty Harbor would soon forget.

"So, there you have it, folks. He finally did it." Gerald chuckled. "Good for him. Looks like you'll have another wedding to plan, Priscilla."

"I'll hang a shingle on my cottage." She laughed. "Though I suspect they'll just head off to the justice of the peace and get this done quickly. That's what I'd do."

CHAPTER TWENTY-SIX

Priscilla kept a careful watch on the time after Hugh's proposal. At five o'clock, she started to gather the troops for the grand finale. Eliza would be so surprised.

With very little time to spare, Trudy drew near. "So, you knew that was coming?"

"Well, not tonight, but I certainly knew Uncle Hugh was trying to come up with a plan. I wasn't very helpful, as he said."

"Oh, I don't know. Sounds like you gave him the courage to do it on his own, which was what he should've been doing all along."

"True. And I'm awfully proud of him."

"Me too." Trudy looked at her. "Do you ever think about it?"

"Think about what?"

"Getting married again."

Priscilla's heart quickened. "It's not really something I spend a lot of time thinking about. It's been such an adjustment, learning how to be single. You know? And getting established in a new place and all. I think I've done pretty well on my own, don't you?"

"Sure. It's admirable." Trudy paused. "But..."

"But what?"

"Just sayin', if you're holding on to any notions that you shouldn't fall in love or get married again because you're worried about what others might think, well..."

Priscilla turned to face her cousin, astounded at what she was hearing.

"I just want you to be happy, Priscilla." Trudy shrugged. "I want everyone to be as blissful as Dan and I are. You know?"

"I do know."

"Maybe God has more out there for you." Trudy gestured in Gerald's direction. "I'm just sayin'."

"Ah. I see. Well, don't marry me off just yet, okay? I'm only fifty-nine. I've got a few good years left."

"I promise not to bring it up again. I'll let you take the lead on that one."

"Good going."

Trudy hugged her. "On nights like tonight, I wish everyone could fall in love."

Priscilla glanced at her watch again and gasped. Five minutes after five. Time to get this show on the road.

Priscilla walked onto the stage at ten minutes after five and took the microphone. She invited the guests to grab a bottle of bubbles and meet her in the driveway. Three minutes later, with the most gorgeous sunset sending rays of gold and red overhead, the bride and groom made their exit.

They walked onto the drive hand in hand as the guests blew bubbles over them. They were so busy gazing into one another's eyes that neither one noticed the car. At first. When his gaze shifted to the convertible, Carson stopped cold. Eliza, on the other hand, burst into tears and began jumping up and down.

"You did it! You did it!" She sought Priscilla out through the crowd and rushed her way for the best hug ever. Then she rejoined her husband in front of the gorgeous vehicle.

Carson stood, frozen in place. "What in the world?"

"Surprise!" Eliza giggled. "What do you think of our getaway car?"

"Whoa." He took a couple of cautious steps toward it and then ran his hand along the hood. "Who did you rent it from?"

She shook her head. "No one."

His eyes narrowed and Priscilla could read the confusion in his expression. "What are you saying, Eliza? If you didn't rent it, then..." He shook his head. "Did someone from the car club loan it to you?"

"Nope." She giggled. "Try again."

"Honey, are you saying this is your car?"

"*Our* car, Carson. Yours and mine. A 1954 Bel Air convertible. We're going to drive off into the sunset, but we have to hurry." Her gaze traveled to the golden skies above.

He shook his head, clearly still in a state of disbelief. "Do you have any idea how long I've dreamed of having this car?"

"Oh, for twenty years or so?"

"You remembered."

"Every detail."

"But, how...when?"

"There are a lot of blanks to fill in, but I promise to do that after we drive off into the sunset." She squinted as she pointed upward. "That was the plan, after all, to drive off into the sunset. Right?"

"Have I mentioned that I love you?" He planted a kiss on her that caused the crowd to cheer.

"Mm-hmm. But a gal always loves to hear it repeated."

"Well, I love you. And this is the finest gift anyone has ever given me, bar none."

"You're welcome. Now, would you please take the wheel, Carson? Folks are waiting. They want to see us off."

Carson waved at the crowd, and cheers rang out. He opened the passenger door for his bride to step inside. Afterward, he took his place behind the wheel. Of course, he had absolutely no idea how much work it had taken to get to this point. He just slipped into the driver's seat as if the whole thing had been a piece of cake. Likely Eliza would tell him the whole sordid story, but hopefully not tonight. Perhaps on the flight to Florida. Or, better yet, on the flight home.

They pulled away at 5:17 just as the sun's colors morphed to orange and pink. The whole thing was like a dream. Priscilla watched it all in wonder and sent up a silent prayer of thanks.

Gerald walked over to her and slid his arm around her waist. "Well, there they go."

"Yep."

"They look as happy as two peas in a pod."

"Two car enthusiasts in a classic, you mean."

"That too." He grinned. "Perfect ending to a rocky story, I guess you'd say."

"No kidding."

He pointed to a familiar young man holding a camera. "Is that the reporter from the *Vineyard Gazette*?"

"Sure is."

"You invited him to the wedding?"

"While you were busy talking with the police, I gave him a call and told him to be at the Bluffs at exactly five minutes till five. Said he wouldn't want to miss this."

"I'm guessing he was thrilled to get that scoop."

"Not as happy as I was to call him." She paused. "I wanted to mark the moment, not just with wedding photos, but for the whole community to see. I wanted people to know that God goes above and beyond to shower us with blessings."

"He does, indeed. He's in the details, for sure."

A few seconds later, Victor joined them. He smiled at Priscilla. "Do you have a minute to chat?"

She glanced at her watch. "Sure."

"Do you believe people can change, Ms. Grant?"

"Of course."

"I just want you to know I'm not the same man who ran for office this past year. I might look like the same Victor Fox on the outside, I might even sound like him with my sales techniques, because, frankly, that's all I know. But I'm not the same guy. Things are changing on the inside. I don't expect people to believe me until they've seen me in action a little longer, but hopefully time will prove me out. I'm different."

"I believe you, Victor."

And she did. For the first time, Priscilla genuinely believed that the man was a transformation in process. And they had Gerald to thank for that, at least in part.

Victor and Gerald turned their backs in a private conversation, and then they excused themselves. Looked like both were in a hurry to get to their cars, the way they sprinted across the parking lot. Not that Priscilla had much time to pay attention, what with the cousins crowding in around her.

"Where are they going?" Trudy asked.

"Yeah, looks like they're off to put out a fire or something," Gail added.

"I have no idea." Priscilla focused on her cousins. "But right now, I only have one thing on my mind."

"Is it a 1954 Bel Air convertible, by any chance?" Joan asked.

"Sure is." She quickly filled them in. "I just can't believe how perfectly everything worked out. And I feel like I've learned so much."

"Oh?" Trudy's brows elevated. "Like what?"

Priscilla paused to think it through. "Well, I guess we can safely say that I've learned—by watching Eliza—that possessions might be valuable, but they are in no way as valuable as the people God has placed in our lives."

"I wholeheartedly agree," Gail said.

"And I dare say, Eliza and Carson would've been just as happy with one another if we hadn't located that car."

"But I'm awfully glad you did," Trudy added.

"Me too," she admitted.

She caught a glimpse of Sally Jenson and Tony Romano standing hand in hand, visiting with other guests. Wow. Looked like things were moving quickly around here.

Sally let go of Tony's hand and joined the ladies for a final hug. "Tony has asked me out for coffee. Someplace quiet. I hope you won't take that as a snub."

"No way," Priscilla said.

"I just want to thank you all for befriending me," Sally said. "This has been an amazing few days. Life changing. Best of all, I met all of you."

"I love how God weaves friendships in and out of our lives," Priscilla said. "Many of the people we spend quality time with are those we've known for years. We've grown to trust them, feel completely comfortable around them. But every now and again God surprises us with brand-new, unexpected friendships. Before long, they're a perfect fit too."

"God is so good." Sally wrapped her arms around Priscilla.

"He is. The truth is, He knows what we need and who we need. And He'll bring those people to us, even if it means crossing miles or bodies of water." Priscilla smiled. "That certainly is the case with you, our new—and hopefully forever—friend, Sally."

The sound of tires against gravel caused the ladies to stop talking. Priscilla looked up to discover Gerald and Victor pulling up in a blue SUV.

The blue SUV.

What in the world?

Victor pulled it to a stop in the driveway and bounded out. Then Gerald exited the passenger side.

"Gerald?" Priscilla squinted, to make sure the setting sun hadn't affected her vision. "What are you doing?"

"Well, I seem to recall a certain lady saying she wished she had a new car, and that she would buy it if Victor would come down on the price."

"Well, yes, but there's no way he would come down five thousand dollars."

"You're right." Victor stepped into the spot next to her. "I came down eight."

"Wh-what?"

"I'm also going to give you a fair price for your trade-in. I'll even make sure it gets back to the dealership for the recall work. If they can't get it in tip-top shape, my mechanics will know what to do. So I think you'll drive away a very happy camper."

Okay, that might've sounded like one of his slogans, but it was a great one.

"Victor, Gerald ... I don't know what to say."

"Say you'll take it for a spin." Victor handed her the keys.

Gerald walked to the driver's side and opened the door. "I've already tried it out and it's in mint condition."

"Should I get in? Now?"

"Of course now."

"But there's a dining hall to clean, guests to take care of, vendors to pay."

"We'll all pitch in, Priscilla," Gail called out.

"Yes, go for a spin," Trudy added.

"See?" Gerald grinned. "You've got lots of help. Your only job is to get behind the wheel of your new car and focus on the road. Life is a journey, you know. Enjoy the ride." He laughed. "And yes, I stole that slogan from Victor's car lot. Now, there's not much sun left. I thought you might want to go for a ride while you can still show off the car."

She settled in the driver's seat, completely enamored with the gorgeous interior, and waited for him to take his spot in the passenger seat.

"I think I'm gonna like it here," she said.

"Kind of thought you might. And here's a real kicker…you don't even have to use the key to start the engine."

"I just have to think about driving and it turns on?" She grinned at him.

"No. Just have the key nearby and push that button right there." He pointed to a small round button.

She pushed it and the car started with ease. Outside, the crowd roared with delight.

"What do you say, Gerald? Trust my driving enough to take a spin around the block?"

"You betcha. Even farther, if you like."

She slipped the car into gear and pulled out onto the road. Her heart wanted to burst into song as the truth of what was happening confronted her.

She and Gerald were driving off into the sunset...
together.

No, the story wouldn't end here. There would be plenty of
adventures ahead. But for now, Priscilla was perfectly happy
behind the wheel of her new car with this handsome classic at
her side.

AUTHOR LETTER

Dear Reader,

Oh, how I love Valentine's Day! As a baker, it's my busiest day of the year. It's not unusual for me to bake and hand-paint as many as six hundred cookies during Valentine's week, and don't get me started on the heart-shaped cakes and pink rosette cupcakes. My whole house smells like sugar. As I penned *Beyond the Sea*, I could envision Candy Lane's bakery smelling that way too, as she filled her cases with sugar cookies, scones, cupcakes, and other yummy treats.

Unfortunately, this past Valentine's Day things went slightly off course for me and nearly brought my baking to a halt. It started when I broke my right wrist in two places. Working with just one hand is tough, but try writing books and running a bakery without your dominant hand! By the time Valentine's Day arrived my wrist was feeling a little better, but I came down with a terrible case of Influenza B. For two weeks, I battled high fevers and upper respiratory symptoms. Fun, right? Somewhere in the middle of all that—and between the cookies, cakes, and cupcakes—I started writing this book.

I wasn't altogether sure the story would come together, but one thing kept me motivated—the Valentine-themed wedding. You see, my oldest daughter got married on Valentine's weekend back in 2004. I helped coordinate the event, with all of its red and gold décor. Memories of that amazing event kept me going as I powered my way through the writing of this story. Reminiscing about her ceremony, reception, food, cake, and so forth, gave me lots of inspiration for Eliza's Valentine wedding at the Bluffs B&B. As always, I pulled from my real-life story to build the framework of this book. I hope you can catch glimpses of that as you read.

This journey would not have been possible without my amazing editor, Susan Downs, and JoAnne Simmons, the skilled copy editor who helped me shape the story to fit the cozy mystery line. I hope you enjoy this Valentine-themed story as much as I do.

Enjoy!

Janice Thompson

ABOUT THE AUTHOR

Award-winning author Janice Thompson got her start in the industry writing screenplays and musical comedies for the stage. Janice has published over 100 books for the Christian market, crossing genre lines to write cozy mysteries, historicals, romances, nonfiction books, devotionals, children's books, and more. She particularly enjoys writing lighthearted, comedic tales because she enjoys making readers laugh.

Janice is passionate about her faith and does all she can to share the joy of the Lord with others, which is why she particularly enjoys writing. Her tagline, "Love, Laughter, and Happily Ever Afters!" sums up her take on life.

Janice lives in Spring, Texas, where she leads a rich life with her family, a host of writing friends, and two mischievous dachshunds. When she's not busy writing or playing with her eight grandchildren, Janice can be found in the kitchen, baking specialty cakes and cookies for friends and loved ones. No matter what she's cooking up—books, cakes, cookies, or mischief—she does her best to keep the Lord at the center of it all.

AN ARMCHAIR TOUR OF
MARTHA'S VINEYARD
Oak Bluffs, Martha's Vineyard

A good portion of *Beyond the Sea* takes place at a bed-and-breakfast on Martha's Vineyard. A location on the Vineyard that's perfect for a real B&B is the town of Oak Bluffs—a resort town known for its beautiful architecture and breathtaking views.

When I visited the area in 2016, I was delighted by the quaint feel. The land mass of Oak Bluffs is only seven and a half square miles, but every bend in the road offers another opportunity to gasp in awe at the scenic delights. Whether you're looking for beaches, ponds, coves, or lagoons, you'll find them here, along with some of the sweetest homes, inns, and colorful cottages on the Vineyard. Nineteenth-century buildings are beautifully preserved and make you feel as if you've stepped back in time.

If you really want to view a piece of history while in Oak Bluffs, be sure to stop off at the Corbin-Norton House, a newly renovated summer retreat home built by turn-of-the-century entrepreneur Philip Corbin in 1891. The luxurious Queen Anne architecture is rich in ornamentation, detail, and color. Known as "the Grand Old Lady of Ocean Avenue," this home is a testament to the beauty of nineteenth-century architecture with its wraparound veranda and overhanging roof and octagonal turret. As I wrote *Beyond the Sea*, I could picture Eliza, the bride-to-be, preparing for her wedding in a building such as this. What fun, to plan for a Valentine-themed wedding in such a quaint, delightful locale.

Of course, Oak Bluffs offers ample shopping and eating opportunities as well. Whether you're in the mood for seafood chowder, lobster rolls, or fried fish, you'll find it in abundance here, along with a host of shops that feature ice cream and other sweet treats.

While in the area, you'll want to see the East Chop Light, a historic lighthouse atop a bluff overlooking the harbor. Built in 1878, it stands as a testament to the Vineyard's rich maritime history.

No matter where you land in Oak Bluffs, be sure to kick back, put your feet up, and breathe in that salty ocean air. It will remind you that life, no matter how hectic off the island, moves at a much slower pace on the Vineyard. Ah, such bliss!

SOMETHING DELICIOUS FROM OUR SEASIDE FRIENDS

Candy Lane's Hand-Painted Valentine Sugar Cookies

Cookie Ingredients:

Two sticks (one cup) butter

1 extra-large egg

1 cup powdered sugar

½ cup granulated sugar

½ teaspoon almond extract

1 teaspoon vanilla

3 cups flour

1 teaspoon baking powder

½ teaspoon salt

Mix butter, egg, sugars, vanilla, and almond extract until creamy. In separate bowl sift together flour, baking powder, and salt. Add gradually to wet ingredients. Put the dough into a freezer-safe bag and chill (in the freezer for 15 minutes or the refrigerator for 30 minutes to an hour). Roll out dough between two pieces of waxed paper to ¼-inch thick and use cookie cutters to cut in desired shapes. Bake at 375 degrees for ten minutes. Do not over-bake. Cool completely.

Royal Icing Ingredients:

4½ tablespoons meringue
    powder

½ cup + up to 2 tablespoons
    water

1 teaspoon cream of tartar

1 tablespoon vanilla

½ teaspoon almond extract

One bag (7–8 cups)
    powdered sugar

Coloring gel

Royal Icing:

Mix meringue powder, 1/2 cup of water, cream of tartar, vanilla, and almond extract until frothy (less than a minute). Add full bag powdered sugar and mix until incorporated. Turn mixer on low and beat for ten minutes until mixture is meringue-like in texture. Immediately cover with plastic wrap (touching the icing) and a damp towel above that. Scoop out about a cup of the icing into a small bowl and add coloring gel. Mix thoroughly. Add water, a few drops at a time, until icing is the desired consistency for piping. Piping/outlining icing should be the consistency of toothpaste. The coating (or "flood" icing) should be the consistency of honey. Pipe onto cookies using piping bags with #2 tips.

Read on for a sneak peek of another exciting book
in the Mysteries of Martha's Vineyard series!

Wider Than an Ocean
by Beth Adams

Priscilla couldn't believe the color of the sky. She thought by now she'd have grown used to the way the light here on Martha's Vineyard seemed to shimmer, the way it cast everything in a gorgeous, glowing radiance. And yet, as she came over the rise, the beauty still took her breath away. The vibrant sky was somewhere between robin's-egg blue and a deep, rich cerulean. The tidal marsh, surrounded by trees stripped bare by the long winter, appeared both beautiful and haunting. Priscilla slowed—a luxury she could afford in mid-March, when the island was down to just the hardiest of locals—and took in the vista. The contrast between the stark, barren tree limbs and the luminous blue of the sky struck her with awe.

Soon, she rounded the bend and the marsh disappeared, replaced by woods on both sides of the road. Priscilla drove along, humming a hymn they used to sing at her church back in Kansas. She was headed out to Menemsha, on the western part of the island, to meet Gerald at the Coast Guard Station, and she always forgot how rural this part of the island was. It was hard to believe she was only a few miles from Tisbury, the bustling village near her lighthouse-cottage home. She passed a few houses, set back from the road and surrounded by stacked stone fences, and a convenience store cloaked in wooden shingles and green shutters, making it the most attractive gas station she'd ever seen. Then, nothing but trees again, and another marsh, filled to the brim with glistening water. The tide was in.

She tried to keep her mind focused on the beauty around her, but inevitably her thoughts wandered, settling on the long list of things she had to do. She'd agreed to help Gerald organize an Easter egg hunt for the community; there were all the little details for Rachel's wedding she needed to check on; her best friend from home, Ruth, was about to have another granddaughter; she still needed to finish the blanket she was making; and . . .

Something caught her eye and pulled her out of her mental list making. A plane. A small plane, flying low in the sky above her. Was that—? She slowed again, trying to get a good look at it. It was silver, with some blue on the tail and—was that a trail of smoke coming out of the back?

Priscilla didn't know much about planes, especially not small ones like this. "Flying tin cans," Gary had called them when he saw them cruising low over the cornfields of Kansas. But she was pretty sure they weren't supposed to be wobbling like that. Its wings shifted up and down as the pilot fought to keep the plane level over the marsh.

The day was still. Calm. It wasn't the wind causing the plane to shake like that.

Priscilla pulled over and stepped out of her car. The low whine of the engine filled the air. She watched as the plane cleared the marsh and swayed back and forth, fighting to stay airborne. She could just barely make out the form of someone sitting in the cockpit. It looked like the plane was about to scrape the tops of the trees, and was slipping lower every second.

Yes, that was definitely smoke coming out of the plane, Priscilla saw now. Grayish-black smoke. And more of it was coming out every moment. She continued watching the plane as it disappeared beyond the horizon, skipping lower and lower over the treetops every second, until it fell behind the tree line, out of sight. She reached back into the car and grabbed her purse. She dug out her phone. Her hands shaking, she dialed 911.

"911, what's your emergency?" the dispatcher asked.

"Hi. I'm out on N Road, headed to Menemsha. I passed the Colonial Market a ways back, and I'm by that marsh with the bridge?" Did they need all those details? She had no idea. The dispatcher waited, and Priscilla decided to cut to the chase. "I just saw a small plane flying really low, and there was smoke coming out of the back of it. I think…" She took a deep breath. "I think it's about to crash!"

Priscilla gave the dispatcher all the information she could about where she was, which direction the plane had been heading, and where she thought it might have gone. She did her best, but she didn't really know where it might have landed—or, more likely based on what she'd seen, crash-landed.

After the dispatcher promised to send an ambulance out, Priscilla climbed back into her car. She wrestled with the idea of going in search of the plane, to see if she could help in any way, but when she looked at her best heels and the marshy reeds she'd have to wade through, she realized she wasn't equipped, in any way, shape, or form, to handle an emergency like this. But there was one thing she could do. She could pray. She closed her eyes and prayed for the pilot, that he had been protected from injury, and for the rescuers, that they would find the plane quickly and bring whatever help was needed. She prayed for God's peace, and for miraculous healing for the pilot, who, if she was honest, was probably not in great shape, even if he had survived the landing.

She opened her eyes and started the car, but then waited a moment. She was shaken. Had she really just seen a plane falling out of the sky? It seemed so awful, so startling, that at first it didn't seem like it could be real. And yet, that was exactly what she'd seen.

She took a deep breath. There was nothing more she could do now, she reasoned. Help was on the way. Maybe she should call Gerald, but as it was, she was about to be late to her meeting with him, and she could tell him about it then. Slowly, reluctantly, she put on her blinker, checked her mirrors, and pulled back onto the road.

A few minutes later, she was checking in at the security desk, early after all. The US Coast Guard station's offices were housed in a three-story white clapboard building with black shutters and a cupola on top. Another tidy white building, which Priscilla knew was the barracks for the officers serving at the station, sat next to the main building, overlooking a small pond, just a short way up from the inlet by the boathouse. The main building's entryway had high ceilings and polished oak floors and lining the walls were black-and-white photos of men in old-fashioned uniforms on antique Coast Guard vessels. Priscilla asked for Gerald at the front desk, and a few minutes later, he came down to meet her. After pulling her in for a hug, he led her up the stairs to his office, passing a number of staff along the way. Having called 911 about the small plane, Priscilla decided she could wait for the right moment to tell him what she had just witnessed.

"Thanks so much for coming out this way," he said.

Priscilla smiled. "Considering this is where the Easter egg hunt will take place, I thought it made sense to get a look at the grounds."

After a couple of recent mistakes—one botched open-water rescue that ended in two near-deaths, and a Coast Guard boat that crashed against the Jaws Bridge at high tide, damaging its pilings and injuring three of the officers on board—the Coast Guard had faced some bad publicity. Those incidents had been followed by a string of articles in the *Martha's Vineyard Times* that pointed out that many people on the island didn't know what the Coast Guard did and found the station foreboding and off-putting. Officers admitted that the Coast Guard had something of a public-relations problem. Gerald, captain of the Menemsha station, hadn't been overly concerned—this was a military base, after all—but he'd been persuaded by his higher-ups on the mainland that his team should do more to interact with the local community. The idea of an Easter egg hunt, where families could come out and have fun and explore the base and get to know some of the officers, had been born, and Gerald had recruited Priscilla and one of the younger officers to head up the event with him.

"I appreciate your help getting this set up, Priscilla. Chloe is finishing up a phone call and will be here in just a moment." Gerald led her into the large, light-filled office. His desk was set against one wall, which was paneled in dark wood and hung with various medals, certificates, and plaques. She sat down in one of the leather chairs across from his desk and looked out the large plate-glass window toward the water far below. The sky was still that bright blue, and the water below a flat greenish-gray.

"That one's new, isn't it?" she asked, pointing at a framed copy of the words to the hymn "Eternal Father, Strong to Save" on his desk.

"Yes, Aggie gave it to me for my birthday," Gerald said, handing it to her. The words were superimposed over the image of a Coast Guard cutter surrounded by water.

"I've always loved this hymn," Priscilla said. She let her eyes run over the familiar words.

> Eternal Father, strong to save,
> Whose arm hath bound the restless wave,
> Who bidd'st the mighty ocean deep
> Its own appointed limits keep;
> Oh, hear us when we cry to Thee,
> For those in peril on the sea!

The choir director at her church back in Kansas had had a soft spot for the old hymn and often chose it whenever there was a baptism, based on some logic Priscilla had never quite worked out. Something about water, she supposed, though the whole thing had always seemed a bit foreign in Kansas. It made more sense here, in Gerald's office, overlooking the vast and raging sea. But she had one question.

"Isn't this the British Naval Hymn?"

Gerald laughed. "It's often sung in the States too. And it seems entirely appropriate for the Coast Guard as well. I've always thought so, anyway."

"That it does." She handed back the frame.

"How are you?" he asked as he sat down behind his desk. His leather chair squeaked as he lowered himself down.

"I'm..." She hesitated. "I'm fine, mostly. But the weirdest thing happened on the way out here."

"What's that?"

She took a deep breath. "I think I saw a plane crash."

"What?" Gerald leaned forward, the springs on his chair creaking. "What do you mean?"

Priscilla told him about seeing the small plane skimming low over the treetops, its wings whipping up and down as it fought to stay level while it dropped.

"Where was this?" Gerald asked, his brow wrinkled.

She told him where she was when she'd seen it, and that she'd called 911 immediately. "But I am worried about the pilot, and I hope he's all right—"

"Hold on a second," Gerald said, pushing himself up. "Let me see what I can find out." He stepped out of the office. Gerald was in communication with just about every emergency response team on the island; he was probably checking to find out more.

Priscilla sat and waited, thinking he would be right back, but he was gone longer than she expected. She looked over each of the certificates and plaques—awards for valor, and for dedicated service. She knew Gerald's dress uniform was also decorated with many medals and stripes, reflecting a long and distinguished career.

Finally, he came back into the office. "I think I have some good news," he said.

"Did they find the plane? Is the pilot all right?"

"No. They didn't find the plane, and aside from yours, there have been no calls about it."

"Oh dear." Priscilla had a sinking feeling.

"The EMTs didn't get any other calls, but it's strange that there weren't any calls on the radio either. Usually, if a plane is in trouble, the pilot will radio for help on 121.5, the radio frequency used for emergencies."

Priscilla had only a vague understanding of how a cockpit worked, but she'd seen enough movies and news programs to know that a pilot communicated with ground control and other pilots using a two-way radio.

"But the stranger thing is that none of the airfields in the area knew about a small plane approaching."

"Okay..." Priscilla wasn't exactly sure what he was getting at. Gerald sat down behind the desk again. He must have seen her confusion, because he elaborated.

"If the plane was planning to land at the main airport, it would have needed to contact the control tower to let them know it was approaching and ask for permission to land."

Priscilla was pretty sure he meant Martha's Vineyard Airport, outside Edgartown, where flights from Boston and Providence and New York landed. Gerald continued. "Then, depending on whatever other planes they had coming in around the same time, air traffic control would let the pilot know when it was cleared to go in for a landing."

"So you're saying that if the plane was planning to land at the main airport, they would know about it."

"Absolutely." He placed his palms down on the leather blotter on his desk. "And given where you think you saw the plane go down, that's the most likely place it was headed."

"But they *didn't* know about it." Had she heard him right? It sure seemed like he was doubting that she'd seen a plane.

"Correct."

Priscilla tried to make sense of this.

"Maybe the plane had just taken off." The plane she'd seen had been going down, but maybe that hadn't been intentional. "Maybe it had engine trouble and was trying to get back to the airport."

He shook his head. "They know for sure no small plane had just taken off."

Priscilla wasn't seeing where this was going. "But I definitely saw a plane. So where could the plane have been heading, if it wasn't going to land at the main airport?"

"Well, there's Katama Airfield, out in Edgartown. It's possible it was headed there."

Priscilla didn't know what he was talking about. "Katama Airfield?"

"It's a small place. It's mostly used for those scenic biplane tours of the island. It started out as a training facility for pilots during World War II, and it's still kind of rough. It's right on the beach, so in the summer, plenty of private planes land there, but it's pretty quiet this time of year."

"And they didn't know of any planes that were planning to land there?"

"No. They had no notice of any plane coming in for a landing."

"Is it possible someone could have planned to land there and not let them know?"

"It's possible…" Gerald said. "But if the plane was flying as low as you say when you saw it, it wouldn't have made it all the way to Katama."

"I don't think it was flying that low *on purpose*," Priscilla said.

Gerald nodded. Something wasn't adding up. Why was he so calm about this?

"Is there anywhere else the pilot could have been planning to land?"

Gerald shrugged. "There's an airstrip out in Oak Bluffs on the Trade Winds Land Bank. But you definitely need to have permission to land there, and I just spoke with the director, who said they hadn't given permission for any planes to land today."

"Okay." Priscilla tried to wrap her mind around this. "So we don't know where the plane was planning to land, but it doesn't really matter, because I'm pretty sure it didn't make it to an airport of any kind. I definitely saw it going down. So we just need to find it, and—"

"The plane didn't show up on any radar, either."

"What?"

"Martha's Vineyard airport and Katama Airfield have radar systems so they can monitor the skies above them. None of them picked up any sign of the plane."

Priscilla just looked at him, openmouthed.

He shrugged. "I don't know what to say, but there isn't any sign of a small plane being anywhere near here."

Priscilla didn't understand what he was getting at. Could he really not believe her? "What are you trying to say?"

Gerald hesitated, and then said slowly, "The emergency crews have been sent out and are searching for the plane, but so far they haven't found anything. I'm sure they'll keep looking. If the plane is out there, they will find it."

There it was again. Priscilla wasn't imagining it. *If* it's out there. He doubted the plane existed.

"What do you mean, *if* the plane is out there?" she said. "I saw it, Gerald. I saw it with my own eyes."

"I have no doubt you did," Gerald said, but his voice had taken on a soothing, calm tone that only made Priscilla more frustrated.

"Then why did you say that? Do you think I am imagining things? That I didn't really see it?"

The look on his face was inscrutable. He was giving nothing away. But he didn't believe her. That was clear enough, and for a moment, Priscilla began to wonder if he was right. *Had* she seen something that wasn't really there?

But—no. She had seen it. She had definitely seen that plane flying low, the trail of smoke coming out from behind. She knew what she'd seen, even if, for whatever reason, he didn't believe her.

"You don't think I really saw it."

"It's not that, Priscilla."

A dozen emotions swirled within her, but she was more confused than anything else. She and Gerald had gotten to know each other pretty well. They'd spent a lot of time together, and sometimes she even thought—well, of course they weren't a couple in any sort of official way, but she'd thought they had been headed that direction.

"I *saw* it, Gerald. It was there. It was about to crash."

"It's not that I don't believe you, Priscilla." His voice now took on an exaggerated calm, which only made her more upset.

"I know what I saw, Gerald. And I know—"

"Priscilla. Listen to me." Gerald pushed himself up and walked around his desk. For a moment, she thought he was going to come toward her, but instead he walked over to the office door and closed it gently. Then he came back to his desk and stood over her.

"I believe that you saw something. I just don't think you saw a plane."

Priscilla reared her head back. "What else would I have seen?"

Before she could stop them, thoughts about government conspiracies and little green men flashed through her head. She'd had an uncle who was convinced the government was involved in some sort of elaborate cover-up involving alien spacecraft. He had wild theories about Area 51 and the FBI and all kinds of odd things Priscilla had never given any credit to. But was Gerald now suggesting something of the sort?

"What do you think it was, then?" She forced her voice to remain level.

Gerald took a deep breath and looked around, as if to make sure they were alone.

"I could get in a lot of trouble if anyone finds out I'm telling you this," he said.

"Go on," Priscilla said. If he mentioned the name *Roswell*, she was out of here.

"I should probably let you believe you really saw a plane and leave it at that. But I don't want to let you believe something that isn't true."

She crossed her arms over her chest and waited.

"The Coast Guard has been doing some tests in the area recently."

She narrowed her eyes. "What kind of tests?"

"Drones."

"Drones?" Priscilla had heard about them, of course. The remote-controlled flying robots had been gaining in popularity and were usually used for taking video footage, she thought. Though didn't the military use them for other purposes? She felt certain she'd read that the military used them in warfare. "Why?"

"I can't tell you that, I'm afraid. All I'll say is that we've been doing some drone testing in the area, and I suspect there's a good chance that's what you saw this afternoon."

She thought about this for a second, and then she shook her head. Drones.

"I don't think so. I've seen drones, and they have four arms with propellers. This was nothing like that."

"What you've seen are civilian drones. Quadcopters, they're called. Not all drones look like that. Some look like… Well, some look remarkably like small planes."

Priscilla let that sink in for a moment. "You're telling me the Coast Guard is flying drones that look like small planes?"

"I'm not telling you anything. And if this conversation ever becomes public, I could be court-marshalled and dishonorably discharged." He leveled his gaze at Priscilla. "But because I care about you, and I want you to know I'm taking your concern seriously, I am"—he cleared his throat—"suggesting that what you might have seen was a drone that didn't look like one."

She processed this for a moment. Was this possible? Somehow, his answer had only inspired more questions.

But above that, was it possible that a drone was really what she'd seen?

"Did you have a drone crash this afternoon?" she asked.

"All I can say is that we were doing tests. And I shouldn't even say that much."

"No," Priscilla said, shaking her head. "There was a person in there. I saw a person inside the plane."

Gerald let out a long sigh.

"I'm not really sure what to say, Priscilla. I really don't want to—"

Just then, there was a knock at the office door.

"Come in," Gerald called. The door was pushed open, and a young woman poked her head in. "Hi, Chloe. Come on in."

This was the officer who had volunteered to help mend the Coast Guard's relationship to the public, then.

"Hi, I'm Chloe Park," the young woman said, holding out her hand. She had a bright smile and shoulder-length black hair. "I'm sorry I'm late. I was on a call and couldn't get off." She rolled her eyes. She talked so quickly Priscilla had to work to keep up, but Chloe seemed cheerful and pleasant, and Priscilla got the sense she would enjoy working with her.

"Priscilla Grant," she said, holding out her hand.

Priscilla understood that the discussion with Gerald regarding what she'd seen was over. But she couldn't stop running it back through her head, trying to make sense of what she'd witnessed, of what Gerald said.

Had she mistaken a drone for an actual airplane?

Had she mistaken a toy airplane for the real thing?

Priscilla really didn't think so. She knew what she'd seen. She'd seen the shadow of a person inside the plane. But Gerald didn't believe her.

Emergency crews were out looking for the wreckage, she reminded herself. If it was out there, they would find it.

If. She realized she had just thought that word too. She was so turned around by this conversation she couldn't even be sure what she'd witnessed anymore. Had she really even seen the plane at all?

A NOTE FROM THE EDITORS

We hope you enjoyed Mysteries of Martha's Vineyard, published by the Books and Inspirational Media Division of Guideposts, a nonprofit organization that touches millions of lives every day through products and services that inspire, encourage, help you grow in your faith, and celebrate God's love.

Thank you for making a difference with your purchase of this book, which helps fund our many outreach programs to military personnel, prisons, hospitals, nursing homes, and educational institutions.

We also create many useful and uplifting online resources. Visit Guideposts.org to read true stories of hope and inspiration, access OurPrayer network, sign up for free newsletters, download free e-books, join our Facebook community, and follow our stimulating blogs.

To learn about other Guideposts publications, including the best-selling devotional *Daily Guideposts*, go to Guideposts.org/Shop, call (800) 932-2145, or write to Guideposts, PO Box 5815, Harlan, Iowa 51593.

Sign up for the
Guideposts Fiction Newsletter
and stay up-to-date on the books you love!

You'll get sneak peeks of new releases, recommendations from other Guideposts readers, and special offers just for you . . .
and it's FREE!

Just go to Guideposts.org/Newsletters today to sign up.

Guideposts.

Visit Guideposts.org/Shop
or call (800) 932-2145

Find more inspiring fiction in these best-loved Guideposts series!

Mysteries of Martha's Vineyard

Come to the shores of this quaint and historic island and dig in to a cozy mystery. When a recent widow inherits a lighthouse just off the coast of Massachusetts, she finds exciting adventures, new friends, and renewed hope.

Tearoom Mysteries

Mix one stately Victorian home, a charming lakeside town in Maine, and two adventurous cousins with a passion for tea and hospitality. Add a large scoop of intriguing mystery and sprinkle generously with faith, family, and friends, and you have the recipe for Tearoom Mysteries.

Sugarcreek Amish Mysteries

Be intrigued by the suspense and joyful "aha!" moments in these delightful stories. Each book in the series brings together two women of vastly different backgrounds and traditions, who realize there's much more to the "simple life" than meets the eye.

Mysteries of Silver Peak

Escape to the historic mining town of Silver Peak, Colorado, and discover how one woman's love of antiques helps her solve mysteries buried deep in the town's checkered past.

Patchwork Mysteries

Discover that life's little mysteries often have a common thread in a series where every novel contains an intriguing whodunit centered around a quilt located in a beautiful New England town.

To learn more about these books, visit Guideposts.org/Shop